"There's

"There are the now, ready to move against key positions at a predetermined time," Castilo said.

"What about the army? Surely they won't just sit by and let their country be snatched out from under them," the Room 59 operative replied as he pressed the pistol's muzzle harder into the man's forehead.

"You have already met our man on the inside. He has given us invaluable information. We know where we will land the rest of the men, what to take first and, most importantly, how to block communication between various army units. There are also dissatisfied elements of the nation's military who will assist with the overthrow of the government at the proper time. Any kind of organized resistance will be disrupted long enough for the internal forces to seize control and order the rest of the military to stand down."

Castilo's eyes gleamed with the fire of the true political radical. "As for the event that will launch the real revolution—my man inside the army is going to assassinate Raul Castro later this very morning. That is when the true liberation of Cuba will begin!"

ROOM 59

THE
powers
THAT
be

cliff RYDER

A GOLD EAGLE BOOK FROM
WORLDWIDE®

TORONTO • NEW YORK • LONDON
AMSTERDAM • PARIS • SYDNEY • HAMBURG
STOCKHOLM • ATHENS • TOKYO • MILAN
MADRID • WARSAW • BUDAPEST • AUCKLAND

First edition January 2008

ISBN-13: 978-0-373-63265-7
ISBN-10:   0-373-63265-7

THE POWERS THAT BE

Special thanks and acknowledgment to
Jonathan Morgan for his contribution to this work.

THE
powers
THAT
be

PROLOGUE

Francisco Garcia Romero's world had been reduced to two sensations: light and pain.

The light came from the bare, wire-caged, hundred-watt bulb in his windowless, four-by-eight-foot punishment cell. Always burning, it turned the already sweltering space into a cramped oven, and had long ago stripped Francisco of any notion of the time of day. It limited his sleep to fitful minutes here and there, throwing his arm over his eyes until it cramped and he moved, which exposed his face to the harsh glare again. Its brilliance burned into his retinas. The light exposed every mark on his naked body, every bruise, every cut, every mosquito bite, every sore in stark relief, revealing the pitiful shell of the man and father he used to be.

Emaciated and filthy, he huddled on the dirty concrete floor of his cell in Quivicán maximum-security prison, with no mattress, blanket or even a concrete bed to sleep on. It had been a good day so far, because the hole in the floor where he relieved himself—when he could muster both the

energy to do so and the fortitude to handle the pain it
caused—hadn't overflowed yet. Also, he had managed to
keep down the cup of watery, unidentifiable soup and
handful of rice that had been doled out a few hours earlier.
But the rattle of his cell door as it was unlocked meant that
time was at an end.

"*¡Número treinta y cinco, salga!*" One of the fatigue-clad
guards barked the order. Since his detention had begun here,
the guards had only referred to him by a number—thirty-
five.

Francisco crawled to the door and out into the hallway,
where the two men grabbed him by the shoulders and
yanked him to his feet, ignoring his whimper of pain as his
shoulder was wrenched back. They placed him against the
wall and searched him—a seemingly useless gesture, since
he was already naked, that was meant to humiliate and further degrade him. Francisco waited with his legs apart, wondering which pair would accompany him this time. There
was only a casual inspection of his buttocks today, so it must
have been Guards Three and Four, as he called them. The
other pair of guards, One and Two, took an unpleasant interest in certain parts of his anatomy, and used every opportunity to torment him with the ends of their batons or other
items.

Satisfied he wasn't carrying any contraband, the two
guards pushed him down the hall toward the interrogation
area. As he did every time this happened, Francisco whispered his usual litany:

"*Padre nuestro, que estás en los cielos,*
Santificado sea tu Nombre.
Venga tu reino,

Hágase tu voluntad,
En la tierra como en el cielo...."

He always tried to finish the Lord's Prayer before being silenced by one of the guards or entering the interrogation room. If he could do that, he believed it gave him the inner strength to resist whatever they had planned for him. And just like every other time he had been taken to these small rooms, a part of him wondered if this time he would break under the endless torture, and tell them everything he knew.

As he shuffled down the hallway, he tried to ignore the flashes of pain from his battered body. Everything hurt, from the deep throbbing of his improperly-healed shoulder, injured in his very first interrogation and beating, to the burning pain in his rectum from the near constant diarrhea combined with torn sphincter muscles and the resulting infection from when he had been sodomized a few weeks earlier. The assault hadn't come from the guards, but from an enforcer for the "prisoners' council"—trustees given limited authority by the warden—when they learned he was planning a hunger strike to protest the inhumane conditions. Those, along with numerous other injuries, were a constant reminder of every minute he spent here, and also what had been stripped from him since his very first night in captivity—not just his limited freedom on the outside, but his dignity, health and free will.

Ever since he had been rousted from his bed in the dead of night so long ago and herded through a bewildering series of prisons, interrogations, torture and starvation, Francisco had clung to the slim hope that he might be released, or at least be allowed to stand trial for his supposed crimes. But as the days had stretched into weeks, and then months, and he had endured the near daily beatings, the deprivation of basic human needs and other mental and physical tortures, Francisco realized that he wasn't going to be saved. Unlike others, such as the poet Armando Valladares, who had gained international recognition for the abuse he had endured, Francisco was just one of hundreds of low-level political prisoners trapped in the grinding wheels of the government's relentless repression of basic human rights— what he had been fighting for every day.

Now, with his incarceration stretching into its sixth or seventh month—he wasn't sure exactly how long it had been—Francisco had lost hope of ever seeing the outside world again. He hadn't seen his wife and son in at least three months, and wasn't even sure they knew where he was anymore, since he had been moved several times before ending up at Quivicán. All he could do now hold one rational thought in his mind. No matter what happened, he would never betray his fellows still struggling to free Cuba from the Communist dictatorship. It was the one goal he still clung to—even though he couldn't be sure, given his semilucid state from hour to hour, that he hadn't already done so.

The interrogators had certainly tried hard to break him. They had taken him from his stifling cell to an air-conditioned room and left him there for hours before questioning him, when he could barely answer through chattering teeth. The beatings and malnutrition were bad, but it was during the third month that they had come closest to breaking him.

Just when he was coming to terms with the cruel conditions, the guards had come to his cell and told him he was being released. They had allowed him to wash up and shave, given him a decent meal, then escorted him to the main doors of the prison. And there, with freedom just a few yards away, the commander of the prison had walked up and told him that it was a mistake, that he was going back to his cell. It had taken three guards to wrestle him back into his cell that day. He had been beaten for resisting them, and that night he had been beaten again by fellow prisoners, who suspected he had made some kind of deal with the government to betray them.

Since that day, Francisco had resisted his captors as much as possible, but he had steadily weakened. He was on the edge of telling them whatever he could to get out of his punishment cell, receive some medical treatment, even just get a bare concrete bed to sleep on. His only solace was that if they ever broke him, he wouldn't be able to tell them much. His mostly bare-shelved bodega had been a drop point for messages among cells of the resistance, but he had never known who any of the contacts really were besides the man who had recruited him long ago. Francisco wasn't a government informer, but obviously someone in one of those cells he had serviced was.

Guard Three opened the interrogation-room door and entered, followed by Francisco, who stumbled in, assisted by a shove from Guard Four. The room looked like every other room he had been questioned in. A rattling air conditioner blew cold air across his fevered skin, and there were the standard two chairs and a small table in the center of the room. What was different, however, was the man sitting in the chair on the other side of the table.

He was a high-ranking member of the Cuban Revolutionary Armed Forces, at least a major, according to his epaulets. He was taller than the usual Cuban soldier. Even seated he loomed over the table. His features were unusual, too. He didn't have the usual dark caramel coloring of the majority of the people. His skin tone was a few shades lighter, almost café au lait. Francisco thought he was mulatto, perhaps part African, but that his nose wasn't broad, but narrow and long, almost patrician. And his eyes—which had locked onto the prisoner with the usual single-minded zeal—were a common light blue, not the expected dark brown.

The two guards came to attention and saluted. The man sitting in the chair tossed off a crisp but casual salute to them.

"Abandónenos." ·

The order to leave made the guards look at each other in confusion. *"Mayor?"* one asked, confirming Francisco's suspicion about the man's rank.

The major waved his hand at the door. "Leave us," he ordered again.

"But, sir, all interrogations are to be supervised in the event of an attack by the prisoner," a guard said.

The major leaned back in his chair. "As you can see, this man is no threat to me. I wish to question him in private. Now." The genial expression hardened in the blink of an eye. "Or must I report this insubordination to your superiors?"

"No, sir!" The two men saluted again, and left, closing the door behind them.

Francisco shivered in the cold, unable to take his eyes off this man who held his life in a black-gloved hand.

"Please, sit. You must be weak after everything you have

endured." The major pushed his chair back and stood, making Francisco cower, tensing in expectation of the first blow.

"No, no. Come, sit, please." The tall man took an overcoat from the back of his chair and slowly walked toward Francisco, holding it out like a matador approaching a nervous bull. He eased it around the wasted man's shoulders, then led him to the second chair and gently pressed him down.

"Thank—thank you." Francisco pulled the lapels of the coat around him and huddled into the cloth.

The major did not return to the other side of the table, but walked around to stand behind Francisco. "No, it is I who should be thanking you, Francisco Garcia Romero. You have survived agony that would have broken a hundred lesser men, yet you have not bought yourself any comfort by providing even a scrap of information about the counter-revolutionaries that plague our great nation. However, all men have their limits, my friend, and I am afraid that my superiors have reached theirs."

The odd choice of words made Francisco start to turn to look up at the major, but as he did, he saw a shadow rise above him, and the last thing he felt was an impact at the base of his neck, then merciful blackness.

The hammer blow to Francisco's neck fractured his second and third vertebrae, causing a piece of bone to punch inward, severing the spinal cord. The shock to his nervous system killed him before the pain impulse reached its final destination.

The major relaxed his interlaced hands and examined the prisoner, satisfied that he had broken his neck and killed him as painlessly and quickly as possible. Turning his back to the door, he quickly made the sign of the cross over the body and bent low to the man's ear.

"The people thank you for your dedicated service. You will be remembered when our nation is truly free."

He walked to the door and knocked on it, looking over his shoulder at the body slumped on the table. *"Vaya con Dios, amigo."*

1

Kate Cochran somersaulted through the air, maintaining enough control to tuck into her fall and roll with it instead of slamming to the mat on her back. Rising, she immediately assumed a defensive posture, feet shoulder width apart, legs slightly bent, arms close to her sides, fists clenched at her waist with knuckles up, ready to either punch or block.

A burst of laughter came from behind her. Kate turned, keeping her fists ready, to confront the man who had just sent her sailing across the room.

"My, my, don't you look tough." The man was a full head taller than her, and all lean, wiry muscle. His ink-black hair was cropped just short of high and tight, making it impossible to grab in a fight—as she had already discovered. He regarded her with amused, dark brown eyes that missed no detail of their surroundings.

"Kate, I'm not training you to fight in a dojo. What I'm teaching you—well, trying anyway—is how to survive on the street. Pure down-and-dirty fighting, where no one is going to wait for you to assume the position. By the time you're ready, your attacker will have already incapacitated or killed you."

"That's what I have you for, remember?" She slowly stepped toward him, keeping her center of gravity balanced, waiting for him to pounce again.

"Well, let's assume for this exercise that I'm already fighting two—no, make that three other guys, and you're on your own." His white teeth flashed in a razor-thin grin, and Kate knew who would win in a three-on-one fight with the man standing in front of her—Jacob Marrs, her bodyguard and instructor. "Now, relax that horse stance of yours, and for god's sake, stand like you're walking down the street, not some extra in a kung fu movie."

Kate straightened up and dropped her arms to her sides, unclenching her fists. She walked toward Jake, maintaining eye contact the whole way, ignoring the spectacular view her floor-to-ceiling town house windows afforded of the Manhattan skyline to the west. Sweat dripped in to her gold-green eyes.

She walked to within a foot of him, but nothing happened. Turning on her heel, Kate strode back across the room, ready for a chokehold from behind, or a grab at her platinum-blond hair or any one of a dozen other possible attacks. Still nothing. Peeking at him out of the corner of her vision, Jake still stood there in loose pants and his sleeveless *gi,* hands on his hips, as if he were carved from stone.

With a sigh, Kate whirled around to ask whether they were sparring or posing, only to find her trainer already in motion. Arms blurring like striking cobras, he took one large step forward and grabbed her arm. Instinctively, she stepped back, using his momentum to yank him off balance. Grabbing the collar of his *gi* with her right hand, she pulled him farther down while her right foot swept his outstretched left foot out from under him. Jacob lurched forward, and Kate directed his fall to the ground, raising a fist to follow up with a blow to his temple—

But Jake wasn't lying still like a good foot-sweep victim. He lifted his legs and scissored them toward her head instead. He caught her between his muscular thighs and snapped her forward, flipping her to the ground. Before she could scramble away, he was atop her, pinning her shoulders to the mat and leaning back so that his weight almost crushed her abdomen, but not quite.

"Two lessons here. One, the most important thing I'm trying to instill in you is to always expect an attack, because the moment you don't, the moment you relax your guard, that's when your opponent will strike." Jake leaned forward, his face inches from hers. "Second, why in the hell aren't you trying harder to escape right now?"

Kate arched her back as high as she could, hoping to throw him off enough to free an arm, but his weight was too much. He simply relaxed and settled down, forcing her back down to the mat. He readjusted his leg for a better pin, and Kate managed to wrench her left arm free and immediately brought her elbow down toward his groin. Jacob blocked it with a low forearm just before it would have made painful contact.

"Better. Let's try that again, and I'll show you another couple ways out of it—"

"Whoa, am I interrupting something, 'cause I could definitely come back later."

The voice from the doorway of the exercise room made both Kate's and Jacob's heads turn. Recovering first, Kate reached between Jake's legs with her free hand and grabbed his crotch while scooting down underneath his legs. Emitting a startled yelp, Jacob reared up on his knees, enabling her to emerge from under him and whirl around, finding him ready for her with a small yet genuine smile on his face.

Framed in the doorway was Kate's live-in housekeeper, Arminda Todd, holding a stack of folded towels and grinning from ear to ear. A couple of inches taller than her employer, she was slender and willowy where Kate was more muscular and toned. She shifted from one foot to another, fiddling with her waist-length hair, currently bound in a thick braid that curled down over her shoulder.

"That's okay, Mindy, we were just sparring. We're done for now," Kate said.

Jake stood and offered his hand. Kate accepted it warily, expecting him to try another takedown maneuver. However, once on her feet, he simply released her.

"I'm gonna hit the shower," Jake said. He walked by Mindy, snagging a towel as he passed. Kate noticed the college student's gaze follow as he left the room, and put on her most disapproving stare as the young woman turned back.

"What?"

Kate shook her head. "Don't be thinking what I know you're thinking."

Mindy's eyes widened in shock. "I just—like watching him leave, that's all."

"As long as that's all you're doing, then we're fine." Kate wasn't the jealous type and Jacob wasn't even close to the kind of man she'd be interested in. However, pretty little Mindy, all of twenty years old and usually wise beyond her years in most matters, seemed to have a soft spot for the laconic bodyguard. Owing to the unusual relationship between the three of them, Kate wanted to make sure that Mindy didn't do anything she might regret later.

She wasn't concerned about Jake. He understood the rules, and wasn't about to bend any of them for anyone, officer, civilian or otherwise. As he liked to say, "This ain't that bodyguard movie with Costner, but real life, and there's a world of difference between the two."

The best way to remind Mindy of that was to get her mind back on the job. "I assume you didn't just stop in here to deliver towels?" Kate asked.

"Oh, right. You had two messages. One from Mr. Tilghman—" Mindy scrunched up her pretty face as she said Kate's soon-to-be-ex-husband's name "—regarding some papers you were supposed to sign and scheduling that conference call to discuss more terms."

Kate rolled her eyes. "Great, he probably wants to discuss dividing the weekends at the Hamptons cottage. Someone ought to remind him that he was the one cheating on me, not the other way around." Noticing Mindy's sympathetic gaze, she shrugged. "Never mind, thinking out loud again. Okay, I'll get back to him—sometime soon. Please tell me you have something more pressing than that."

"The other message is from Judy."

Kate's internal antenna went up. Judy Burges was the liaison between Kate and her superiors—the men and women who headed up Room 59—and the various division heads and agents around the world.

"What did she say?"

"I asked if she wanted to wait while I got you, but she muttered something about you being indisposed and just said to pass along this message. She was very specific, as always." Mindy smoothed out a crumpled piece of paper and handed to it to Kate. On it were two lines of neat script:

Contact soonest you receive this.
Trouble in Paradise.

Although it sounded cute, Kate knew instantly what Judy was referring to. "Paradise" was their current code name for Cuba, and trouble meant something had happened to their asset there. Without a word, she grabbed a towel from Mindy and wiped her face and neck, then draped it around her shoulders as she headed to her home office.

When Kate had been appointed as the director of Room 59, the town house she lived in had been swept and cleared by the agency, and modifications had been made to every room, particularly this one. As she pulled her chair up to the glass-topped desk, Kate slipped on a pair of MicroEmissive Displays eyescreen glasses, enabling her to access and surf the Web not only wirelessly, but without a keyboard. With precise eye movements, she selected where she wanted to go and blinked to activate programs. She quickly logged in and sent a page to Judy.

Judy Burges was the consummate diplomat. Recruited from England's diplomatic service, she was the only person, besides the shadowy heads of the agency, to have been with Room 59 since its inception. As always, she looked perfect, from her sleek, highlighted brown hair done up in a simple chignon to her immaculate navy pantsuit. Kate smoothed her rumpled *gi* and thanked her lucky stars that she could only be seen from the neck up.

"Good to see you, Kate." There was a barely perceptible pause. "I hope I'm not interrupting anything?"

Kate berated herself for assuming that Judy wouldn't notice anything out of the ordinary. "Not at all. I was just working out when I got your message."

"Naturally." Her clipped tone made clear what Judy thought of Kate's excuse. "You have my message. Our asset in Paradise has not made any of his drops in the last seventy-two hours. Given the rumors of increasing instability there, there is concern that he has been compromised. The heads would like a sitrep and proposed plan of action in an hour. I've downloaded all of the pertinent information for you. Shall I expect you in the conference room at eight-thirty?"

"I'll see you then." Kate broke the connection and leaned back for a moment, taking a deep breath while frowning at the wall. She knew as well as Judy that they had to work together, but that didn't mean they had to like each other. Kate was proud of the work she did, but she couldn't help getting the feeling that the polished Ms. Burges sometimes considered her nothing more than glorified middle management just because she had come to her position through her intelligence-analysis work at the CIA. Kate was extremely aware of the difference in her current position. *If I screw up in this business, it's not just that an operative dies. Hundreds, maybe thousands more could die with him,* she thought.

Kate brought up her instant-message screen, finding Mindy online as usual.

"Hey, what's up?" Mindy typed in response to Kate's greeting.

"Just coffee and a plain bagel this morning—duty calls."

"Right away."

"And let Jake know I'll be in conference until at least nine."

"You got it."

Rising, Kate walked into the adjoining master bath. Shucking the *gi,* blue belt, white cotton pants and her undergarments, Kate stepped into the shower, already analyzing and discarding plans and possibilities. Assuming he has really been compromised, and given the island's current state, will they go for an insertion to get real-eyes intel, or just write him off and move on? If the former, who's available with the necessary background? She reviewed dossiers in her mind, until a likely candidate popped up. Marcus would be the perfect choice, if he's finished with that mission in cattle country.

2

Shit, this is not how it was supposed to go down, Marcus thought, eyeing the meth-cranked biker brandishing a meter-long rusty iron pipe.

"I'm tellin' you, guys, we got a fuckin' rat in the house, and we're all looking at him right now!"

Robbie "Horse" Jenkins shook with the conviction of his drug-fueled suspicions. The biker was a long-term user—in his case, several years, and his face and body showed the ravages of his addiction. His words sprayed out from rotting teeth and his lips, along with the rest of his face, were scabbed and cracked, a by-product of the constant thirst and poor hygiene methamphetamine induced in addicts. His limbs trembled from the damage to his nervous system, but his grip on the pipe was as solid as a rock. The pungent odor wafting from the biker's filthy jeans, T-shirt and grimy leather vest made Marcus think of summertime on his godfather's ranch in Texas, where dead cows would bloat and burst from the heat. Given the choice, he'd rather have smelled one of those stinking carcasses than Horse at the moment.

Marcus adjusted the do-rag atop his curly black hair and grinned. "Hey, Horse, take it easy now. Maybe Terry's a rat and maybe he isn't, but before we pass judgment, let's hear his side of the story, huh?"

The good news was that Horse wasn't inciting the rest of his gang to beat or kill Marcus. The bad news was that he was directing the others' drug-heightened psychosis at their chemist. The skinny, long-haired guy holding both his hands out in front of him had used his two semesters of college chemistry to produce batches of the most potent meth around, which the Death Angels had been distributing to unsuspecting college kids and hard-core addicts throughout a four-state area.

With the government cracking down on the base ingredients for cooking the drug, a pipeline for pseudoephedrine from Asia had been flooding the Pacific Northwest during the past year. Assigned by Room 59 to track the flow back to its source, Marcus was wearing the same pair of jeans and leather jacket he had on when he'd first infiltrated the Angels two months earlier, insinuating himself up the chain of command. He tried hard not to think about what he'd had to do to get there—serve as muscle as the Angels got their shipments and payments, stand by and watch helplessly as the bikers spread their chemical death, inwardly seething with anger as he saw kids with their whole lives ahead of them trading it all for an insidious, deadly addiction. He'd worked through it by concentrating on the end, not the means used to get there, and finally he'd won enough trust for the Angels to take him to the source.

They were in a converted warehouse in the deserted plains of Montana, their drug lab, manufacturing base and the next link in the chain across the Pacific. But his potential link to the supplier was about to get his head bashed in because their strung-out leader was riding a paranoia high.

"For Christ's sake, listen to Smooth, man. I haven't ratted on anybody." While Horse and the rest of the Angels reeked like month-old dirty laundry marinated in sweat and beer, Marcus smelled the fear oozing out of Terry's pores ten feet away.

Horse whipped his head around, wild eyes fixing on Marcus. "Yeah? Why you standin' up for him, man? Maybe you're in on it, too. You and him got a sweet deal goin'? Sell us all out and take over yourself!" He moved toward Marcus, the pipe held in front of him like an orange baseball bat.

Although Marcus knew at least four ways to disarm Horse, six ways to disable him and more ways than he could count to kill him, that was the last thing he wanted. "Hell no, man, I roll with ya, you know that. Just sayin' you want to think a bit before you cap our cook. He's a wizard with the rock, that's all. Be a long time 'fore we find anyone that good at baking again, y'know?" And if you splatter his brains against the wall, my connection goes with him, Marcus thought.

"Yeah…yeah, maybe you're right…." Horse said.

The thing about meth addicts was that their addiction was so powerful, if they could be distracted from their train of thought for a few seconds, they often forgot what they were doing in the first place as the gnawing need made its demands known. Marcus waited. Horse started lowering his pipe.

"Why don't you go take a ride on that M-train and chill?" Marcus relaxed his shoulders and hands, blowing out his breath and shaking his head in mock disapproval at the biker's antics.

Unfortunately, Terry—who was still smart enough to not use his own product—put two and two together at that exact moment. "Holy shit, Horse, that's why he was asking about our supplier last night and angling for a meeting! Smooth doesn't want to take over—he's the goddamn rat!"

For a moment, everyone froze, including Marcus, who maintained his composure even as his mind shifted into overdrive. *I can't believe a dropout college punk just blew my cover—and after I saved his ass, too.*

Before he could say a word, everyone turned to stare at him. And as fast as Horse's rage had dissipated, he whirled and charged, his drawn face twisted in a mask of hate, the pipe raised overhead to crush the other man's skull.

Instead of ducking or dodging out of the way, Marcus stepped forward to meet the biker's wild lunge, pistoning his cowboy-booted foot up and out in a front kick straight at Horse's chest. The heel slammed into the junkie's sunken ribs with a sickening *crack,* and Marcus felt two of them break under his foot. The sudden impact made Horse fold over Marcus's leg, and the pipe came down slowly enough for Marcus to catch it and twist it out of the collapsing biker's hands.

As he pushed off Horse's suddenly limp body, Marcus planted his right foot and brought the pipe down in a diagonal arc, blocking the punch coming from another Angel on his right and breaking the man's arm. He screamed and fell to his knees and Marcus kept turning, tracking his next target. He saw Terry bolt into the depths of the warehouse, but he still had four crank addicts between him and the chemist.

With a wheezing Horse on the ground and another biker moaning and clutching his broken arm, Marcus had only a few seconds until the rest got it together and rushed him. He snapped the pipe out again in a wide arc, keeping them back, but saw them psyching up to charge, so he moved first. Stepping near the guy to his left, he feinted at the biker's head. When the man flinched and leaned back, Marcus swept the pipe down into the Angel's knee. The punk dropped with a howl, clutching the shattered joint, his riding days over for a long time.

The other three all moved at once, the far pair trying to rush Marcus's flank while the nearest one grabbed at his leather jacket. Sliding his right hand to the middle of the pipe, he jerked it up, the capped end thudding into his attacker's solar plexus. The biker's breath whooshed out and he started to fall, but Marcus kept him upright and shoved him back into the other two, both of whom aborted their attacks to dodge their injured buddy. The stunned Angel plopped to the ground on his back, trying to draw breath into his reddening face.

Marcus faced the last two, who had regrouped and now exchanged uneasy glances, having just seen him take down four of their buddies in less than fifteen seconds. Marcus tucked the end of the pipe under his arm, held his other hand out at low guard and stared at them. "If you don't want to end up like them, get the hell out of here right now," he growled.

The pair glanced at their prone comrades and took off, their boots clattering in the cavernous warehouse as they ran for their bikes. Marcus straightened up and turned toward the back of the building, scanning for Terry. The roar of an engine starting warned him of danger even before the pickup truck's headlights came on. The speeding vehicle surged right at Marcus, making him dive out of the way, skidding to a stop on the oil-stained floor. He heard a scream as the truck barreled by, followed by a thump, and then a shriek of shearing metal as the warehouse doors were torn away by the truck roaring out of the place.

Marcus got up and took a step toward the bikes outside, but stopped as he heard the explosive whoosh of fuel igniting behind him. Glancing back, he saw a bright blue flare of natural gas. Damn it, he set off the fuel supply. He looked at the receding pickup truck, then back at the bikers and ran back to them. Even though they were drug-dealing junkie scum, no one deserved to die like that, he thought.

One look at Horse told Marcus he was the one who'd been killed by the truck. The impact had sent him skidding across the floor, his chest and face a bleeding broken mass. The broken-armed biker had gotten to his feet and was trying to help out his stunned buddy, leaving the guy with the blown knee for Marcus. He grabbed the guy's leather collar and dragged him across the concrete floor, barking, "Get the hell out of here!"

The other two Death Angels staggered out behind him just as the volatile chemicals in the warehouse began cooking off, exploding in bursts of shattered glass and metal. "You two keep going, this whole place is gonna blow!" Marcus said. "And take gimpy with you." He patted his man's vest pockets, coming up with the keys to his bike, then shoved him at the other two. "Go!"

Running around to the front of the warehouse, Marcus found the motorcycle that fit the key, switched it on, kicked the starter over and gunned the powerful engine. The straight pipes blatted as he shot away from the burning warehouse and past the trio of bikers, now about forty yards away. He had just shouted "Get down!" when the entire building went up in a huge fireball, spraying sheets of metal and timber framing everywhere.

The shock wave rolled out around Marcus and the motorcycle, forcing him to fight to retain control. Once he had stabilized his ride, he glanced back to see the trio of bikers sprawled on the ground, but all still moving, and none of them on fire. He shifted into second until he hit the dirt road leading away from the warehouse, then opened the bike up, trying to eat up the distance between him and his prey. With less than ten miles to go before the highway, there was a good chance the chemist would reach the main road and be long gone before Marcus got there.

Cresting a small rise, the Room 59 operative caught sight of the pickup as it bounced along the rutted hardpan a half mile away. He twisted the throttle hard. The bike's back tire sprayed gravel as it thundered down the hill. The truck had no chance of outrunning the powerful bike, and Marcus soon drew within a few yards of the pickup, hunching as Terry slewed the vehicle back and forth, kicking up rocks and dirt and forcing Marcus to keep his distance.

He blinked through the cloud of dust thrown up in the truck's wake, his eyes tearing. Okay, I've found him—now what? he wondered. The answer came in the next fifty yards. The dirt road curved sharply, and Terry was forced to slam on the brakes or lose control as he headed into the turn.

Seeing his chance, Marcus aimed the bike left of the truck and pushed the road bike up to the truck's rear fender. He hopped up on the seat, balanced there for a moment, then leaped into the open bed of the pickup.

Though he tried to keep his legs under him and his body loose, Marcus landed hand, falling to his hands and knees and banging his ribs on the wheel well. He shook off the stars and crawled to the back window, rising up and enjoying the sight of Terry's wide, terrified eyes as he saw the scowling biker coming for him in the rearview mirror. The kid slammed on the brakes, pitching Marcus forward to crack his head on the window. Then he jammed the gas pedal to the floor, sending him skittering back across the bed to slam into the tailgate.

"This son of a bitch is pissing me off," Marcus muttered. Using the side of the truck bed, he pulled himself toward the driver's side of the cab. He wedged himself into the corner and yanked off one of his boots, then popped up again and swung the heel at the side window, which exploded across Terry in a spray of safety-glass pellets. The kid shouted and jerked the wheel to the right, the pickup fishtailing as he wrestled for control.

Marcus tossed his boot into the cab and reached in, grabbing Terry by the throat. "Stop right now, or I'll tear your goddamn head off!"

The terrified kid hit the brakes, but Marcus was braced for it this time, and rode with the truck as it skidded to a stop. "Turn it off, slowly," he ordered.

Terry did so, unable to protest due to the steady pressure on his windpipe. Marcus released the scared chemist, then popped him in the jaw, sending him flopping over on the bench seat, out cold.

"Damn, kid, didn't think I hit ya that hard." Marcus swung down from the bed, opened the door and pushed him over to the passenger side. He retrieved his boot and slipped it on, then started the truck and headed for the interstate. "Lost the lab, and the bikers got away. At least I got the guy I came for—and he's even still alive. Asia pipeline, here we come."

He ruffled the unconscious kid's lank hair, then Marcus's expression turned cold for a moment, thinking of that Indian Chief motorcycle he'd had to ditch to get him. Even though he stank like body odor and felt like chopped roadkill, he had enjoyed the riding, the wind in his hair, the feeling of freedom on the open plain. Maybe when all this was over, he'd get himself a bike. But before that, he wanted a long, hot shower, although he doubted the stink would ever wash away—and the wounds to his soul were another matter entirely.

Marcus shook his head as he turned onto the Montana highway. "The things I do for my job."

3

Showered and dressed, with her still damp hair brushed away from her face, Kate had just swallowed the last bite of her toasted bagel when what she liked to call her "analyst alarm" went off—that feeling in the back of her head that something wasn't right.

Why would the agency call a full meeting just to discuss a possible compromised turncoat? she wondered. Something bigger's in the wind. Opening her notebook computer, Kate assessed the file Judy had sent and scanned the contents quickly. The summary title told her everything she needed to know.

"Evaluate Potential of Cuban Exiles Raising PMC Forces for Force Insertion into Homeland."

Kate skimmed the report, whistling at what she read. Now, this definitely calls for our intervention, she concluded. She checked the clock in the corner of her monitor. Ten minutes until the meeting. Calculating the time difference, she placed an overseas call that was answered on the second ring.

"Good morning, Kate."

She smiled at hearing the polite tone, with just a hint of a German accent coloring the man's words. "Keeping Eastern Europe quiet for us, Jonas?" she said.

"Other than your country and Russia still squawking about planting antimissile systems along the bear's border, everyone's either concerned with their own problems or keeping an eye on the Southeast. I gather this isn't a social call, however."

Kate had liked Colonel Jonas Schrader, their Eastern European section head, from the moment she had met him. A fit, no-nonsense, career law-enforcement man, he had made his mark with GSG-9, the antiterrorist arm of the German Bundespolizei, or Federal Border Guard. He had retired several years earlier, but his stellar career had brought him to the attention of Room 59's spymasters. He was an invaluable resource in keeping an eye on all things east of the Rhine, particularly when Russia had started flexing its new energy-backed might.

Unlike Jake, who could often be blunt to the point of rudeness, Jonas retained that European sense of pragmatic calm every time she'd seen him, although she had no doubt he could take care of himself when the time came for deeds instead of words. And, as always, he had gotten right to the point.

"I know this might not be your normal field of expertise, but have you heard anything about exiles making a move on Paradise—whispers of European or other PMCs involved, anything like that?"

She didn't get the reaction she had hoped for—there was

an indrawn hiss of breath, then Jonas's calm voice returned. "I haven't thought of Paradise in a long time. Officially, I've never even been there. I would have thought Denny would be your go-to man for this."

"I figured your background would give you more expertise, given your former company's interest in antiterror operations." Kate checked her watch. Eight minutes left.

"Since the Bay of Pigs failure, there have been militant organizations, such as Alpha 66 and Assault Brigade 2506, that have advocated a violent overthrow of the government. But there hasn't been anything large scale other than the attacks by the now disbanded Omega 7 group in the late 1970s. Over the past three decades there have been small-scale events, the occasional bomb threat or kidnapping, but nothing indicating a bigger operation lately. There are always rumblings of varying degrees, but as far as I know, there hasn't been any real movement on a grand scale, just guerrilla operations, small hit-and-run and sabotage missions. I take it things have changed?"

"Apparently, since I'm heading to the conference room to discuss that very possibility. I'll probably be convening a meeting of the department heads afterward, so don't go anywhere. In fact—" she tapped a few keys on her computer "—I'm making the file available to all department heads now. Take a look while I'm getting approval, and if you'd care to draw up some plans, I'd appreciate whatever input you can provide."

"Kate—" Jonas paused, as if he was thinking about what to say, which she found odd. The ex-commando was never at a loss for words. "As I've said, I was never officially there. But if something is happening, I'd like to be involved."

"No offense, Jonas, but I thought you were retired. And

besides, isn't Paradise a bit far from your normal field of operations?"

He chuckled, a warm sound through the phone. "Kate, what the world doesn't know about some countries' special-forces missions could fill a hundred books, and still not tell everything. Besides, do you remember how we got that particular asset in Cuba? He was on a training junket in Spain when our man made contact. As the agent in charge, I was closer than you might think. Just keep it in mind, if you would."

"Of course, Jonas. I'll be in touch afterward. Goodbye."

Kate broke the connection and paced, pondering the conversation. Jonas had probably already been to Cuba, as GSG-9 had operated around the world, and he'd also been involved in some kind of elite search-and-recovery team inside the organization. Although she knew he kept himself very fit, and could probably still handle himself in most situations, he wasn't an operative in his prime, either. Still…he would be an excellent lead for the operation, particularly if an extraction was needed. Marcus could be the operating pointman, with Jonas gathering intel in the Cuban population in Miami. He could serve as backup if needed.

Kate sat in her desk chair again, mulling over the sketchy plan. It was a risk—typically, Room 59 missions were carried out as clandestinely as possible, using local resources as available. Sending not one, but two officers with direct agency ties into an area could prove extremely hazardous if the mission failed. Kate imagined the look on Judy's face when she gave her the news, as well as the one on the British woman's face if it all went wrong. *I'll just play this by ear and see what comes of it,* she decided.

Slipping on the viewscreen glasses again, Kate scrolled

through her options until the conference room was highlighted. Activating the connection with a blink, the projected computer desktop faded away, replaced by a comfortably appointed meeting room, with nine leather chairs arrayed around a hardwood conference table. Judy was already there, nodding curtly as Kate established her presence through the virtual private network that let her meet with the heads of the International Intelligence Agency, the overseers of Room 59.

Even though she had been the director for more than a year, Kate always felt a thrill whenever she came before the IIA board. Every time a mission was approved, she knew this was why fate or circumstance or maybe even her own dogged persistence had placed her here—to cut through the red tape of partisan opinions and complacency and do what needed to be done.

After the 9/11 disaster, governments around the world had tightened their intelligence and security protocols in many different ways. Some, like America's white elephant, the Department of Homeland Security, were in vain, public attempts to show that the wounded superpower was actually doing something in response to the blood that had been shed with the fall of the Twin Towers. It didn't take long, however, for the organization to become just as compartmentalized, overgrown and slow to act as the rest of the intelligence community. The bickering and partisanship began all over again, only with a brand-new participant scrabbling for its slice of the budget pie and squabbling over duties and powers, instead of doing the job it had been created for—protecting the nation from all threats, foreign and domestic.

Kate had often thought that if the President had really

wanted to utilize his post 9/11 goodwill effectively, he'd have summoned all the heads of Washington's alphabet soup—CIA, FBI, NSA, DOD, DIA, Joint Chiefs and all the rest—together in a room, locked the door and placed armed guards in front of it. He'd tell them they were staying there until they came up with a comprehensive plan to improve intelligence gathering and sharing among all of their agencies, both at home and abroad. Of course, that would have required independent thought and a will to actually get something done on Capitol Hill, Kate thought. Instead politicians did the next-best thing in their minds—spent billions of dollars on a very public but useless solution that couldn't even help its own citizens in a time of national emergency, like a hurricane striking the Gulf Coast.

Fortunately, a group of like-minded individuals from around the world saw the need for an organization that could accomplish what the Homeland Security was supposed to do, only on a global scale. They also recognized that, despite the tremendous cost, they had been given the perfect opportunity to create such an agency. Room 59 was the result of that consensus. It was a completely decentralized agency with the power and ability to go wherever it was needed and do whatever was necessary to defuse, derail or otherwise prevent a potential or growing threat from becoming a full-blown crisis situation. Operating with the secret mandate of the United Nations, and the unofficial approval of every major espionage agency around the world, Room 59 handled the blackest of black operations, and viewed its operations with an eye toward protecting the world and its population, not simply one country, region or continent.

Naturally, this required a special kind of intelligence officer to execute the wide-ranging and hazardous missions assigned to Room 59 operatives. Having the absolute authority to go anywhere, any time, and take any measures necessary to accomplish a mission could corrupt the noblest of motives. Kate was determined to ensure that didn't happen. The one adage that stuck in her mind was a well-known.

"Who watches the watchers?"

From her first day, she had assumed that mantle, and while she would take whatever measures necessary to protect both her operatives and the agency, she also knew that there had to be safeguards in place to ensure that the board or a department head didn't take on a personal vendetta or crusade.

That, she thought, is what Judy doesn't understand about my position. Judy was the operational liaison. She moderated between the spymasters and the operatives in the field, but felt more of a kinship with the department heads and other personnel—hence her thinly veiled view of Kate as a detached, bureaucratic middle manager. Kate, on the other hand, had to balance mission information, parameters and necessities with the desired goals and oversee operations with a minimum of overt agency involvement while giving the operative the best chance of coming back alive.

But, as Room 59 had been designed to operate independently of all known governing bodies, that also meant that there was no one to call for help when a mission went bad. If an operative was caught or killed while on a mission, Kate was supposed to walk away. That had taken some getting used to. She had a mind-set like many military special-forces units—never leave a person behind. However, she also knew that sacrifices were sometimes required to protect the whole, and had reconciled that part of the job as a necessary evil paired with the opportunity to accomplish so much more.

Like we're about to do right now, she thought as the leaders of the IIA convened in the virtual conference room. Unlike Kate and Judy, the ranking members were not visible. Instead, computer-generated avatars in the form of nine black silhouettes represented each member of the board. A small national flag floated above each dark form, representing the United States, United Kingdom, France, Germany, Israel, India, Russia, Japan and China. Neither Kate nor Judy knew who made up the IIA board, and Kate, at least, preferred it that way—if she was ever captured and interrogated, no matter how remote the possibility, she couldn't reveal their identities.

The IIA board approved every mission undertaken by Room 59. Potential operations could be brought up by Kate or other division heads, or by individual members of the board, but in the end, the board voted on each mission, its members presenting various pro and con arguments until a three-quarters vote, either yes or no, was achieved. Even then, the Room 59 heads themselves had the power to veto a mission, but that was rarely exercised, and Kate had never used it during her tenure.

The flags glowed when the person they represented spoke, and the shadow below the Stars and Stripes began the meeting. "All members of the International Intelligence Agency board are present. This meeting is now in session."

Every board member's voice was unaccented, gender neutral and electronically modulated to prevent recognition. As she looked around the table, Kate wondered about these anonymous people who put their personal or political loyalties aside to look at doing what was best for the world in general, and what they brought to the table in terms of knowledge or ability. All the members present had shown a remarkable ability to look at the big picture, and not just at a single region or nation. They were the global policemen of the new century, and they did their job very well. And Kate was determined to do her job equally as well—or better.

The Russian flag flashed. "This discussion is in reference to the potential situation in the Third World country, Cuba. Recent intelligence has suggested that there is a growing movement by exiled hard-liners hiring foreign private military contractors to launch an incursion to overthrow the current Communist dictatorship and install a more democratic government."

Although Judy had referred to Cuba in code across unsecured lines, in the conference room there was no way the conversation could be spied on, as some of the best hackers and electronic security personnel in the world had programmed pieces—with none of them ever knowing the entire project they were creating—of the electronic suite and the secure countermeasures that enabled all of them to meet in perfect seclusion.

The silhouette under the Union Jack responded. "Although on the surface this could be viewed as the fastest way to introduce change, since the human rights abuses that occur in this country have been numerous over the decades, recently reports indicate that with the current leadership in declining physical health, and the infrastructure in growing disrepair, the population is taking steps to establish a more representative government model. A military incursion now could provoke a response by Cuba's armed forces, which are on high alert. The resulting power struggle could create a civil war that could further destabilize the nation."

The U.S. flag picked up the narrative. "Recent exploration of Cuba's coastal waters for oil reserves has drawn attention from nations around the world, particularly those in the Western Hemisphere. Some refining is already happening, and if more resources are found there, the nation's standing will increase dramatically. Certain interests in world government have expressed their desire to slowly relax embargoes and open trade relations with Cuba again."

Kate pursed her lips but refrained from commenting. The more things change, the more they stay the same, she thought. Everything—security, freedom, basic human rights—still followed the money.

"The IIA has determined that it is in Cuba's best interests to assist the peaceful transition to a democratic government, and therefore to investigate and prevent any possible threats to that ongoing process."

The U.S. flag continued. "In our ongoing investigation, we had established contact with a military asset inside the country. Our most recent report indicates that contact with this asset was recently lost. Is that correct?"

Kate cleared her throat. "At this time, there has been no verified contact with our asset in-country for the past three days. We are trying to ascertain whether he has been discovered by the government, or has been captured or eliminated by other factions within the country."

India's flag glowed. "If the threat is coming from an

external source, isn't the asset less important than verifying that a party is indeed planning to launch an incursion?"

Judy intervened. "The asset has been a valuable source of information regarding current events, including the government reaction to what is happening. If he has been compromised, while there is nothing to connect him with us, a valuable source of information will have been lost. And if he reveals surveillance activities under interrogation, the military could be activated again, creating potential blowback onto the civilian population."

The golden stars on China's flag twinkled as its representative addressed the group. "Also, is there the possibility that this asset was a triple agent, and has simply returned to the fold?"

"A hazard of our business," the voice under the Russian flag said, drawing murmurs of assent from the rest.

The Union Jack shone. "Kate, your thoughts?"

Kate leaned forward and made sure to look at each country's silhouette as she replied. "The proposed mission would consist of two parts—locating the elements behind the possible buildup of a paramilitary force and preventing them from launching such a mission, and also the insertion of an operative into Cuba to ascertain whether the asset has been compromised, determine whether an extraction or termination is necessary and learn whether a faction on the island is involved in his unknown status, as well. If there is an internal aspect, and it isn't stopped, it could foment more resistance at a later date, further hampering the progress toward democracy."

The board members all seemed to concur with her reasoning. The Israeli flag glowed. "What external assets do we have that can be utilized?"

Whenever possible, Room 59 tried to use third parties to accomplish a mission goal—whether the person or group being used knew what their true goal was or not. Some of their best missions had been accomplished with no one knowing that Room 59 had been involved in the first place. Sometimes, however, the most effective way of handling a task was with their own people.

Kate placed her hands on the desk and rolled the dice. "Given the sensitive nature of the insertion, we suggest using one of our own operatives, since it would be not only time-consuming to bring in an outside element, but the chance of them being an informer or double agent would be high. As for the mainland operation, I think we should assign a lead operative to this, as well, someone who hasn't been on that scene and can go undercover and extract the necessary information. I already have some of our department heads working on likely candidates who could provide support for such an operation, as well as possible access venues to make initial contact." She saw Judy's eyebrows rise at this, but the British woman said nothing. I'm sure I'll hear about that later, Kate thought.

"Are there any other questions?" The U.S. representative asked, but no one spoke. "I propose that we move to vote on the mission."

Usually, the missions were prepared in a way that almost ensured acceptance, although there were times when the discussion ranged from polite to heated over whether Room 59 should get involved. Kate knew that the American representative had brought up business interest in Cuba as a tacit way of acknowledging that other factors were at play here. She was interested in seeing how the Chinese and Russian members would reply, since Cuba had been establishing relations with both countries after the collapse of the Soviet Union and the post–Cold War chill of the 1990s. Ultimately, the board was supposed to take a world-view of the missions that they put forward or accepted, but Kate also knew that personal or national politics could undermine even the best intentions.

For the vote, all the representatives would signal their position by activating one of two lights above their flag— green indicated approval, red indicated disapproval. Abstention wasn't allowed—a representative could be for or against an action without explaining why, but there was no sitting on the sidelines.

This time, the outcome wasn't in doubt. All of the board members flashed green.

Apparently no one wants another potential civil war breaking out—at least, not in such a high-profile area, Kate mused.

"The board votes unanimous approval of this mission." The lights disappeared and the U.S. flag glowed one last time. "Kate, Judy, good luck."

4

The U.S. Marine, Springfield M-1 rifle at the ready and steel helmet pushed back on his head, advanced across the windswept, snowy ground, his ice-blue eyes scanning for any sign of the enemy. Upon seeing a Chinese Communist soldier, the Marine lifted his rifle and took aim. He froze in place, allowing the grunt to mow him down with ease.

"Scheisse." Jonas tapped his keyboard in frustration. The bug in his program, a real-time computer simulation of the Battle of the Chosin Reservoir during the Korean Conflict, was preventing his units from engaging, or even reacting to a nearby enemy. Jonas had tried everything he could think of to eliminate it, but the fact was that his mind simply wasn't on programming at the moment.

Jonas leaned back in his chair, letting his gaze wander around his sparsely furnished Munich apartment. He had told a white lie to Kate during their conversation, one he was pretty sure she had seen through. But certain things from the past simply couldn't be revealed. He ran a hand over his close-cropped, salt-and-pepper hair as he thought about the first time he had been to Cuba and what he had done there.

June 19, 1973

HIS MOUTH WAS AS DRY as the rubber raft as he approached the night-shrouded Cuban coastline. He glanced at the other members of his insertion team, each dressed from head to toe in black fatigues with HK assault rifles slung over their backs. A thousand yards out, their leader cut the engine, and the other four men broke out paddles and propelled the raft silently toward shore.

After the massacre of Israeli athletes by members of the terrorist group Black September during the 1972 Summer Olympics in Munich, the GSG-9 had been formed to combat terrorist actions within Germany. They had also been tasked with the top-secret mission of tracking down the remaining three members of the terrorists and either terminating them or capturing them for extradition to Israel.

Israeli intelligence had let them know that one of the survivors, Mohammed Safedy, had gone underground, and their resources had reliable information indicating he had appeared in Cuba, for reasons unknown. Jonas and his team had been airlifted to a German freighter off the Cuban coast with authorization to infiltrate the island, locate and extract Safedy. They had a twelve-hour window to accomplish their mission, so every second counted.

With powerful strokes the team made landfall, pulling the raft onto a narrow strip of rocky shore that was almost immediately swallowed by the thick jungle. Jonas got out with the rest to haul the raft ashore, but as he jumped over the gunwale into the water, his foot slipped between two rocks and he felt a sudden stab of pain shoot through his ankle. Gritting his teeth, he didn't make a sound, but hobbled ashore instead, still carrying his section of the raft. He tried to assist with camouflaging it, but his team leader, a small, tough man named Aurel Reinmann, noticed Jonas limping. When he found out what had happened, he decided they would make their initial contact as scheduled, then head inland and find a spot to hole up while figuring out how to best proceed.

Their pointman, Hans, signaled that there was a dim light coming toward them. Everyone froze, and Hans and the man next to him carefully raised their rifles, aiming them at the bobbing light. Jonas extracted his brand-new HK P-9 9 mm from its holster, quietly chambering a round. His breath was fast and rapid in his ears, and he did his best to ignore the pain in his leg, straining to draw a bead on the light as it approached. The flickering light stopped, then vanished, reappeared, then vanished again. Reinmann straightened, waving at his team to stand down.

"Our contact is here." He held up his own compact flashlight and flicked it on and off twice, waited, then flicked it on and off three times. The light answered in kind, and Reinmann motioned for Hans to go out to guide the person to them.

When the tall man returned escorting their contact, Jonas was hard-pressed to conceal his shock. The person who was to provide cover for them was a slender young woman, her hair concealed by a tightly bound kerchief, perhaps twenty years old. She didn't smile, but looked at each man intently.

"One of my men is injured," Reinmann said in German-accented Spanish, pointing at Jonas. "We are continuing the mission, but he will have to stay somewhere while we are gone. Can you hide him?"

The young woman glanced at Jonas, her lips tightening in a thin line at the change in plans, then nodded toward the jungle behind her. *"Vámonos."*

A STEADY BEEPING SOUND made Jonas shake his head, banishing the memory back to the distant past. He thought he'd left all that behind him, buried as part of the things he'd had to do for his country. But judging by his reaction when Kate had told him where the trouble was, that wasn't the case. Deep down, he'd known that someday, what he had done so long ago would come back to him, and now it looked as if it was finally happening.

He had kept an eye on the country, following its slow decline, especially after the Soviet Union disintegrated. Information, even from government sources, slowly dried up as Castro tightened his already suffocating hold. Gradually, Jonas had turned his attention to more-pressing matters, but every so often, a part of him remembered that first mission. He'd been a green recruit tossed halfway around the globe to a place that was completely foreign to anything he had known before. And when the chance had come to acquire a high-ranking mole in the Cuban army, he had led the operation to successfully bring the man into their fold. Now it seemed that was going to extract a price, as well.

He picked up his chirping cell phone, the tone indicating a text message was waiting. He flipped it open to read: "R59 ops room. Five minutes."

No time like the present, he mused, slipping on his own pair of viewscreen glasses and navigating to the Room 59 virtual opps center. Two people were also logged in and Jonas nodded to Denny Talbot, the operations director for North America, and Samantha Rhys-Jones, his counterpart in the United Kingdom.

Kate and Judy appeared in the virtual space. Unlike the board meeting, people were linked face-to-face, and Jonas spotted immediately that something had gone down since he had spoken to Kate earlier that morning. Her expression was grim, her lips compressed together in a tight line. Judy, on the other hand, looked even more reserved and unflappable than ever, a sure sign that something was bothering her, as well, since the stoic side of her came out primarily during a conflict.

Kate started without any preliminaries. "Thank you all for meeting on such short notice. Directors Planchard and Ramon are attending the Middle Eastern crisis conference and Director Kun is observing the China–North Korea summit meeting, so we're it. I trust you've all had a chance to review the dossier on the mission that's just been approved. It's a two-pronged mission, with an insertion into Cuba, as well as an undercover operative going to Miami and finding out who's behind a possible invasion."

"Pardon my skepticism, but are we actually going on a hypothesis that someone is actually going to attempt a Bay of Pigs sequel?" Denny crossed his long legs and leaned back, cradling the back of his head in his hands. "The Cuban army can field anywhere from forty-five to sixty thousand soldiers, probably double that with conscripts, along with artillery and land armor to match, including tanks. They don't have much of an air force nowadays, but can probably put some gunships up to pin down a force long enough for the army to engage at will. Bottom line, while they wouldn't stand up to any first world nation, they certainly ought to be able to pound the hell out of even a sizable insurgency force."

Jonas leaned forward. "All good points. However, based on what I've seen in this dossier, there is a good chance that this group of exiles will have contacted resistance cells in Cuba, and will coordinate with them around an event that would shake the government there to its very core—like an assassination."

Denny snorted. "Of Castro? The man's bulletproof, for god's sake. His own head of security estimated there's been more than six hundred attempts to kill him over the past forty years, so what makes anybody think this time will work?"

"Yes, but when something is tried six hundred times and fails, that makes those who try the next time all the more determined to succeed," Jonas replied.

"Yeah, I'm more fond of the maxim that no battle plan survives contact with the enemy." The agency director stared at the virtual ceiling. "Sounds like a lot of running around and risking necks for one missing double agent," Denny said.

"Gentlemen, I think the main point is being missed here." Samantha Rhys-Jones, recruited straight from British intelligence, regarded them all with her limpid, dark brown eyes. "As I'm sure Mr. Talbot and Mr. Schrader would agree, an invasion of Cuba will likely not resemble other fourth-generation-warfare scenarios, such as the Iraq debacle. The fact is, anyone with enough money can now field a well-equipped, suitably armed force to take over a small Third

World country. If the right preparations are made—and I would certainly include assassination of the current leaders to be among those preparations—along with a sizable force already there turning against the current government, then the resulting confusion could allow the overthrow of the regime. Castro certainly accomplished that with his own ouster of the Batista regime in '59. From what I've seen, so far, this threat is real and should be dealt with before it gets out of hand."

"Thank you, Samantha." Kate brought the meeting back on track. "Recent intel indicates that some of the army generals have grown irritated at the scaling back of the military, as well as their own reassignment to oversee the country's economic holdings. We hadn't any more details before we lost contact with our man. However, we believe there are groups in Cuba that are considering revolution regardless of where it might lead the country, figuring that any change is better than the status quo."

"Which could lead to regional warlords carving the country up into spheres of influence, or an even more totalitarian, corrupt, influence-peddling system arising, where bribes and threats are the only way to get things done—well, more so than they already are," Denny pointed out. "While I'm as cynical as the next intelligence agent—it's hard to believe that their current system is still the way to go."

"As Raul Castro had begun training officers in the military in successful business techniques—before his brother shut it down—it's not that far-fetched. Change can happen internally—look at Libya," Samantha replied.

Kate's gaze swept the virtual room. "We have an operative in mind to handle the insertion onto the island, but need a second to handle the Florida end of things. Denny, I expect you have someone to put forward?"

Jonas cleared his throat. "Actually, Kate, I've been giving this some thought, and would like to volunteer my services on the American end."

Everyone turned to Jonas, who glanced around at each of them, returning to Kate to find her narrowed eyes locked on him. He saw Judy stiffen slightly, but didn't let it phase him. There was something already going on that he didn't know about, but that wasn't his problem.

"I wasn't aware that this was what you meant by being involved, Jonas. It's highly irregular to let a department head undertake a field mission, especially on such short notice." Kate's gaze dropped to the table, and Jonas knew she was thinking furiously. "Denny, this is your theater of operations—therefore, it's also your call."

Now Denny leaned forward in his chair. "Sell me, Jonas."

Jonas smiled, knowing the ex-Navy man would give him a fair shake. Kate, on the other hand, might be a different story. "There are several advantages for me to be the point agent on this mission. First, the majority of our American agents are ex-military, and therefore listed as such on rosters everywhere, despite the agency's best efforts to remove or suppress that information. Even with an excellent cover provided by us, the exiles will most likely be suspicious of an American wishing to provide goods or services, whereas a native German who does not appear on any foreign or domestic military service registers might have an easier time of it."

Denny stroked his chin as he weighed the possibilities. "What cover were you thinking of going in under? Not a mercenary?"

"If the exiles already have an existing contact with a PMC, that would simply cause unnecessary tension. But there is something that both of these groups will want for their operation."

He glanced at Denny, who pointed his finger at Jonas and simply said, "Bang."

"Exactly. An arms dealer will be the perfect cover, and if necessary, we can set up a ship in international waters holding the rest of my supposed wares—all with the right papers and registration, of course. Restricting this to a simple business transaction should lower their guard even further."

"There are several vessels available to us that could serve that purpose," Judy said. "If this moves forward, Dennis, you and I could review suitable ones after we're done here."

"Lastly, any agent that you send in will very likely not be familiar with Cuba, given the risks of insertion in the first place. I have been there several times—" Jonas glanced at Kate and saw the corner of her mouth quirk up in a wry smile "—and am familiar with the locations where our operative is likely to be during his investigation. I would be happy to advise in a mentoring capacity, as well on site if needed—no offense in that regard, Denny."

"None taken. Well, Kate, I don't know about you, but he's got me hooked." He looked expectantly at their director.

Jonas knew Kate was no fool, and figured she was wondering why a department head would volunteer for a mission like this when there were those who were equally or more qualified for the job. He didn't feel the need to explain anything to her, although he wasn't sure what he would do if she asked.

Judy broke the silence first. "What about the current operations you're overseeing? My primary concern is if there is an emergency while you're on assignment and you are unavailable to handle your primary duties."

Jonas had expected Kate to bring this up, but his answer was ready nonetheless. "The current assignments can be routed to headquarters, and I will have up-to-date dossiers prepared on all of them before I leave."

Kate glanced at her liaison. "Judy brings up a good point, however. I'm still having a difficult time reconciling the idea of assigning a department head to a field mission, leaving his ongoing missions in the lurch, possibly to be compromised. I have to think of what's best for everyone, both here and in the field."

"I have an idea." Denny had been leafing through virtual operative dossiers while keeping one ear on the exchange. "I think I know who you want to put into this assignment on the Cuban end—Marcus Ruiz, right?"

"He was one of several candidates on my list. However, he just finished his current assignment and was supposed to have some downtime," Kate replied.

"Yes, there is that, and also the rather explosive way that his last mission ended, even if it was successful. Perhaps it would be a good idea for him to go into the field again, this time under the eye of a more experienced man, learn a few techniques on covert operations. Get back on the horse, so to speak. I can think of only a few better men to learn from than Jonas," Denny said.

Samantha frowned. "From what I read, he stated that the destruction of the warehouse wasn't his fault, given the highly volatile chemicals stored there, as well as the sabotage by one of the drug dealers. Do you have doubts about Mr. Ruiz's capability to handle himself? Given the sensitive nature of this mission, perhaps it would be best to go with someone new, perhaps already in place."

Kate shook her head. "One, it sounds like there's no time, and two, given the high levels of secret police and informants on the island, we wouldn't know if we could trust anyone there. Regardless of his past performance, Marcus is an excellent choice. He's an American-born Cuban, speaks the language with the proper accent and will blend in like a native, which is exactly what we want—someone who won't arouse suspicion."

Judy smiled tightly. "Very well. If Jonas can reroute or clear his schedule, and Denny, with your approval, as this still falls under your oversight, by the way—"

"Then let's get to it," the rangy Tennessean replied. "Jonas, let's conference about setting up your identity after this."

"Then it's agreed," Kate said. "Denny, please contact Marcus and offer my apologies, but I'm afraid we'll need him to be ready to go in the next twelve hours. After this, however, he'll receive the mandatory month off—he has my word. Jonas, looks like we'll be seeing you stateside soon."

"I'm looking forward to it."

"Any other questions?" Kate asked.

"Just one more, if I may?" Jonas leaned forward. "The double agent on site—I assume it is the same one that we turned in Spain?"

"Correct. Is there anything else?" Kate rose from the table. "That's all, people. Let's get to work."

Jonas cut the connection and slipped off the glasses,

wincing at the slight headache they always gave him. He stared at the frozen Marine on the computer screen in front of him and, with a sigh, saved his progress on the program and turned it off.

He envied that young agent who would be heading to Cuba, for a moment even wishing he could take his place. *And what do you think you would do then, old man? Charge over there and invade Cuba yourself? Maybe you should just let the past remain as the past and not go chasing old ghosts.*

Jonas walked to the steel-and-glass bar on the other side of his living room and poured himself a drink—Maker's Mark bourbon, his first and last of the day. As he swallowed the fiery liquid, he considered the real reasons for going over there.

I do have the knowledge and it's extremely unlikely that any of the players would make me for anything other than who I'll pretend to be. And even Denny said it was a good idea to keep an eye on this young agent, he told himself.

But as he drained the glass, he ignored the voice in the back of his mind that was quietly telling him it was all bullshit—that the reason he was putting himself in harm's way again was entirely personal.

His cell phone chimed again, and Jonas looked at it for a moment, then shook off his doubts and got down to business. "Hello, Denny… Yes, it will be good to get back into the field again."

5

With a huge yawn, Marcus Ruiz opened his eyes and reveled in the sensations all around him—a real bed and clean sheets, the aroma of frying ham and toasting bread from the kitchen below, the feel of his hair without weeks of sweat, oil and grease in it. Marcus rolled over and basked in the bright sunshine streaming in through the windows, one thought on his mind.

It's good to be home.

After delivering Terry to his superiors for interrogation, Marcus hadn't wasted a moment getting out of Montana on the first available flight to Florida. Along the way, he had been debriefed by Denny Talbot, and had taken some heat over the destruction of the warehouse and the meth lab evidence. Marcus had defended his work, saying, "Hey, it was six on one, and I still managed to get the guy out in one piece. Now, if you had told me you wanted the place intact, well, I would have done what I could, but you guys said get the link to Asia, which I did—alive—which I also did. Sorry if the locals are stuck sifting ashes. If they wanted to build a case against the Death Angels, someone should have told me. And by the way, the best news I can deliver is that gang won't be pushing crystal meth on anyone for a long, long time."

Denny had said that he would have to take up the mission's parameters with his superiors, and Marcus had replied that he had to do what he had to do, but, "If there's nothing else you need from me right now, I'm heading home." Denny had assured him that he'd certainly earned some downtime and told him to enjoy it.

And now, twenty-two hours and three flight changes later, he was relaxing in his parents' house in Little Havana, his rumbling stomach telling him it was time for some real food for a change. Not like the junk or fast food eaten on the run—when the gang had eaten at all. Marcus suspected he had lost about twelve pounds running with the meth-snorting Angels over the past eight weeks. Time to put some of that back on, he thought with a grin, rolling out of bed and heading for the shower. He had taken one when he had gotten in late last night, but wanted another, just to enjoy it.

Seven minutes later—his Army training still in full effect—dressed in loose cotton pants and a two-pocket guayabera shirt, Marcus ambled downstairs just in time to see his two younger brothers, wrestling in the living room, about to crash into the coffee table.

"*¡Párese!*" Without waiting to see if they would heed his command to stop, Marcus leaped forward to intercept the twins before they damaged themselves or the furniture. "*¡Venga en!* Mother has breakfast waiting."

The trio trooped into the kitchen. The cheerful room was

painted bright yellow with a pattern of blue-and-green curls decorating the walls. Marcus gazed around at the kitchen he had grown up in and where his parents were now raising another generation. They had planned on only having Marcus, but had been surprised with the twins a dozen years ago. Marcus suspected his father, Reynaldo, had secretly been pleased at his virility, as he doted on the boys, often mentioning his plans for them to join the family business.

Their mother, Maria, scolded them, her tone teasing as she delivered the piping-hot, traditional breakfast she always served when Marcus was home—*tostadas, coquetas,* rolls of ground pork and ham dipped in egg batter and fried until golden-brown and strong, sweet *café con leche.*

Marcus had two helpings of everything, then tipped his chair back and stifled a belch. "*Gracias,* Mama." Even though he had his own apartment in the neighborhood, Marcus loved his family and always tried to spend as much time with them as possible, especially after a mission.

"Marcus, will you take us to the movies this afternoon?" Esteban pleaded. He was fascinated with the cinema, and was already making films in the backyard, intending to be the next Steven Spielberg or James Cameron.

His twin brother, Ismael, glared at him. "No, he doesn't want to stay cooped up all day. We should go to the marina, see the speedboat exhibition." A budding speedboat racer, he was as addicted to ESPN and other boating channels as his brother was to film. He could recite statistics on famous powerboat pilots, either current or past champions, with ease.

"All right, that's enough from both of you." Maria silenced the chattering boys with a raised finger. "Marcus has just gotten here. It's not right for you to demand such things from him like this."

"It's all right, Mama, but I wanted to talk to Papa first." Seeing her turn back to the sink, he waved at the boys to head outside and play. Clearing the table, he brought the stack of dishes to her. "How is the store doing?" His father ran the same neighborhood grocery store that he had founded when they had first arrived in America. Marcus had been born three months afterward, making him the first Ruiz to be a natural-born citizen.

"It seems all right, although he says that the big box stores keep cutting into his business and taking his workers, and he doesn't know how he's going to stay open if this continues." She turned to face him. "I've told him that he needs to talk to the chamber of commerce about organizing some kind of referendum, but so far he hasn't listened." She turned away again, rattling dishes as she worked. "Oh, Marcus, you aren't here to listen to me prattle on so."

Marcus took his mother's hand, warm and rough from years of housework, and brought it to his lips for a kiss that left the smell of lemon detergent in its wake. "Mama, that's exactly why I come here, to talk to you. I'll head over to see Papa a bit later, but first I'll take the boys off your hands for the rest of the after—"

The shrill chime of his cell phone interrupted Marcus, and he glanced down in surprise. He shouldn't have heard that tone for another twenty-nine days. He looked up to his mother's face, who also recognized the sound, and now she took his hand, clasping it between hers. "Go on, answer it."

He flipped the phone open. "Hello…Yes, sir… No, I'm available. It's where?… All right, I'll pick him up tomorrow afternoon… Yes, sir… It's all right, but let her know I'll hold her to that. Thank you, sir."

He closed the phone and slowly replaced it in his pocket. For a moment, he stood there with his mother, neither of them saying anything. The chatter and shouts of the twins playing outside reached their ears.

"They need you again."

It wasn't a question. Marcus's parents hadn't been exactly thrilled when he had joined the Army, and less so when he had applied for the Ranger program. But they had learned to respect his passion for the military, and when he had taken this new job, which he described as "government consulting," he knew his mother wasn't naive enough to think it was simple travel and advising. But in their conversations, he had told her that this was what he wanted to do, to give something back to his homeland and their adopted country. Unfortunately, that also meant that there was only one answer he could give her.

He nodded.

"Oh, Marcus, you were gone so long this last time. You tell us not to worry, but I cannot help it—"

He put a finger to her lips. "I know, I know. They wouldn't have asked if it wasn't necessary. At least it shouldn't be too long. They said perhaps five to seven days, so I'll be back before you know it."

"Do you have time to stop by the store and see your father? He would be upset if he didn't see you before you left."

Marcus had spoken with both his parents when he had first arrived, but he'd been so tired he didn't remember much of the conversation. "Of course, Mama. I don't actually start until tomorrow, so at least we'll have this day together. I'll be sure to spend some time with the boys, as well." He walked to the door, then turned in the archway. "At least I'll be doing something you always wanted for me this time."

She frowned in confusion.

"I'm going back home."

6

Major Damason Valdes sat alongside several soldiers from his brigade in a small, sweltering room, pressing headphones to his ears, straining to hear the hushed conversation in a room a few blocks away. He ignored the sweat, the smell and the restlessness of his men, concentrating instead on picking out the vital words that meant he and his unit could go in and do their job. While most other high-ranking officers in Cuba's Revolutionary Armed Forces would have assigned this job to a sergeant, Damason was a firm believer in not ordering his men to any task that he wasn't willing to oversee personally. As a result he'd wound up perspiring in a closed room, listening to a smuggling transaction at two in the morning.

Since the government had been forced to relax the strict sanctions against foreign trade and investment, Cuba had recovered somewhat from the crippling economic blow dealt to it by the breakup of the Soviet Union, their only benefactor since the early 1960s. However, with that inflow of trade had come side effects the country had been ill prepared for, such as an increase in crime. From street violence and robbery to drug and human trafficking, the police were hard-pressed to stem the sudden rise in illegal activity.

Well, they cannot do that and continue to monitor and report on our citizens at the same time with the efficiency the government demands, Damason thought sourly, wiping the sweat from his forehead. Since much of the military had also been reassigned to civilian business projects, he had come up with the idea of using his trained soldiers as an adjunct to the police force when necessary. Formed into handpicked units, the additional men had been paying dividends in the form of a marked decrease in overall crime in the areas they patrolled. But even now he faced rising lawlessness in areas not doubly patrolled, as if the criminals had learned of the combination of police and military, and simply set up shop elsewhere. His commander, General Alejandro Marino, was putting increasing pressure on him to not let the crime spill over into the high-profile tourist areas. The vice squads already had their hands full trying to contain the prostitution that had infiltrated the luxury resorts. If our great revolution would allow educated people to earn an honest wage, then our great leader wouldn't have joked about the prostitutes having college degrees to that American filmmaker a few years ago, he thought bitterly.

Pressing the earphones tightly to his head, Damason heard the words he had been waiting for. "Here is the money—fifty thousand dollars. Now, let's see the merchandise."

What sounded like a cargo door of a panel truck was opened, the racket nearly deafening in his ears. He held his hand up, index finger pointing up, and felt all of his men straighten to attention. Pistols and rifles were quietly checked as he listened for the signal to begin the raid.

The small microphone he had cannibalized from a drug dealer's karaoke machine last year transmitted the frightened whimpers of the "merchandise" the dealers were haggling over—women. They were to be transported to Mexico and used there or in the United States as sex slaves, then killed when their usefulness was at an end. The inhumanity made Damason's blood boil. These men were dealing in human lives as casually as if they were selling cattle, inflicting degradation and suffering on hundreds, maybe even thousands of women. Until tonight.

Damason's middle finger popped up next to his index. The deal was almost consummated. The money was fake, of course. Real dollars had to be pumped into Cuba's flagging economy, to prop up the claims of excellent health care and free education, both of which were provided, but at a terrible cost.

Just when he was about to order his men to move out, a distant rattle caught his attention. It was the sound of another door opening, the garage door to the building. Shouts of *"¡Policía!"* and *"¡No muévase!"* rang in his ears.

"¡Mierda!" He yanked off the earphones. "That pig Gustavo went in too soon! Come on!" Drawing his .45, he yanked the slide back and led his men out the door and down the narrow alley to the crumbling building where the transaction was supposed to be taking place, berating himself for letting the police sergeant in on the raid in the first place. Damason knew how ruthless these slave traders were. He'd seen the report of them throwing their living cargo overboard when accosted by Cuban or U.S. Coast Guard

patrols, hoping the ship would stop for the former captives and allowing them and the rest of the cargo to escape. And even now, as he led his men to the garage, he heard gunshots as the smugglers tried to blast their way out of the trap.

Damason assigned two men to head around the back to see if they could catch the thugs by surprise, while the rest of them took positions at the front of the building and readied their AK-47s. "The truck can only come out this way. Remember, if they try to escape, shoot only at the tires unless you have a clean shot at one of them. They'll still have the women as hostages in the back." It had gone ominously silent inside, with only a hanging light swinging crazily.

He pointed at two more of his men. "Take cover across the street at the corners and make sure that truck doesn't leave." To the other two men he said, "Follow me."

Damason bent over and trotted to one side of the door, his two men right behind him. He smelled gunpowder and blood and heard a truck engine turning over. He ran to the other side of the closed door, then motioned his men to pull it open.

Headlights pierced the darkness as they did so, lighting up the alley as the truck rumbled forward. Automatic-weapons fire strobed the night as a man leaned out the passenger window, spraying bullets into the street. As the truck swerved into the narrow road, Damason stepped up onto the running board and slammed the butt of his pistol into the driver's head. The man fell over, rendered unconscious by the blow. On the other side, the shooter slumped half out of the truck cab, his chest spouting blood from the gunfire of his men.

The truck, still in gear, lurched toward the other side of the street. The two men there ducked back into the alley as

Damason wrenched the wheel to the left, turning the vehicle down the street with the barest scrape of a dented fender against the nearby building. He popped the door open and shoved the smuggler over, grabbing for the gearshift and kicking at the clutch to bring the truck to a stop before it plowed into something. With a screech of clashing gears, it shuddered to a stop in the middle of the street.

Damason turned off the engine, grabbed the motionless driver and dragged him out of the cab, handcuffing him. His men gathered around, and after Damason found keys on his prisoner, he assigned a soldier to guard the man and the rest to come with him to the back of the truck.

They unlocked the doors and opened them to reveal about two dozen women from the ages of fourteen to midtwenties, all dressed in filthy T-shirts and underwear and suffering from dehydration and heat stroke. The cargo area stank of sweat and feces, and Damason spotted a five-gallon bucket in the corner with a hole cut in the top. The majority seemed to be Cuban or Latin American, although there were a few Asian girls, and Damason saw a flash of red hair in the back, which meant at least one European or, heaven forbid, American was inside. They were all huddled together, staring dully at the fatigue-clothed men.

"Get water for these women," he ordered. Two of his men trotted off. Damason turned to his second in command, a smart black sergeant named Elian Garcia Lopez. "Sergeant, make sure these women are given water and treated respectfully. Above all, they are not to be transported from here without my approval."

"*Sí*, Major, it will be done." Elian assigned one man to go in to talk to the women, leading them out one at a time, then began doling out water, cautioning the dazed women to drink slowly.

Another soldier ran up to Damason and saluted. "Major, Sergeant Lopez-Famosa y Fernandez wishes to see you inside."

Damason stifled a sigh as he walked to the building. The police sergeant's name wasn't the only flowery thing about him. He was a preening cock of the walk perfumed with aromatic hair oil and aftershave at all times. The scent drifted around the room in a sickly-smelling cloud. That's probably what gave them away—the smugglers smelled him coming, Damason thought.

He spied Fernandez standing with three other police officers near a prone form that immediately drew his attention. The sergeant prattled on about the good work, but Damason hardly heard him as he knelt next to the body.

The man who had volunteered to act as the buyer for the sting operation had been a quick-witted, genial young man. Santiago Cantara had seen his mandatory army service as a way to learn business skills that would help his family start their own venture someday. In the meantime, he had been the joker of the unit, and morale had soared when he had joined the men. Damason had to talk to him about becoming an officer, as he had possessed all of the skills the army was looking for. Now he was lying on the floor, dead.

Damason put his hand on the man's chest, feeling the stillness of the body, knowing the heart inside would never beat again. He closed his eyes, trying to tamp down the rage coursing through him at this senseless tragedy. He swept the staring eyes shut and muttered a brief prayer over the body, not caring if anyone heard him. Then he stood and turned on his heel, fighting the urge to plant his fist in the oily sergeant's face.

"An excellent job. Everyone will be commended in my report." Sergeant Fernandez nodded with satisfaction.

"What happened to your man?" Damason's voice was low and calm. Cantara had been paired with a veteran undercover police officer, who was nowhere to be found.

"Ah, Officer Garcia was wounded in the leg during the heroic struggle. He was taken to the nearest hospital and is being cared for now. Unfortunately, there was nothing that could be done for your man," the police officer said.

Unfortunately? It should be you lying there in a pool of your own blood, you arrogant bastard! Damason fought to keep his thoughts to himself. He took a step toward the police sergeant, staring at him with his cold blue eyes, knowing his intense stare often unnerved those who weren't used to it. "Why did you order your men to come in before my soldiers were in place?"

The slender, immaculately dressed sergeant didn't quiver, but flicked an imaginary bit of dirt off his uniform lapel and shrugged. "We thought we heard a struggle, so we came hoping to stop these criminals before anyone was hurt." He glanced down at the body and shook his head in feigned sympathy. "Alas, we were too late. When they saw us, they started shooting, and we had to defend ourselves. By the time it was over, I'm afraid your man was already dead."

Damason knew the man was lying—whether it was for glory, or just, as he suspected, simple stupidity, the officer had bungled the raid, and one of his best men had paid the price.

"You did stop the truck, correct?" Fernandez asked, as if the reason for their mission had just occurred to him.

"Correct, and we captured the driver alive." No thanks to you. "With a bit of persuasion, he should lead us to the group that supplies him with the women," Damason said coldly.

"Excellent work, Major! I shall note your men's bravery in my report, as well." He strode to the door. "All that remains is to collect the women and make sure they are secure until preparations can be made to return them to their homes." He turned to walk out of the room.

"My soldiers will help escort the women to a safehouse," Damason said.

Sergeant Fernandez halted in the doorway. "Pardon?"

Damason slowly walked toward the sergeant. "I said my men will assist with escorting the women to a safehouse. There is a large number of them, and they have been through a terrible experience. We want them to feel safe now."

Fernandez half turned, so that his profile was visible in the moonlight. "Major, although I appreciate your offer, it is not necessary. The presence of soldiers has no doubt already confused and frightened these poor women. It will be best for all concerned if we handle them from here." He turned to exit the building.

"Sergeant!" Damason enjoyed putting the steel tone of command in the title.

Fernandez stopped again.

"I must insist, I'm afraid. As this is a joint operation between the police and the military, we all must do our duty and see it through." Besides, if I leave those girls in your hands, they'll likely end up raped or resold, and that isn't going to happen, Damason thought. "I would hate to have to report to my superior that you were not cooperative in this simple matter. We must all do our part in the struggle against crime, you know."

The police sergeant's handsome features twisted in an ugly scowl. "Very well. Your men will accompany us during transport."

"Good." Damason pushed past the police sergeant to his men. "You four will accompany the police and escort these women to their safehouse." He lowered his voice. "Sergeant?"

Elian patted a small notebook in his breast pocket. "Names and nationalities have been recorded. A couple had even memorized their passport numbers."

"Excellent." In the morning, he would make sure that the various consulates had been contacted, so representatives could help the girls get proper identification and travel home safely. He glanced back at Fernandez, who was glowering with his two stooges a few yards away. "Soldiers, make sure that nothing happens to these women during transport or after their arrival, and I will give each of you an extra day's leave."

Brightening at the carrot included in their boring guard duty, the men saluted with pride and returned to the truck. Damason pointed at the building. "Elian, get a detail in there. Cantara didn't make it. I will visit his family later this morning."

His sergeant's shoulders slumped. *"Sí, Mayor."* He headed inside to collect the private's body.

Another truck arrived to take the women. As Damason watched them go, he couldn't stop thinking of the lives that had been lost to free them. Cantara would have said it was right, that it was just, he thought. But if I had known what would have happened beforehand, would I have sacrificed him to save them?

Although he knew what his answer should have been, it brought him no comfort as his men brought the sheet-wrapped body outside.

7

Kate paused in her review of after-mission reports and rubbed the bridge of her nose. *Even with all of the red tape we can cut through, the paperwork never ends. I don't know how any of the normal agencies ever get anything done,* she thought.

"You look like you could use a break." Like magic, Mindy appeared in the doorway, holding a frosted glass. "I brought you some honeysuckle-lemon iced tea."

"How do you do that?" Kate flipped the viewglasses up on her forehead as she accepted the cold glass. The tart-sweet liquid was heaven sliding down her throat, which she hadn't even realized was dry until that moment.

"Do what?" Mindy asked.

"Read my mind when I need something."

Mindy shrugged. "Suvi-Tuuli says it's my gift, that I sense when people I care about are hurt or in distress, and try to help—that's all."

Suvi-Tuuli was Arminda's Estonian grandmother. Kate had met the wizened woman once, and was still trying to decide if she was a contemplative philosophical genius, or simply buck-nuts batty. Whichever it was, at least the good side of her genes ran true in her granddaughter. "That's why I hired you," she said.

"What can I say, serendipity is a wonderful thing." Mindy beamed, and Kate smiled with her, enjoying the pleasant moment.

The room's silence was shattered by the clamor of multiple electronic devices going off. Kate grabbed for her cell phone and slid the glasses down over her eyes. "Yours or mine?" she asked.

Mindy checked her tiny phone. "Not mine. Laundry's done and the *Dr. G: Medical Examiner* marathon is starting. If it's okay with you, you're on your own."

Kate stared at her glasses, reading the message she didn't want to see: "Incoming from Judy Burges."

"Ah, crap. Go, get out of here while you still can. This might not be pretty," Kate said.

Mindy slipped out of the room as Kate steeled herself for the call.

Judy's handsome—no one would ever call her pretty—face appeared on the screen. She was pristine, as always, and stared at Kate like a disapproving nanny would regard a misbehaving child. *How does she do that—she's only five years older than me?* Kate thought, trying not to squirm under the other woman's stare.

"Judy, how are you?"

"Fine, Kate, thank you. I was wondering if you had a moment to discuss this afternoon."

"Well—" Kate looked at the virtual pile of reports to review, and then there was a conference with Denny to follow up on that meth assignment, as well as a half-dozen other operations in progress that needed attending to.

I don't have time to hand-hold my liaison right now, she thought, and then was instantly annoyed at her reaction. No, it's better to deal with this now, rather than letting it fester.

"What's on your mind?" she said pleasantly. She had the satisfaction of seeing an inkling of surprise cross the other woman's patrician features, as if she had expected to be brushed off.

"There seems to be some confusion over the duties that people are carrying out in certain departments. I thought we should discuss it and see if we could clear things up a bit."

"Please, go ahead," Kate said.

"Simply put, a liaison is a person who facilitates communication between one group or office and another," Judy stated.

"True, although I don't have my dictionary handy to confirm the definition." Kate's attempt at humor fell faster than the first and last time she had tried to cook a soufflé.

"Quite. Regardless, in this case I think that the person designated as the liaison isn't being allowed to perform her duties to the best of her ability."

Kate had a master's degree in psychology, but also knew when the time came to cut through the double-talk. "If I can summarize, you don't think you're being utilized effectively?"

To her credit, Judy's expression didn't change an iota, although her voice could have frosted glass. "Correct."

"I see." Kate raised her eyebrows. "Well, how would you like to see the situation changed?"

A lesser woman would have been caught off guard by the verbal lob, but Judy didn't hesitate. "Kate, quite simply, you have a lot on your plate. Directors around the world answering to you, the board calling you at a moment's notice—like this morning—"

"And I appreciated the heads-up there, too," Kate said.

"You're welcome, and that's the perfect example of what I'm getting at. Over the past several months, I've seen a tendency, and I hope you forgive me for implying anything, for you to micromanage things."

Instead of flying into a rage or cutting the other woman off with a cold retort, Kate grinned. "You've noticed, eh?" This time she was rewarded with an answering smile. Finally cracked that frosty reserve, she thought.

"It has come to my attention. A liaison isn't any good if there is no one to liase between. Although I do admire your aggressive attitude toward this job, which is often exactly what's needed. But there isn't a need to take on *everything*. The board has chosen the best men and women from the top down, or else neither one of us would be here. I can help, if you'll let me."

"My God, you must have crushed your opposition at the Oxford debates," Kate said.

"I was part of the Cambridge team, actually, but we did all right."

Kate had the advantage in the conversation, since she had had varying versions of it with almost everyone she had ever known for more than a month or two. Some ended well, like the dialogue with her mentor at the CIA, Herbert Foley, who had been instrumental in her getting her current position. Others, like the colossal throw down with her then husband, Conrad, hadn't ended nearly as well. But through it all, she had let others come to their own conclusions and then moved forward accordingly. Just as she had with Judy.

"While I understand where you're coming from, my main concern is that I certainly don't wish to be cut off from the directors or our operatives in the field," she said.

"Naturally, however, like every other organizational structure, there is a chain of command. Operatives report to their directors, who would then report to HQ, such as it is. There the decision would be made to either handle a situation or bring in more oversight. I can certainly prepare action briefs, or whatever you would like to call them for your review, and of course, if you request a status briefing on a particular mission or region, then we'll crunch the data and present you with whatever is needed, within reason," Judy said.

"Don't worry, Judy, the one thing I'm not is a power-mad office dictator, although sometimes it can be tempting." Kate laughed.

"Then, of course, your decisions would flow down the chain, as well, to be disseminated as necessary," Judy said.

Kate tried to minimize her triumphant smile. It wasn't that she was gloating; everything Judy had said made sense. In a way, she wished they had had this conversation about eight months ago, since all of this could have been dealt with and over a long time ago. "I think we have an excellent way to move forward, and I'm looking forward to it. And I think I'll also take you up on those summary briefs you mentioned. That sounds like a perfect way to start each morning."

"Excellent." Judy's smile was genuine.

"There is one catch, however."

"And that is?"

"I can't promise I'll adapt to this change right away. I'm more of a take-charge-and-charge-ahead kind of person," Kate said.

"Of course, and indeed, there are times when the circumstances may warrant that. I would just hope that you would request assistance at the earliest opportunity."

"I'll do my best. So, speaking of intel flowing up the chain, how are things proceeding with Jonas's cover?"

"What is the term the kids are using today? Ah, yes, he'll be the dopest arms dealer in Florida." Kate almost choked on her tea when she heard the slang come out of Judy's flawless mouth. "The allocation-request program has been extremely useful in this regard."

When Room 59 had been established, one of the tenets that had been struck was that its operatives could use anything from another agency, no questions asked, as long as the resource wasn't slated for the agency's own use at the same time.

"The DEA has a lovely luxury yacht that will serve our purposes very nicely," Judy said.

"I'm sure Jonas will enjoy that, and our other operatives can get a bit of sun as the deck crew. You'll make sure they're all familiarized—" Kate trailed off when she saw Judy's eyebrow rise. "Okay, okay, hey, it's what I do."

"I've already organized a list of operatives with the necessary experience and background to handle the ship. From the captain to the cabin boy, they will all be our people."

"And the ordnance?"

"Oh, we've got something that is sure to pique the interest

of any PMC that's worth their guns. On loan from Defense, but they didn't seem particularly thrilled about it, so we do have to get everything back to them intact," Judy reported.

"Jonas will make sure it all goes out and comes back in one piece," Kate said. Both women checked their watches. "He should be touching down about now, with Marcus greeting him at the airport. Say, Judy, did you ever get nervous when you were in the field?"

The British woman smiled. "Every time. But you learn to deal with it. I've got to run. I have a meeting with Denny on Jonas's cover, and we're putting together the regional comm cell to handle traffic. I'll let you know when that's set up, as well as let you know if anything else comes up in the meantime."

"Great. And thanks for coming to see me. I appreciate it," Kate said.

"You're welcome." Judy's visage winked out, and Kate leaned back in her chair, sighing with relief. *Much better than I had expected.*

A shadow at the door made her look up. Mindy stood there, her hand over the cordless phone. "Remember that message I gave you? About you-know-who?" Kate's blank look spurred the college student on. "Conrad—the paperwork—you were supposed to call him back."

Kate let her head thump back against the top of the chair. She pointed at the phone. "Of course. Let me have that so he can let me have it in general." *If it isn't one thing, it's another,* she thought as she raised the phone to her ear. "Conrad?… I wish I could say the same…."

8   II II65 III II ■ I 59II II ■■ III II ■ I■

Jonas leaned back in his business-class seat and drained the last swallow of complimentary champagne, which he had specifically requested be brought to him before they came in on their final approach. A trim, neatly dressed flight attendant approached, and he handed the empty glass to her.

"Will there be anything else, Mr. Heinemann?" she inquired, using his cover name for this part of the mission.

"Nein, danke." He settled back in his seat and looked out the window, watching the endless, blue expanse of the Atlantic Ocean give way to the bustling metropolis of Miami. Ninety miles south, not visible, but its presence felt all the same, was Cuba. An impossible distance for some, Jonas thought, and a lifetime away for others.

June 19, 1973

THE SLENDER WOMAN LED them through the thick jungle to an abandoned sugar mill that must have been a hundred years old. Its ramshackle buildings were overgrown with jungle foliage, vines and colorful flowers slowly reclaiming the entire area.

Jonas limped in, leaned his G3A3 sniper rifle against the wall and sat down on a pile of canvas sacks before the young woman could say anything. A squeal erupted from the cloth as a half-dozen angry rats boiled out of it and scurried around him, chittering all the while. The rest of the team took up positions around the perimeter while his team leader probed Jonas's injury with gentle fingers.

"It's nothing, sir. I can continue with the mission." Jonas tried not to gasp as his leader pressed on his ankle, sending a bolt of pain through the rest of his foot.

"We cannot risk you slowing us down going there or back. You will have to remain here while we head out." Reinmann stood and turned to the woman, explained the situation and told her to remain, as well, that the team would be in touch once they had ascertained whether Safedy was actually where their contact had said he would be. Then he signaled to his team, and the group melted into the forest, gone in seconds.

With a hangdog expression Jonas watched them go. He tested his foot, but even sitting, the moment he put any weight on it, pain lanced up his leg, and he bit back a groan.

The young woman returned to stand over him, her arms crossed. "Shouldn't you remove your boot?" she asked.

"If I take it off, the swelling will make it impossible to get back on again. Also, it is holding my foot in place, more or less, so there is less chance of causing further damage." He eyed her, sensing her displeasure. "Believe me, I'd rather not be sitting around uselessly. I should be with my team right now, not—" he waved at the ruins around them "—stuck here."

She nodded, then knelt by him. "Your government must want this man very much, to come all this way for him."

Jonas's eyebrows rose at what she knew, although he figured that their contacts here wouldn't have let them in unless there was a damn good reason. Apparently Cuba had enough of its own problems that its people didn't want an international terrorist holing up in their country. "What he and the rest of those animals did was unforgivable." His eyes narrowed as a thought struck him. "Do you know the story?"

She shrugged. "The government tells us only what it thinks we should know, particularly about the outside world."

"Then let me." He related the story of the Summer Olympics and the invasion into what was supposed to be the world coming together in peace and celebration as the best athletes competed against each other. Jonas spoke of the Black September members, and how they took eleven of the Israeli athletes hostage, killing two of them in the Olympic Village. Even though the hurt was still relatively fresh, he told of the botched interception attempt at the airport, which left the nine remaining hostages, five terrorists and a German policeman dead.

"That is why I am here now. My unit was created to prevent something like that from ever happening again." He'd heard rumors that the Israelis were sending their own agents to track down and kill the organizers in the Middle East, but kept that information to himself.

"But to send you and the others on such a dangerous mission. You are just a boy."

"I am older than you," he said.

Her smile was shy. "Perhaps."

"Besides, from what I've heard about your country, your government trains children from the time they are little, indoctrinating them into an obedient, programmed state of mind to follow the orders of the people in charge."

"Much like the Nazis and their Hitler Youth guard of World War II, yes?" the woman said.

Jonas didn't have a comeback for that one.

"But what you say is true, unfortunately. That is why I'm here, risking my life to stop this madman so we can get help against—" She trailed off and cocked an ear, listening to the jungle.

Jonas took the cue and strained his senses, too, trying to catch what had put her on guard. Then he realized it—the animals in the surrounding foliage had gone quiet. Even when the team had been there, the area was filled with the noises of insects, birds and other nocturnal animals. Now they could be heard in the distance, but the nearby cacophony had suddenly gone still, as if the creatures were hiding—or fleeing.

Then he heard a completely different sound—the distant growl of a rough-running engine. Jonas and the woman exchanged glances. "Come on!"

She grabbed his hand and tugged, trying to pull him to his feet. Snatching up his rifle and pack, Jonas managed to get up on his good foot and was surprised when she slipped her head underneath his shoulder. "I can manage," he said.

"Uh-huh, I watched you on the way in. No talk, just walk." Together they hobbled out of the ruined sugar refinery and into the nearby jungle. Just as they edged into cover, pushing broad leaves aside, weak yellow light flooded the clearing.

"Down!" Jonas dived to the ground, taking her with him. She struggled free of him, but remained close, her smooth forehead now smudged with dirt. Eyes blazing, she didn't say anything, but simply watched what unfolded before them.

A large, olive-drab truck came to a stop in the middle of the area. It had barely halted before a dozen men poured from the back, all dressed in military fatigues and carrying AK-47s. They fanned out and searched the area, covering every inch of ground. Jonas held his breath as a man swept past only a few yards away. Two of the men entered the tumbledown building, rifles ready in front of them.

The woman put her lips next to Jonas's ear. "I hope you didn't leave anything in there."

Jonas shook his head, concentrating on the men, assessing their numbers and ability. The pair left the building and spoke to the driver, who turned the truck around and drove back down the road. Men immediately began erasing any evidence of the vehicle having been there.

It was obvious to Jonas what had happened. The mission had been compromised, and these men were here to capture—or more likely kill—the team when they returned.

He got the woman's attention and motioned for her to move farther into the jungle. She crawled away, lifting one limb at a time, checking with every movement to be sure she hadn't been noticed. When she was a few yards away, Jonas began his withdrawal, keeping his eyes on the clearing and the men waiting there.

THE THUD OF THE JET'S WHEELS hitting the tarmac jarred Jonas out of his reverie. He glanced out the window to see the bright, flat runway baking under the Florida sun. Even though the airplane cabin was pressurized and air-conditioned, he already sensed the heat outside, as if it were waiting for him to emerge.

The ten-hour flight had been uneventful, save for some minor turbulence. Jonas had tried to sleep on the way over, but his restless mind kept returning to the same old thoughts. In the decades since that mission, he had returned to Cuba more than once, but had never found any way to lay what had happened that night to rest. And now it looked as if he was going to come face-to-face with the results of that evening, one way or another.

The flight attendant welcomed the passengers to Miami, and he let the words skate over him as he waited for the plane to stop moving, looking like any of the other European tourists or businessmen coming to America. The plane taxied to a stop, and Jonas got out of his seat and removed his small overnight bag from the overhead compartment. Slinging it over his shoulder, he waited for the door to open and walked through the airport to the baggage claim.

Miami International Airport bustled with the start of the tourist season, but Jonas didn't give the assorted wildlife, animal or human, a second glance, scanning the crowd for his contact instead.

A young Hispanic man, dressed in sandals, khakis and a brightly colored shirt held a simple cardboard sign with his cover name on it. Jonas walked over and looked him up and down, then started walking again, the younger man falling into step beside him. "I didn't expect it to be this warm," Jonas said.

"It's not the heat but the humidity that gets to most

people. You'll get used to it soon enough," the young man replied.

"I suppose a good night's sleep will help." The conversation was innocuous enough, but Jonas had given the proper initial code phrase, and more importantly, his contact had given the correct reply, word for word.

Jonas held out his hand. "Pleased to meet you, Mr. Azul."

His new acquaintance took it and shook briskly. "Likewise, Mr. Heinemann. But don't you think this is all rather melodramatic?"

"How so?"

"This back and forth we just did, like something out of the movies. I'd have thought our handlers would have sent a photo of me to your cell to compare faces."

Actually, Jonas did have that, but he knew that his adversaries could always disguise themselves, as well. "Tell that to one of my friends in Europe back in 1987. During a trip behind the Iron Curtain, his contact was made, apprehended and replaced with a government agent. The man said one wrong word when he gave the counter, but my friend passed it off as nervousness and went with him."

"What happened?"

"He spent five years in a Bulgarian prison before being swapped in a trade. His career was over, his health was shattered and he died soon after. All because of one simple wrong word."

"Point taken." The younger man glanced up at him. "I have to admit, you're not what I expected."

"Oh, you were thinking someone younger?"

"No, I read your file. You just appear to be in much better shape than your picture would indicate. Taller, too."

Jonas glanced sidelong at the young man, but got no hint of animosity or insult from him; he had just stated a simple fact. "I do my best."

"Any baggage?"

"Just what you see here."

"You didn't bring any clothes?"

"My wardrobe wasn't appropriate for this assignment." In response to the younger man's quizzical look he said, "I don't own a two-thousand-dollar suit. Yet."

"So we'll need to go shopping?"

"At the best tailor in town."

"That's gonna be expensive."

"Don't worry." Jonas patted his pocket. "It will all be taken care of. In a couple of days it will be time for me to make my entrance into Cuban-exile society."

Damason rested his head on one hand as he held an ancient black Bakelite telephone receiver to his ear. Stifling a yawn, he tried to pay attention to his commanding officer's stream of orders and questions.

"Yes, colonel. I have followed up on all of the freed women, and their various consulates are working on getting them back home, as well. No, at this time I have not yet received a report concerning the interrogation. I will get it as soon as possible. Yes, of course we wish to eradicate this loathsome pestilence of human smuggling. I will keep you informed at all times. Thank you, colonel. *¡Sí, viva la revolución!*"

He replaced the receiver and rested his head in his hands. Since the morning's activity he'd had about two hour's sleep, and now felt as if the smugglers' panel truck had run him over. However, there were still a few hours to go until he could rest. Even then he knew his respite might be brief, for army officers were supposed to be "vigilant and ready to fight for the revolution at all times," according to one of their leader's interminable, three-hour speeches he often inflicted on the military.

Indeed, if the man spent as much time working on the problems of our nation as he did haranguing its citizens, we would be the most powerful country in the world, Damason thought. He pushed back on the two legs of his chair, feeling the old wood creak beneath him. Like everything else in his tiny office, the furniture was worn to its breaking point. Every time he leaned back, he half expected to end up on the ground as the battered piece of furniture, used beyond its ability, finally collapsed under his weight. So far, however, it hadn't happened.

If only my faith in our leader was as strong, he mused. In the beginning, it had not been that way. Indeed, there had been no other way but the revolution. Raised as an orphan during the turbulent 1970s, Damason had gone to a state-run school, where he had been indoctrinated into the Communist philosophy and, having nothing else in his life, had embraced it fervently, becoming one of the revolution's most ardent supporters. For him, the only way forward was to join the army of the revolution, pledging to fight against all oppressors of the glorious Cuban state. His ascent through the ranks, first as a member of Castro Rebel Youth group, then as a full-fledged member of the army at age eighteen, was rapid and distinguished. Too young for service in Angola, Ethiopia or Nicaragua, Damason became a *soldado* just two years before the U.S.S.R. collapsed in 1991, cutting off all funding to Cuba.

At the time, Damason had still believed that Castro would find a way to enable his country to regain its footing. Even through the crippling recession, blackouts and food shortages, the struggle to create industries and goods to export for much-needed technology, medicines and other supplies, he had believed El Comandante's assurances that Cuba's health care was supreme, and that their country would weather this "special period." Like the rest of the army, Damason spent much of his time ferreting out traitors, political dissidents and informers, anyone who could be working against the revolution. He had sent many to his nation's infamous prisons.

But even then he had seen signs that there were problems with Castro's idea of a peaceful, content Communist nation. The hasty trial and execution of Arnaldo Ochoa Sánchez in 1989, one of the finest generals Cuba had ever known and a hero of the revolution, had forced Damason to reconsider his blind faith in Castro and his vision for Cuba. The *soldado* had heard nothing but praise for "El Moro," as his soldiers and other officers had referred to him, yet suddenly he was on trial for drug smuggling, corruption and treason. His swift execution, and the widespread rumor that it was because he was a realist who agreed with many of Mikhail Gorbachev's reforms instead of an ideologue toeing Castro's inflexible party line, had caused the first crack in Damason's previously unshakable dedication to the cause.

Then he, along with several dozen other officers, had been sent to Europe under a pilot program spearheaded by Raul Castro to learn accounting and business practices. They were to return to the island and use this new knowledge to improve the infrastructure as the military began its steady takeover of many Cuban business sectors, including agriculture, the tourist trade, air transportation and much more.

Although Damason did learn much about how to run a profitable business, what was even more valuable to him was the time spent with the people in other countries. He was stunned to discover the many personal freedoms that people enjoyed in places like Spain and Sweden. The cultures, opinions and philosophies that he was exposed to only served to illustrate the wide gulf between the Cuban people and the rest of the world. When he had naively tried to explain that Cuba was the greatest nation in the Western Hemisphere, he was astonished at how quickly others dismantled his arguments. Most piercing was a piece of advice from a Spanish professor who said, "When you return home, try to look at it not from the viewpoint of a Communist, or even a Cuban, but simply as a human being, and ask yourself, 'Is this how human beings should live?' A leader truly dedicated to his people would put them first, not his cause or ideology."

When he had returned to his homeland, he had taken a good look around and saw, as if for the first time, the crushing poverty, the unemployment or menial jobs available to many people, the high education level yet the scarcity of appropriate jobs for white-collar workers and, increasing more and more every day, the tourist apartheid, as it was referred to by many outside the nation, where resorts, beaches and other areas were available only to foreign travelers and off-limits to Cuba's own people. The law was even enforced by the police officers, putting the foreign dollars before their own countrymen.

When Castro eliminated the reform programs his brother had instituted, he announced that those changes were counterrevolutionary. There was an increase in crime and corruption, but no change in the everyday life of the average Cuban citizen, who still existed on only a few dollars a day. When he heard that message broadcast to the people,

Damason had realized an inescapable fact—Castro and the state-controlled media said one thing, but the neighborhoods and people of Cuba showed the exact opposite. He had gone out and seen the truth with his own eyes.

And if Castro was wrong, then what did that make him? What did that make a man who had spent his entire life following the orders of a leader he'd respected and trusted, a leader who had ordered him to spread fear, to punish the innocent, to brutally oppress those who were simply trying to improve their lives and the lives of those around them?

A lesser man would have broken under the weight of having his world so completely shattered. Growing up in the streets, Damason had learned to rely on himself, and only himself, to survive, and when this reality was forced upon him, he turned from Castro, turned from Communism and turned inward to survive. Outwardly, he was the same person that everyone else knew—a dedicated soldier, a loving father, a staunch Communist. On the inside, however, he was a seething storm of rage at what was being done to his country, to his fellow citizens, all in the name of a failed ideology that should have died out with its creators in the previous century.

It happened one night at home, when Damason was playing with his two young daughters. As he watched them chase each other around their bare, crumbling, three-room apartment, he had realized a second vital truth. He did not want his daughters growing up in the same environment that he had. He wanted them to have the freedom to choose what to do with their lives, not have things forced upon them. He did not want to see his daughters, the twin joys of his life, turned into subservient Communist lackeys, working all their lives for someone else's outmoded ideal of a disintegrating social model.

Damason decided that night that something had to be done. The only question was, what? The entire island was riddled with informers and secret police. A wrong word to the wrong person could land him in prison next to the very men he had persecuted for years. It was nearly impossible to figure out who might be willing to gamble everything on a desperate bid for freedom and everything—good and bad—that might bring.

There was a bigger problem that affected his decision— his family. Damason had fallen in love when he was a corporal, and married a wonderful woman who had borne him two lovely children. The path he was considering would put them in terrible danger and could very well mean their deaths. It was just another aspect of what he wrestled with every day, trying to reconcile what he could do for his country with the realities of the situation.

There had already been some attempts to initiate change—of that he was sure. While in Spain, he had been approached by a university student who had put him in touch with a small division of the State Department of the U.S. government, requesting information about Cuba's government and its military. At the time, he had rebuffed the man and even let the people at the university know what had happened. But he hadn't told any of his fellow officers, nor had he let his superiors know about the incident upon his return home.

When he had come to his realization, he managed to contact that same student, who put him in touch with an American contact. He had fed information to that contact for over a year. He would drop the most recent data he had, and would receive confirmation that it had been received, but nothing was any different. Damason had come to the realization that something more needed to be done.

Then, one sultry night Damason had been walking home in civilian clothes, thinking, as always, about what he could do, when he came upon what appeared to be a simple street mugging. Stepping in to break it up, he met an American businessman named Samuel Carstairs, who had thanked him profusely and had insisted on buying him a drink. Initially wary—although he couldn't see the Cuban government using an American to entrap its own citizens—he had agreed and took the balding, sweating man to a local watering hole, where Damason was a regular, and more importantly, they wouldn't be bothered.

Carstairs leaned back and fanned himself with his hat. "I'll have a rum and cola, *por favor.*"

Damason ordered the same, and sipped his drink, nodding when Carstairs handed over crisp U.S. dollars instead of pesos to the bartender, who made them disappear in a second. "You know what we call this back home nowadays?" Damason shook his head. "A *mentirita.*"

He chuckled, and Damason tried not to show his hackles rising too much. The term meant "*a little lie*" and was used by both Cubans and Americans as a derogatory reference to the island's politics.

Is he a spy? Is the government trying to entrap me? Damason wondered. He decided to play along for the time being. "Where are you from?" he asked politely.

"My company does business all over the world, but I

work at its headquarters in Miami. I handle foreign accounts, which is why I'm here. And what do you do?"

The rum had loosened his tongue, and Damason figured he had nothing to lose. "I'm a major in the Cuban army."

The American leaned forward and fixed his new friend with an appraising stare. "Are you going to arrest me for buying you a drink?"

The straightforward question was so ludicrous that Damason roared with laughter and ordered another round. The ice broken, their friendship had progressed along with the evening, until they both stumbled back to Carstairs's hotel, located in the resort area, hours later. They had talked of many things—baseball, U.S.-Cuban relations, the embargo, politics. Damason had known that he had probably told this man too much—his despair at Cuba's current situation, and the knowledge that nothing was likely to change until the government did. A part of his mind screamed at him during the conversation that he was committing treason, that what he was saying would land him in prison, but he didn't care. The opportunity to talk to someone, anyone about what had been gnawing at his soul for months was simply too good to pass up, even if it meant he might suffer as a result.

At the end of the evening, Carstairs shook his hand and pressed a small cell phone into it. Suddenly he did not seem as intoxicated as he had been earlier. "There is someone that I want you to meet. He will send you a message on this phone, and you can reply to it at your convenience. I think you and he would have much to talk about."

Damason's paranoia was too muted by the alcohol to grasp the import of the other man's words. The next morning, with his head aching and his tongue fuzzy, he stumbled across the small cell phone and tucked it into his pocket before his wife and daughters returned home from their trip to see her parents. All day he carried it, its insignificant few ounces of plastic and electronics weighing him down like lead in his pocket. His thoughts were consumed both by guilt at what he had done and the danger he might have put his family in. He wondered if this was a new kind of trap, if using the phone would bring the secret police to his door. But at last, when he was alone and sure he wasn't going to be bothered, he made his decision; if he didn't take this chance now, he would never be able to do anything to help free his country. He flipped open the cell phone to read the text message on the screen: "Do you wish to help your country change its direction?"

There were two options: yes and no. Damason didn't hesitate. He pressed the button for yes. A number appeared on the screen, and gave him instructions when to call. Damason made sure his office door was locked, then dialed that number, waiting with bated breath for the connection to be made. After several clicks, he heard a voice: "Is this the person who wants to change his country's direction?"

Damason swallowed, then committed himself. *"Sí."*

Before he knew it he was involved in the greatest operation that was going to occur to his country—the retaking of Cuba from the Communists, and placing it squarely in the hands of the people. And once he had proved he was who he claimed to be, Damason was assigned an integral part in this new revolution.

Unfortunately, that also required sacrifices from people like Francisco Garcia Romero. Damason had received a message that Romero was in prison, and had to be eliminated before he could go to trial, or more importantly, before he revealed any details, no matter how minor, about the upcoming operation. Damason had reviewed the case, and didn't believe there was any reason for alarm, but the voice on the other end of the phone had assured him that Romero had information that could cripple, or even expose their plan. He had to be removed. "Besides, after eight months in prison, most likely you will be doing him a favor," the voice had said.

After seeing the state Romero had been reduced to, Damason had been inclined to agree. He was even more upset at the indignities and torments that were inflicted on people who just wanted to speak their minds. Those, along with the death of good soldiers like Cantara, were consequences that had to be accepted if Damason truly wanted to help his country. And he wanted that more than almost anything else in the world.

Damason shook himself out of his reverie. Just like that first day, he made sure his door was locked. He lifted his desk onto its side. The right desk leg was loose, and he pulled it out, revealing a hollow just big enough for the phone. He had made the hiding place himself, a bit at a time over several weeks, carrying out the wood shavings in his pockets bit by bit every day. The internal batteries had died long ago, so he relied on a jury-rigged battery pack that could be plugged into the phone's power jack. It only lasted for about ten minutes, but would do the job.

He plugged the batteries in, flipped the phone open and smiled. There was a message. Damason dialed the number given and waited for the connection, savoring the fact that the countdown was about to begin, heralding a new dawn of freedom for a nation that had been suffering for over forty years.

10

Kate stood staring at a large screen in a virtual surveillance suite, surrounded by men and women all in front of computer screens, each monitoring or researching possible illegal activity around the world.

Along with its other perks, Room 59 had been granted carte blanche back-door access to many computer systems, civilian and military, around the world. Any they didn't have immediate access to, a pool of brilliant, determined hackers could break into at a moment's notice. Although they didn't know the true identities of the others, as Room 59 kept them isolated just like everyone else, the young programming turks had formed a loose cadre and had a running bet to see who could hack an approved site in the shortest time. The current record holder was a girl—at least Kate thought of her as a girl—whose online handle was Born2Slyde. She had cracked a multinational online security company's mainframe in under five minutes. She was now leading an operation, providing electronic backup and intel to an operative tracking a large former Russian army weapons ring.

Kate leaned over the girl's virtual shoulder. She was viewing three monitors while watching some kind of incomprehensible *anime* program that featured a schoolgirl in a short dress running around feudal Japan with a guy dressed in red robes and carrying a huge sword who had either white or black hair, depending on whether he was a human, half-dog demon or something else completely. B2S had tried to explain it to her once, but Kate's head had spun after hearing two minutes of the vast, complicated plot.

As her system sensed Kate's presence, B2S acknowledged her with a small nod of her head, her multiple earrings tinkling softly, but her mascara-ringed eyes not leaving the main screen, which showed a meeting in progress on a remote army base in Siberia. B2S was piggybacking on a French telecommunications satellite to record the movement of vehicles and people and also monitoring the surrounding area to make sure no one was planning an ambush. All the bases were covered, Kate saw with satisfaction.

A soft chime in her ear signaled that the Paradise operation room was ready. Kate popped up an instant messaging screen in front of B2S. "You got it covered here?" Kate typed.

"GTG," Kate read—hacker slang for "*good to go.*"

"Okay, contact me if anything happens, or afterward," Kate signed off.

The girl nodded, intent on the crime unfolding before her. Kate smiled and headed for the Paradise op room, thinking that the U.S. intelligence agencies' loss was her gain. It was doubtful that B2S would even make it in the front door of any of the alphabet-soup agencies, but she was one of the best hackers anywhere in the world. The fact that she lived in Saudi Arabia would have bothered some people, but Kate had insisted on the best of the best, no matter where they lived, and once she gave them the recruiting spiel, almost everyone wanted in. They could never talk about what they did and were monitored constantly from a secondary location, just in case of attempted subversion, but so far there had never been a leak on-line about any covert activity. In fact, the hackers often brought Kate intel on possible security violations before any of the directors even knew there might be a problem. They were also paid extremely well for their work through several dummy companies set up for just such a purpose.

The muted activity around her faded out of sight, replaced by a room with a row of three terminals, all occupied by avatars of the three hackers readying their programs. Once activated, they would work in shifts so that at least one was always on duty.

Judy was also in the room, and greeted Kate with a nod.

"Who's heading this one?" Kate asked.

"We've got KeyWiz as team lead, with El Supremo and NiteMaster as seconds."

Kate shook her head. "Boys will be boys. Speaking of, where's ours?"

Judy contacted KeyWiz, who was running his op out of a bedroom in Alameda, California. "Key, please show us the operatives."

He raised a finger and a moment later a map of Miami appeared, with two tiny green blips representing Jonas and Marcus, traveling south on Forty-second Avenue toward

Coral Gables. They pulled into a side street a few blocks from the Miracle Mile.

"Operatives are entering a custom tailor's clothing store."

All the operatives who agreed to work for Room 59 were implanted with a small passive microchip that wouldn't show up on any body scans or airport security equipment, but would enable Room 59 to track them wherever they went. The chips had saved the lives of several operatives in the past and were mandatory for anyone in the field or their handlers—Kate, Judy and Denny included.

"Jonas must be getting outfitted." Kate shrugged. "I suppose you have to look the part."

"I just hope he upgrades his wardrobe enough for the yacht he's going to be playing arms dealer on." Judy brought up a picture, and Kate's eyebrows shot up in disbelief. "This is what one of the Bogota cartel was running around in a few months ago," Judy explained.

"I think my entire town house can fit on the bow, with room left over for something small, like, oh, Yankee Stadium," Kate said.

Judy stared at the picture. "It's times like this when I find myself reconsidering the decision to leave the field."

"Maybe so, but then again, we won't be facing Cuban exiles forming their own army to try and take back their homeland, either, and I can have a great piña colada at any one of a dozen places in New York City." Kate paused. "That is, if I ever took a night off."

Another chime rang, and a moment later Denny appeared in the room, knotting a black tie around his neck. "Kate, Judy, good to see you both. I've got the information requested on one of the leaders of this exile group for you to pass on to Jonas."

Before replying, Kate isolated their conversation from the hackers. "Wonderful. Got a minute to give us the highlights?"

"Sure, the Ingersoll Rand party doesn't start until five." Denny finished knotting his tie and straightened it, staring off into space as if he was looking into a mirror. "Our most likely suspect is a man named Rafael Castilo." He brought up a photo of a stocky man with thick dark hair and wearing a tailored, tropical-weight silk suit, shaking hands with another suited gentleman. "The man on the right is Castilo. He's shaking hands with the mayor of Miami as they celebrated the twenty-fifth anniversary of the founding of his very first business, a delivery service he started when he was seventeen. It's the largest intracity delivery service today, holding a near monopoly on the trade."

"A self-made man." Kate studied the picture. Mr. Castilo was the poster boy of American prosperity. "What's his background?"

"He came to Florida in 1967 at age fourteen, a victim of the purges during the 1960s. His parents were both killed in Cuba. He landed in Miami right after the U.S. passed the Cuban American Adjustment Act, intended to give exiles and refugees a leg up in making a life for themselves. Castilo is certainly one of the success stories—entrepreneur at seventeen, branched out into real estate at age twenty and engineered his first hostile takeover, of Miami Imports/Exports, at twenty-four. That business has grown twenty times larger in size in the past three decades. He has a master's degree in business administration from the Warrington College of Business Administration. Even though the Ivy League courted him, he said he wanted to learn where he had grown up. Estimated net worth, approximately 1.2 billion."

Judy pursed her lips. "Surely he has a few tens of millions available to give to Cuba's poor, right?"

Denny chuckled. "He might have tried that, if Congress hadn't made it illegal for U.S. businesses to deal with Cuban businesses. He does send money through his overseas branches, but that's a drop in the bucket. Apparently he's decided to raise the stakes a bit. Representatives from all of the major PMCs have recently taken meetings with his people. In fact, the folks at one of them passed this info on to us. Castilo's rep was always very careful not to say anything incriminating, but he was just looking for a PMC that could field a force as large as two battalions, with equipment for an overseas mission in a tropical climate for up to six months, citing foreign expansion into potentially dangerous markets. Since there's no way any American group will take this on, most likely we'll be looking at foreign PMCs, probably operating on the shady side, since they will basically be invading a sovereign country, for all intents and purposes."

"Great, the first attempted takeover by a private army since William Eaton captured Derna in Tripoli in 1805, only this time it's about to happen in our own backyard." Kate shrugged as both Denny and Judy stared at her with their mouths open. "What—I like military history. So, Jonas drops Marcus off to find our contact, and he goes after Castilo. One question—if Jonas is an arms dealer, why wouldn't he deal with the PMC directly?"

Denny nodded. "That's a good one. Jonas and I discussed that, and we both believe that Castilo's flamboyant nature and overwhelming desire to help his countrymen will make him take unusual risks, even for a prominent businessman, such as setting up a meeting between his PMC and a seller. The trick will be to appeal to his revolutionary side, as it were."

"Well, Jonas and Castilo are close in. I'm sure he'll come up with some points in common that they both share—the oppression of communism, for example," Judy said as she clasped her hands on front of her. "How are you getting those two face-to-face, by the way?"

"One of Castilo's hobbies is greyhound racing. We've set up Mr. Heinemann to casually run into him at the Palm Beach Kennel Club. Of course, that's once he drops Marcus off in Paradise."

"I wonder what Marcus will think of his homeland today." Kate turned back to the three hackers and opened a voice link to them. "Everything ready here?"

KeyWiz responded immediately. "We've got scheduled satellites orbiting over Cuba and the surrounding waters, providing coverage for the next seventy-two hours, and we're on top of your man in Miami, as well."

"All right, it's show time." Kate crossed her arms, resisting the urge to nibble on her nails, a nervous habit she acquired whenever one of her operatives entered the field. "Let's do it."

11

Marcus couldn't stop staring. "It's unbelievable."

"And I thought I was the tourist here." Jonas nudged him. "Close your mouth—the flies will get in."

They both gazed at the luxury yacht that Jonas would be using for his cover while in Miami. The *Deep Water* was a custom-built, 180-foot yacht with a plush interior that could comfortably sleep ten passengers. The quad-deck design featured a gymnasium, sun deck, hot tub, Jet Skis, Wave Runners and Windsurfers. It carried a crew of eleven, plus the captain. With a top speed of twenty-one knots, the ship's clean white hull and aerodynamic lines made it look as if it were cutting through the water even while at anchor.

"Unfortunately, you will not be accompanying me on it, as getting you to your destination will mean relying on speed and hopefully stealth, not opulent luxury," Jonas said.

"Too bad, I've always wondered what the interior of one of those looked like."

"Make division head, and you'll find out."

"Yeah, speaking of, that does bring up a question, sir—just why are you overseeing this operation?" Marcus asked.

Jonas stared at him from behind his sunglasses. The kid's not just charm and good looks, he thought. "Our superiors felt that I was the right person to handle this op, and that's all you need to know. Now, come on, let's get you ready for your insertion."

FIVE HOURS LATER, Marcus called out, "This is more like it."

They were riding in the cockpit of a Tiara 4200 Open yacht as it knifed through the calm Atlantic Ocean at thirty knots. Twin Caterpillar C-12 diesel engines rumbled behind them, propelling the pleasure craft through the darkness toward Cuba.

"I thought we'd be using a cigarette boat for this, you know, something more *Miami Vice*." Marcus wriggled into his one-piece, black, three-quarter wet suit.

"It's bad enough that I'm dropping you off as it is, but just how much attention do you want to attract?" Jonas sat at the helm, dressed in khaki shorts, a short-sleeved shirt and a light windbreaker. His face was lit in a greenish tinge by the radar array and control board. "This way, I can claim to be just another European tourist lost at sea."

"Yeah, if they don't nab you on suspicion of ferrying illegals." Marcus checked the regulator of his scuba tank, then measured his weights out. Nearby was his water-proofed package of gear, along with the small, battery-powered underwater sled that would carry him to shore.

Jonas reached under the console to reveal the butt of a HK P-30 V1 9 mm pistol. "I'm ready to repel boarders.

Besides, current military reports say the majority of Cuban patrol boats are inoperable."

"Now who's looking to draw attention?" Marcus asked with a grin. "It's not the regular patrol boats you should be worried about, but the confiscated ones they've been using against the smugglers." He peered out at the darkness, searching for the island he'd be stepping on for the first time in his life—his homeland. "Thousands of people try to flee every year. Only in this job would I actually be trying to get *into* Cuba."

"Don't worry about it—you'll do fine." Jonas checked his watch. "ETA to drop point twenty minutes. You're sure you can handle the insert?"

"Ranger training made us swim for hours carrying full gear. With the sled, this won't even count as exercise."

The two men fell silent for the next few minutes, each concentrating on the job he had to do. For Marcus, a water incursion was simple enough, although he'd have preferred a HALO drop over the island—less risk to everyone. However, if Mr. Heinemann was as adept at nautical excursions as he had been at ordering his wardrobe at the tailor, then he could more than handle himself. He glanced over the older German, who sat at the yacht's controls like a steady stone pillar, making minute adjustments to their course. Marcus thought he had a good idea why their handlers had chosen him—the man looked as if he'd seen it all, but could still handle anything the covert life threw at him. And the ease with which he handled navigating down to Cuba made Marcus suspect he'd been there before.

"Hey," he called as he slung the air tank and vest on his back. "Sorry about the third degree earlier."

Jonas's eyebrow rose as he glanced over. "Accepted, but unnecessary. Were our positions reversed, I would have wondered the same thing myself."

"But…?" Marcus waited for more.

The corner of Jonas's mouth crooked up in a half smile. "But I would have left it at just wondering."

"Touché." Marcus put on his weight belt, adjusted it, then tested his regulator again. He spit in his mask and rinsed it out with water. Next he checked his fins, making sure they were snug and comfortable on his feet.

"Ten minutes to insertion point." Just as he said that, Jonas saw a flash of light from the southwest, which rapidly grew larger. "You weren't kidding—they are patrolling tonight." Although they had chosen an area that should have been deserted, the boat approaching proved otherwise.

"Damn, must be Cuban Border Patrol. No one else would have lights on out here." Marcus crouched down as the spotlight played over the pleasure boat. "Looks like I get off here."

"No, we're too far out. The currents could sweep you completely past the island. Let me go a bit closer. Get on the port side and stay as low as you can," Jonas said.

The boat was much closer now, and was a similar style to what Jonas was piloting, although about fifteen feet shorter. Three men dressed in olive fatigues stood in the cockpit, one piloting the boat, one next to him holding an AK-47 rifle and the third with a megaphone to his lips.

"*¡Pare el barco!*" he shouted.

Jonas held his hand to his ear and shrugged.

"These guys don't have any compunction about shooting suspected smugglers, you know," Marcus hissed.

"Just a few more seconds—go when I turn hard to port."

"Are you sure—it's three to one—"

"Go on my mark. That's an order."

Marcus dropped his mask and gave Jonas the thumbs-up.

"¡Pare el barco inmediatamente!" To punctuate the request, the armed Cuban fired a short burst across the pleasure yacht's bow.

Nodding his head vigorously, Jonas waited another five seconds, bringing Marcus a hundred yards closer to the island, then spun the wheel hard left, making the forty-four-foot craft gracefully turn away. "Go," he whispered.

As soon as he felt the yacht lean, Marcus popped up and out, following his gear into the warm water.

12

"He's dead in the water. Second agent is away from the craft."

"You know, I would appreciate it if you didn't use phrases like that at this exact moment." Kate steepled her hands, keeping them still while giving her something to do. This was a part of the job she despised: sitting safe and sound while watching operatives risk their lives in real time, and knowing if something happened, she would be absolutely powerless to help.

"Yes, ma'am," KeyWiz said. He was a cyberjock, not a fool. Recognizing the clipped tone in Kate's voice, he dialed down a bit.

"Show us who's interdicting," Kate said.

KeyWiz tapped his namesake, and the picture on the large holographic screen zoomed in closer on the region, with the peninsula of Florida jutting down from the north and the curved island of Cuba arcing through the tropical water like a lethal serpent.

This could claim two operatives before it's all over. Kate shook off the foreboding thought. She had no doubt that

Jonas could handle himself—the man probably had more experience in covert ops than any two of her people. In fact, the more she had thought about it, the happier she was that he was overseeing the mission—it freed up Denny to concentrate on the myriad threats Room 59 was keeping tabs on in the States. Also, Jonas could be counted on to make sure that the operation didn't turn wet until absolutely necessary. Even now, as they were being boarded by potential hostiles, Marcus had left the boat and was executing his assignment. Which is great, except that leaves Jonas alone against three—

"I've got it." NiteMaster had used the satellite's imaging capability to zoom on the two boats bobbing in the middle of a watery nowhere.

The detail was so good Kate could make out four figures, the one in the larger boat rising from his chair, keeping his hands in plain sight. Three men in uniforms and billed caps, one holding what was obviously an assault rifle, came on board.

"Looks like Cuban Border Patrol—must have spotted them coming in," NiteMaster said.

"I knew we should have gone complete stealth on this." Kate kept her eyes glued to the screen, but her gaze wavered when she heard a snort from KeyWiz, who had pulled up a composite photo of Jonas and had matched him to a severe, official-looking photo.

"Are you kidding? Have you read this guy's jacket? A founding member of GSG-9, served thirty years before retirement, plus he's a sniper with seventy-plus confirmed kills. He's done things I only role-play. If you gave him a Swiss Army knife, a can of SPAM and dropped him in there by himself in just his underwear, he could probably bring back Castro's head on a plate, gift wrapped."

"Less talking, more stalking, Key." Judy appeared on-screen beside Kate. "Couldn't sleep, either, eh?" she asked.

"No, and before you say it, I do know the old intelligence saying, the more people watching an operation—"

"The quicker it goes to hell. I think they meant the eyes-on-the-ground kind of watching. I doubt those young men—or that older one—have any idea who's keeping tabs on them in America," Judy said.

"Something's going down," NiteMaster interrupted, and all eyes in the room watched what unfolded next in complete silence.

JONAS FINISHED the 180-degree turn, then pulled the throttles back, dropping the diesels from a roar to a whispering idle before cutting them completely. He rose, keeping his hands at shoulder level as he turned to face the three Cubans, who'd brought their boat alongside and made it fast to his. A flick of his eyes to the stern showed no obvious trace of Marcus's entry into the water—the yacht's wake had already broken up any ripples.

"Um—*Buenas noches, señors. Wie sagen Sie—¿Hay un problema?*" Knowing there was a good chance one of the men might speak English, Jonas mixed clumsy Spanish with his native German.

"*¡No muévase!*" Without asking permission, the three men came aboard, the man with the rifle covering him, motioning for him to step away from the captain's chair and sit in the passenger's seat, which Jonas did. He eyed the distance to the hidden pistol, then calculated his odds of disarming the officer and holding him hostage. Even though the man was about six feet away, Jonas was confident he could do it in less than two seconds.

The man with the bullhorn stood in front of him, while the third one went belowdecks presumably to search the cabin.

"What are you doing in Cuban territorial waters?"

Jonas let his features go slack in bafflement. "You mean—that is not Florida?" He gestured at the island and the scant lights in the distance.

The officer frowned. "No, you are within our sovereign waters now. Let me see your passport and registration papers."

Jonas handed over his fake German passport, listing him as one Werner Buehler. His cover for the drop was that of a businessman on vacation, and he played it to the hilt. "*Ach du Lieber,* my wife will be so upset that I won't get back in time to meet her tonight. We were supposed to go to the Miami Beach for drinks, and now she will be very angry indeed."

He kept wringing his hands and rambling like a worried husband as the third man came up from the galley and reported. "No contraband or stowaways aboard."

"You own such a magnificent vessel?" the officer asked.

"Yes, here are my papers." Jonas forced a smile, knowing the man's interest was anything but recreational. "I come to the U.S. every year to fish and sail on the water."

The officer glanced at Jonas, then around at the boat, addressing his men in rapid Spanish. "This is a wonderful powerboat—it would be very useful against the smugglers."

One of his men smiled. "Yes, and we could trade up from that piece of shit we're using now."

"Then we are agreed." The third soldier's eyes flicked to Jonas, who kept an uncertain smile on his face as though he couldn't understand what was being said. "The only question is what happens to him?"

The officer shrugged. "Too many questions for our leader if we bring in another foreigner to prison. Better that he just have an accident, and then we say we found the abandoned boat out here."

The officer turned back to Jonas, papers extended. "Well, Mr. Buehler, you are free to go. However, there is the small matter of a fine for crossing into our waters—"

Jonas smiled and nodded so hard he thought his head would fall off. "*Ja—sí, sí,* I pay, I pay. One moment, please." He reached out for the sheaf of registration papers, taking them from the officer's hand, but let them slip through his fingers to the deck. "*Ach,* I am sorry, so clumsy—"

With a thin smile, the officer leaned over to snatch the papers off the deck. As soon as he bent forward, Jonas brought up his knee, smashing it into the man's face, feeling the man's nose pulp under the blow and sending him reeling back, clapping his hands to his ruined features.

Jonas immediately turned to the second soldier, who had been bringing his AK-47 down from a sloppy port arms hold. He tried to bring his weapon to bear, but Jonas was already too close and grabbed the barrel, pulling it down even farther. Surprised, the soldier tightened up on the weapon, trying to pull it back to him. As soon as he did that, Jonas lunged forward, striking the bridge of the soldier's nose with his forehead. The man doggedly clung to his weapon and squeezed the trigger, spraying a long burst of bullets into the night. Jonas butted him in the nose again, breaking it and forcing him to release the rifle. He then jabbed the butt at the soldier's forehead, dropping him to the deck.

Jonas was about to whirl to take out the third attacker when he felt strong arms clamp around his chest, pinning his own to his sides. Still gripping the rifle, Jonas arced his head back, smashing his skull into the man's face while kicking back with his heel into the Cuban's left shin. The dual attack made the soldier release him, and the operative immediately spun and slammed the AK-47's butt into the man's solar plexus, staggering him back against the captain's chair, howling in dismay.

The soldier clawed the Makarov 9 mm pistol out of its holster as Jonas stepped forward and lashed out again, shattering his cheekbone and rendering him unconscious.

Jonas looked around, his hands tight on the assault rifle. His pulse pounded in his ears as adrenaline coursed through his system. Two soldiers were down and out, but the leader had recovered enough to try for his side arm, making soft, whuffling noises as he bled on the deck.

Stepping over, Jonas brought the butt of the rifle down hard on the man's head, silencing him. He looked at all three of the Cubans bleeding on his deck and sighed, then grabbed the leader and dragged him on to the other boat, disabling its engine while he was there. He transferred the other two soldiers, then untied the boat and pushed it off. When the watercraft had floated far enough away, he started his yacht's engines and pushed the throttle forward until it danced across the waves.

Several miles away, he pitched the AK-47 overboard, then stopped the boat and got out the cleaning supplies.

Before he began cleaning up the mess the three men had left behind, he called in.

"It could have been worse," he grumbled to himself as he waited for the connection. "At least there are no bullet holes to explain."

13 ıı ıı&s ıı ı ■ ı ss1ı ıı ■ı ıı ı ■ ı■

"Wow."

The simple exclamation, uttered by a slack-jawed El Supremo, summarized everyone's thoughts. In mere seconds, they had all watched Jonas disable three armed men without getting a scratch. The trio of cyberjocks chattered among themselves while Kate and Judy watched in the background.

"The man certainly can get the job done," Judy said, her tone pure admiration.

"He wouldn't be working for us if he couldn't." Kate glanced at the three hackers still staring at their screens. "Gentlemen, give me a status report on our two operatives in the next ten seconds."

They stopped reviewing Jonas's moves on a high-definition digital file, and each turned to their separate keyboards.

KeyWiz informed them, "Alpha is heading toward target insertion point at approximately 305 miles per hour. Estimated time of arrival fifty minutes, twenty minutes later than our original estimate, due to being dropped off farther away from destination than planned."

NiteMaster chimed in next. "Beta has transferred hostiles to their boat and is about to leave the area. Do you wish to transmit any operational orders?"

"That won't be necessary," Kate replied.

NiteMaster was really asking if she had wanted to change the operation in any way, including termination of the three men. If Jonas didn't think he needed to kill them, she wasn't going to argue. Operatives in the field made split-second, razor's-edge decisions all the time, and knowing a director was breathing down their neck who would second-guess their every step wouldn't help anyone.

NiteMaster continued his report. "Beta is proceeding due north at approximately thirty knots per hour. He will most likely make landfall in two hours, fifty minutes, unless detained again."

"That won't be nearly as much of an issue," Kate said. She knew that Jonas wouldn't get picked up by the Coast Guard, and even if he attracted their attention, he'd be able to slip out of their grasp with ease. They watched the two dots grow farther apart, the operatives heading their separate ways.

Judy cleared her throat. "Waiting for the incident report?" she asked.

"Of course. Aren't you?" Kate replied.

"I'm still here, aren't I? If you'd like, I can have a summary ready for you later this morning."

"Thanks, Judy, but I'll take it now, if you don't mind. I imagine it won't be long before he calls."

As if on cue, a ringtone sounded. "Secure channel. Hello, Beta," Kate said.

"My ears are burning," Jonas's voice came over the line.

Kate smiled—of course he'd know they were watching; he'd certainly done enough of it himself overseeing Eastern European operations. Still, protocol had to be followed. "Report."

"Alpha and Beta operatives entered Cuban waters at approximately 2342 hours. Although the area was supposed to be clear of government patrols, we were sighted and intercepted. Alpha deployed safely and undetected, then I stopped and let the hostiles board. After completing their search and questioning me, during which I utilized the cover story, I overheard them planning to kill me and seize the boat. I incapacitated them, transferred them back aboard their vessel, disabled its engine and left the area."

"Thank you. That was very nice work," Kate said.

"*Ach,* you are too kind. I'm slowing down—ten years ago I could have had them all on the floor in less than three seconds. I think it took me about four this time."

Kate and Judy exchanged impressed glances. "Regardless, we're just happy that you're all right and that Alpha is safely deployed. Return home and prepare for the next phase."

"Beta out."

Kate cut the connection with Jonas and turned to Judy. "I just hope our man in Havana does, as well."

14

Once Marcus hit the water, he descended to about sixty feet, then achieved neutral buoyancy, floating in the pitch-black ocean as the yacht passed by, the pounding of its engines reverberating through his skull. He made sure his gear was intact, then uncovered his dive computer and got his bearings. When he was facing south, he activated the Torpedo 2000 Diver Propulsion Vehicle and let the battery-operated craft tow him toward his destination. After five minutes of hurtling blind through the warm currents, he turned on his dive light, which only penetrated about ten feet of dark water at this depth. For his part, Marcus kept his legs as still as possible, trying not to think about a shark attack.

It took over an hour, but at last his personal sonar indicated that he was approaching a large land mass. Marcus angled the DPV up, breaking the surface about one hundred yards from shore. Inflating his buoyancy vest, he checked the area through a night-vision monocular, scanning the brilliant white beach through the green-tinted amplified light. Satisfied he was alone, he let the Torpedo pull him to the beach, then took off his fins and ran for the jungle.

Jonas had let him off near the Matanzas province, about ten miles from its main city of the same name. Marcus removed the rest of his equipment, buried it deep in the sand and erased all evidence that anyone had been there. He slipped on a pair of cotton drawstring pants along with a loose, short-sleeved guayabera shirt and sandals. Checking his digital compass watch, he headed south again, knowing there was a main road nearby that led into Matanzas, where he could catch a bus to Havana.

The jungle was thick, but he had only gone about fifty yards when he hit the Via Blanca Highway, a well-maintained, four-lane asphalt road. Turning right, his sandals slapped the pavement as he trudged along, shoulders slumped, looking like any other weary Cuban forced to walk to his destination.

MARCUS LET GO of the outside rail of the bus and stepped onto the Havana street. He had been here for less than half a day, and already he was weary. It wasn't a physical weariness, but rather an emotional one.

His tour of Cuba had begun well enough. When he walked into Matanzas, he found a relatively clean city, with several neighborhoods and business sections connected by attractive bridges. Although the buildings were mostly small, one story and crowded together, they were also neat, as were the paved streets they lined.

Asking the locals for directions, he found the bus station, and was surprised to find that he would be riding in an air-conditioned bus to Havana. The trip was very comfortable, as they passed over the Ponte de Bacunayagua, an incredible bridge built over a massive chasm. Marcus stared at the carpet of lush, green jungle that stretched out and up the hillsides below him.

Once they hit the outskirts of the capital city, however, things changed rapidly. Although he saw the high-rises of Havana's financial district in the distance, all around him were blocks of crumbling buildings, their facades worn and fading, with missing windows, doors and sometimes even roofs and walls, lending an eerie, war-torn ambiance to the streets. Many buildings were little more than gutted ruins, long abandoned. Even the splashes of once vibrant paint, greens and pinks and blues and yellows, were faded and flaking away from years of neglect.

People either sat on the stoops of their houses or walked wherever they had to go. The traffic in the city was sparse. Large buses were packed full of dozens of people, with more hanging on to the outside and riding on the roof. The old, overloaded vehicles labored to haul their human cargo around the city. No one looked particularly ill or hungry, but they also didn't look particularly happy. Marcus saw many furtive, downcast gazes as his bus drove past slowly disintegrating neighborhoods. It seemed that everyone was concentrating on getting through the day so much, they didn't have time to think about the future, or even what tomorrow might bring. Here and there he spotted small flashes of normalcy—an abandoned lot transformed into a working garden, laughing children darting back and forth as they played a pickup game of stickball in the street. But overall Marcus felt a sense of oppression, of needs and wants, of hopes, dreams and desires clung to until they stagnated, rather than their holders being able to fulfill their wishes.

The only people who looked even remotely comfortable were the police, who were interspersed with occasional small units of army personnel. They all looked well fed and content in their uniforms, and Marcus saw them detaining and questioning people who didn't look as if they were doing anything wrong or even out of the ordinary. Once, as he watched two police officers interrogating a young black man, they both looked up, their dark eyes following him as if they knew something was amiss, as if they knew he didn't belong there. Marcus didn't drop his gaze, but stared at them until they passed out of view.

He leaned back in his seat, trying to make sense of what he was seeing. He'd known going in that things wouldn't be pretty. While growing up, Cuba had been the subject of many conversations around the dinner table, and he had heard the arguments on all sides—capitalist, Communist and socialist. He had seen the pictures, went on the exile Web sites and even marched in a couple of lift-the-embargo protests in Miami when he had been in high school. But nothing had prepared him for actually being there, for seeing the seamy conditions that people experienced every day.

It wasn't the fact that the neighborhoods existed, or even that the people who lived there seemed so bereft of hope. During his years in the Rangers, Marcus had traveled to places that made Cuba look like a true paradise. He'd been to Darfur, walked through the smoldering remains of villages after the genocidal militias had swept through, slaughtering and destroying everyone and everything in their path.

At least, he thought, the majority of the Cubans still had all their limbs intact. He was also well aware that America didn't have a glorious record of upholding human rights, either, particularly in areas where they had a vested interest, like the Middle East.

What stunned him was the idea that Castro kept claiming to be a progressive leader of this nation, preaching that he was helping his people in the first place, that they were still fighting the *revolución* despite the fact that the opposite was so obviously true. Cuba had slipped closer to capitalism as it became more dependent on tourism as its economic base. That was just fine with Marcus, since the introduction of free-market, capitalist ideas often opened doors for more democratic and personal freedoms. However, the trickle-down theory of a wider economic base improving the everyday lives of the nation's citizens had dried up before it could even get started, leaving most of the populace still thirsty for the chance at a decent life.

Even more amazing to him was the fact that no one had ever been able to stop Castro. Marcus knew of the many attempts to destroy the man over the decades, by the U.S. government and others, but none had ever come close to succeeding.

It's tempting to take a shot at him myself, he thought. After all, I'm here, and it would be the one thing no one would expect. I don't think the home office would be pleased, however.

The bus ground to a stop at the main Havana station, and everyone piled out. Marcus took it all in for a moment, the buses arriving and departing, crowds of people swarming around them. Marcus had no desire to pack himself in like cattle on a city bus, but he knew his final destination was still several miles away.

A familiar if rough-pitched rumble echoed through the station, and Marcus turned to watch a vintage Harley-Davidson Electra Glide rumble up. Its passenger, a long-limbed young woman, got off and gave the driver a long hug and kiss before picking up a small bag and disappearing into the station. Marcus walked over to the bike.

"Very nice," he said, checking out the motorcycle. Every painted surface of the bike gleamed. "And your friend isn't bad, either."

The rider polished his Ray-Ban sunglasses on his shirt-tail. "She's not my friend—she's my sister, asshole."

"And she's lucky to have a brother like you to look out for her." Marcus let his gaze stray to the bike again. "The reason I came over is that I don't feel like sardining it in the buses, but I have to get downtown. Could I pay you for a lift?"

"Sure, sixty pesos."

"Whoa, man, if you're going to rob me, then at least take me to a dark alley first. All I got is twenty," Marcus said.

"Man, that won't even cover my gas."

"Yeah, but you're already out here anyway. If you head back in alone, that doesn't get you anything."

The biker watched two slender women stroll by, their colorful skirts swirling around their legs. "Yeah, but I could find a fine lady who wouldn't mind the wind in her hair as she rode on the back of my hog, either. I might not even charge her, and she'd be a damn sight better looking than you!" The stranger smiled as he spoke.

Marcus laughed with him. "All right, all right, I can do thirty pesos, but that's it."

The biker looked him up and down. "You got a ride. Now, where to?"

"Take me to the Plaza de la Revolución, please."

15

Damason drove through the streets in a rusty Lada, the car he was forced to use after Castro had ordered all of the more modern cars—anything European and made in the past twenty-five years—confiscated for the state's use. He thought the faded, red, 1970s Soviet-built car he was crammed into was horrible. It puttered along on a wheezing, seventy-five horsepower engine, bald tires and no air-conditioning. Damason's head brushed the ceiling, even when he hunched over the steering wheel, and driving on the inner city's rougher roads, he often found himself taking more than one knock as he jounced over scattered potholes.

But none of that mattered. The message he had received told him to go to a building on the corner of Placencio and Maloja Streets. On the second floor he would find a package crucial to his upcoming mission. Damason wiped his sweating forehead on his shirtsleeve. Although his army uniform would command more respect from the local populace, it would also attract attention, and that was the last thing he wanted.

As usual, traffic was light except for the buses, and he had no problem reaching the address. Like most other inner-city neighborhoods, this one had seen better days about half a century earlier. The rows of two- and three-story buildings were barren, empty shells of their former magnificence. Damason locked the car and crossed the street, looking up and down to make sure no one was watching him.

Checking the address again, he wasn't even sure he'd be able to get to the second floor. He was impressed that the building was still standing, as its bottom walls leaned in different directions, half the roof was missing and the entire structure looked as if it was about to collapse the moment anyone touched it. Damason crossed the street and pushed aside a rotting sheet of plywood blocking the crumbling doorway. It fell with a damp thud on the litter-and-brick-strewn ground.

Sunlight streamed in through empty window frames, revealing what had been a large open room, perhaps a cantina or restaurant once. Now, there were just piles of mortar, broken rocks and moldy, rotting wood. A large portion of the ceiling was missing, and he saw more wreckage on the second floor. Spotting an open doorway at the back of the room, Damason walked over to find a narrow, gloomy staircase leading up. Kneeling, he saw footsteps in the dust on the steps. He cocked his head and listened, but heard nothing upstairs save the cooing of mourning doves. Selecting a fist-sized rock from the floor, he started up, testing each step before putting his full weight on it.

It looked as if the second floor had been an apartment before time and the elements had ravaged it. The remains of an iron-framed bed rusted in one corner under an ancient, ragged bullfighting poster. The hole he had seen from below had devoured a full third of the floor, leaving a yawning pit behind. The remaining boards creaked ominously when Damason stepped on them, and he knew he'd have to get what he came for and get out before the whole place came down on his head.

Edging around the perimeter, he scanned the floor and walls, looking for a loose board, a broken section of wall, anything that would give a clue as to where the package was hidden. Other than a crumbling, weakened wall above the staircase, he saw nothing out of the ordinary. He searched to the lip of the hole on one side, then went back and examined the other side, as well, to no avail.

It has to be here somewhere he thought nervously. Damason walked back to the doorway and looked around the room again. Nothing looked any different this time around, the collapsed bed, the poster—*the poster*—surely that would have rotted away long ago. He walked over and examined it closely. The paper looked old, but wasn't stained or wrinkled as it should have been if it had really been hanging there for months. He pulled it down to find a head-sized hole behind it. Banging on the sagging wall to make sure no rats were lurking, he carefully reached inside. His questing fingers pushed past spiderwebs and flaking plaster to touch a narrow, cloth-wrapped package. After some maneuvering, he extracted the long, heavy parcel from the hole, and knew he was holding some kind of firearm.

A shout from the street brought Damason's head up, and a burst of answering laughter confirmed his suspicion. Creeping to the window, he peeked out to see three young men approaching his car, the only one parked on this street. He cursed his luck under his breath. The message had been very specific, warning him that he shouldn't be seen by anyone when he went to retrieve the package. He waited in the shadows, hoping they were just walking by, but the three circled the vehicle, peering into the windows and testing the hubcaps, prying one off with a twist and more laughter.

Damason didn't think they'd steal the car—that was a major crime, and would send them to prison for years if they were caught—but he didn't want to sit around and wait for them to become bored, either. He hefted the package in his hands, immediately dismissing the thought of using it as a deterrent. Glancing around the room again, he saw a long crack on the wall facing the street, running parallel to what remained of the roof. It gave him an idea.

Grabbing one of the bed frame's iron bars, Damason worked it free and made his way over to the wall. He braced it against the crack and pushed with all his might. At first nothing happened, but then the entire section groaned, split and toppled to the street with a crash that echoed off the surrounding buildings.

Damason ducked behind the wall until the noise of the destruction had died away, then peeked over the wreckage. Instead of chasing the three youths off, the collapsed wall seemed to have piqued their interest in the building. They were walking toward the entrance. Scowling, he watched them skulk around the doorway. Their laughter and boasts carried up to him as each dared the others to go farther inside. Another inspiration came to him, and Damason grabbed a pebble and tossed it through the back doorway, the rock rattling down the stairway. The trio fell silent, then all of them crept through the room. Lying next to the hole in the floor, Damason poked his head through, trying to see where they were.

The three young men were clustered around the doorway. Damason got up and tossed another rock at the door. The three whispered among themselves, then one began climbing the creaking steps, with the other two watching.

He crept back to the rotting wall that formed part of the stairway and listened to the slow footsteps as the boy approached. When he judged the intruder was close enough, Damason put his shoulder to the wall and pushed again.

The weakened wall crumbled and gave way, collapsing on top of the boy, who screamed briefly as dozens of pounds of mortar and dust rained down on him. The other two scrambled to assist him, shouting his name and digging through the rubble. Damason checked to make sure they were completely occupied, then slid through the hole with the package in his hands, landing in front of the doorway. He raced to his car, placed the package in the backseat and drove away.

Damason wound through the narrow streets of Havana until he found a deserted alley. He got out, put the package into the trunk and, after another circuit of the city to ensure that he wasn't being followed, he headed south, getting on the highway that would eventually take him past the military base at Managua. He didn't give much thought to the three youths he had left behind. If their curiosity hadn't gotten the better of them, their friend would have been fine. It was a minor sacrifice compared to what he had gained.

Risking pushing the Lada beyond its limits, Damason pressed the gas pedal down harder. He had to be back in the city for a rare speech that Raul Castro was giving in the plaza later that afternoon, but first he wanted to see what he had recovered, and to do that, he needed total privacy.

A dozen miles outside the city, he found one of the innumerable side paths that led into the jungle. They were little more than trails that had once led to fields or an old sugar mill, now long overgrown. He pulled onto it, wincing as the Lada bottomed out in the ruts. He prayed not to get stuck, for it would impossible to explain why he had come out all this way. The little car seemed to sense his need, however, for it rose to the occasion and didn't bog down once.

When he was sure he wouldn't be seen by anyone, Damason pulled over and got out. Walking to the trunk, he opened it, removed the package, then closed it and placed the bundle on top. He carefully unwrapped the cloth to reveal a slender, long-barreled rifle with an unusual, skeletonized stock featuring a built-in pistol grip. A long scope was mounted on top. Included with the rifle were two magazines full of 7.62 mm ammunition.

Damason lifted the Russian-made Dragunov SVD sniper rifle, feeling its weight, its balance, relishing the texture of the wood and stamped steel. It felt right in his hands.

It felt like a weapon that could kill a dictator.

16 ‖ ‖₆₆ ‖ ‖ ▪ ‖ 59‖ ‖ ▪‖ ‖ ‖ ▪ ‖▪

Jonas sipped an excellent Australian Zinfandel and dabbed his mouth with his napkin, then placed it over the remains of his delicious blackened-snapper lunch. "There is something about everything in America, although I enjoy my homeland, everything here somehow just tastes better." His accent had thickened, the guttural Germanic tones coming through on each word.

He was dressed in a new, tropical-weight, beige linen suit with a white, raw silk shirt underneath. A pair of Christian Dior sunglasses covered his eyes, lending a cool gray tone to everything he looked at. His dining companion—a Room 59 operative on temporary loan from a long-term assignment in the Florida Keys—was dressed in a strapless, light blue, hibiscus-print sundress and a straw hat.

"Glad you think so. Has our target arrived yet?" Karen Mulber was tall, blond and tanned—the perfect accessory for a foreign businessman on vacation. She also had a mind like a titanium trap, which made her the perfect partner to watch his back during this meeting. While Jonas was making contact, she would be locating Castilo's car to plant a minuscule tracking device on it.

They sat on the topmost tier of the five-level restaurant, which had been built to allow all of its guests an unobstructed view of the track below. The bright Florida sun bathed the arena in golden light, making it a perfect racing day. While pretending to discuss the day's races, they casually scanned the rest of the restaurant.

Jonas finished his wine. "Not yet, but the matinee begins in twenty minutes, so unless he's stuck in traffic, I expect him to walk in any moment now." The Room 59 hackers had accessed Castilo's computer calendar. Every Wednesday afternoon was blocked off for the greyhound races.

Karen pressed a slender finger to her ear, making the movement look perfectly natural. "Hold on—his limousine has just arrived, along with another car. Looks like he has company."

"What about the driver?" Jonas asked.

She leaned forward, revealing a lush swell of cleavage along with a wicked grin. "Just leave him to me."

"Say no more." Jonas studied the racing program for that afternoon. "Let me guess, Mr. Castilo's animal is number six in race ten."

She followed his pointing finger. "Cuba Libre? Nothing like displaying certain political views in plain sight."

"Let's just hope he's a winner. It's a Class B race, and old Cuba Libre has just slipped a ranking, so he should outclass the others. Unfortunately, he got box six, but he's an inside dog, so he'll need to do some hard running to get ahead of the pack before the escape turn." Jonas slid three one-hundred-dollar bills across the table. "Put this down on him across the board."

"Am I your beard now?" Karen asked.

"Someone's got to stay and watch for him. Besides, it won't seem suspicious if you head out to bet and also scout the parking lot to see where their car is."

She scooped up the bills. "And here I thought you'd only go for the win—you know, that kind of all-or-nothing macho bullshit."

"A smart man hedges his bets whenever he can," Jonas said with a smile.

"Looks like he's coming in."

Both Karen and Jonas kept up their idle chatter while watching the party of three men and three women enter the restaurant. The maître d' greeted Castilo effusively and escorted the party to a pair of reserved tables on the first tier, a good distance from Jonas's table. They were all dressed well, but Jonas only had eyes for one man.

Rafael Castilo had a bit more gray hair than in the picture Kate had sent to him, and his suit was probably tailored to hide a few additional pounds, but otherwise he'd aged well. He laughed and talked with his party and was affectionate with the woman at his side, a beautiful Cuban-American woman at least twenty years younger, and from the looks of it, trying not to age any faster than necessary. She was Castilo's second wife, his first having passed away seven years ago. Jonas noted that the man's eyes were always in motion, sweeping the room as if constantly evaluating who was there.

Jonas swept the party with his gaze, while his Dior sunglasses recorded everything through a quarter-inch color, closed-circuit lens built into its frame. Unlike other spy glasses, which still required relatively bulky battery packs, this model, reverse engineered by a cutting-edge technology firm in California, had modified lithium batteries installed into the temple bars, so that the glasses were ready to go when put on.

"Hope you're getting all this, Kate," Jonas muttered.

Everything was being transmitted back to Room 59's on-line suite for analysis. He hadn't bothered to bug the reserved table, as it was doubtful that Castilo would be discussing anything regarding his personal crusade there.

Loudspeakers around the track blared into life, the sound distorted and muted by the thick glass windows. Jonas kept an eye on the small LCD screen at his table as the greyhounds came out for the post parade, guided by the lead outs. The people at Castilo's two tables cheered and clapped when Cuba Libre appeared in the lineup. By the time the last dogs were walked out, the first ones were in the boxes, ready to go.

With ten races before the action would really begin, Jonas still kept an eye on Castilo's group, but his thoughts kept returning to that long-ago mission. Seeing the island last night, even through the darkness, had brought back more memories, and they were proving increasingly hard to dismiss.

June 19, 1973

THE BACK OF JONAS'S NECK itched as rivulets of sweat ran down it and his sprained ankle throbbed, but those were the least of his worries at the moment. The twelve men taking up ambush positions around the clearing a dozen yards away were another matter entirely.

After squirming far enough through the jungle to be sure that they wouldn't be seen, Jonas and his contact took cover in a copse of blue mahoe. He turned to the woman. "What's your name?"

"¿Qué?"

"Your name. Or should I just say 'Hey, you' when I need your attention?"

"Marisa," she whispered.

"I'm Karl." Jonas hated having to lie to her, even under the circumstances, but his team couldn't be connected with this operation in any way, so he needed the alias. "We have to alert my team." He eased out his radio, but turning it to the secure channel only got him static. He hit the squelch button three times, the prearranged signal for contact, but there was no reply. Jonas tried again, with the same result. He switched it off. "I cannot raise them," he said.

"That isn't surprising—there are too many hills around here. Radio transmission is spotty at best. Why don't we strike out and find the route they are going to return by? Then we could warn them off and head right for the coast," Marisa said.

"That assumes they'll be coming back via the primary route. Anything might cause them to deviate to a secondary. Without communication, I cannot coordinate a rendezvous. No, it is up to us to neutralize these soldiers before they return," Jonas said.

He felt her stare, even in the darkness. "Has that injury affected your brain, as well? There were at least a dozen men back there. We have you—crippled—and me, and I'm not throwing my life away in a fruitless gesture for anyone."

Jonas shifted position, scratching his back against the tree trunk. "Believe me, I don't want to be buried here, either. I'm not advocating a frontal assault. We just need a distraction, or to trick them into thinking they're being attacked by a larger force—anything to make them give up their position. If only I hadn't gotten injured."

"If you hadn't, then you and your team would be walking into an ambush, and I'd be dead right now." Marisa put her hand on his arm. "What about the truck? If we could gain control of it, perhaps that could be put to use."

"Perhaps—if we can find it." Jonas took out his compass, taking bearings. "They're to our left, about fifteen yards away. Here, hold this." He took her hand, which still rested on his arm, and pressed his compass into her fingers. Shrugging off his pack, he opened it and carefully removed his night-vision scope. Turning it on, he waited for it to warm up, then looked through it at the clearing, watching the jungle night appear in grainy green and black. Through the trees he could just make out the larger image of the sugar mill, with the Cuban soldiers still moving around it. He also took a long look around their current location, fixing trees and other foliage in his mind. He switched the scope off and rewrapped it for protection before putting it away. "All right, we have to walk parallel with the road until we find the truck, then we'll reconnoiter and figure out a plan." He sliced off a few tree fronds to cover his pack, taking his canteen, radio, the spotting scope, rifle, pistol, ammunition for both, a machete and his double-edged commando knife.

Marisa didn't say a word, but slipped her head underneath his shoulder again. "It's going to be a long walk."

"Not this time." He handed her his machete. "See what you can do to clear a path while making as little noise as possible."

"Where will you be?"

Jonas eased himself to the ground. "Crawling right behind you. It's the best way. Otherwise we'll both be exhausted by the time we reach our objective."

She nodded, then began slicing her way through the foliage. They carefully made their way through the thick jungle, with Marisa wielding the razor-sharp blade like a tree surgeon, clearing enough of a path so that Jonas could follow without getting caught in the low bushes.

The insects, however, were another matter. Each time Jonas put his hands down, something crawled over them, and he spent as much time trying not to get bitten or stung as moving forward. Every ten yards or so, he sat up and took another look through his scope, comparing their surroundings with what he remembered.

When they had covered what he thought was about one hundred yards, Jonas hissed at Marisa to stop. He tried his radio again, but got nothing. Then he removed his commando knife and tapped the young woman on the shoulder. "Here. This is going to be dangerous, and I don't want you unarmed."

She strapped the sheathed blade on her belt. "Thank you."

Jonas took another look around with the scope. "I don't know how far they might have gone to be sure they wouldn't be seen."

"Why don't I cut over to the road—surely we're far enough away now—and see what I can find out." Before he could stop her, Marisa darted off between the trees without a sound, her lithe form swallowed up by the darkness.

Jonas hissed in frustration and hunkered down, his pistol drawn, for all the good it would do him. One shot would bring the soldiers running. Every sense alert, he sat and waited for her to return—or for her to be discovered.

"HEY, YOU ALL RIGHT? The tenth is about to start." Karen slid back into her seat.

Jonas tuned back into his surroundings with a blink. "Just waiting for the lead to go. Any problems?"

"Nope. The GPS is in place, and if I were that kind of girl, I'd have a date for the weekend." She smiled. "But I'm not."

"He'll be very disappointed, I'm sure." Jonas focused on the monitor as the tenth race started. Cuba Libre got off to a quick start, but was caught on the outside coming into the escape turn, and couldn't make up the lost ground. It was in the middle of the pack on the far turn, and put on a final burst to finish second. Castilo's table celebrated quietly, accepting the second-place finish with good humor.

"At least you didn't lose," Karen offered.

"True, true." Jonas handed her several more hundreds. "Go collect my winnings, would you? When you return, hand me the whole thing at their table."

"Just make sure you're there when I come back." Karen stood again and pecked him on the cheek, then walked through the room, her poised stride drawing stares from every man she passed.

Jonas flagged a passing waiter. "I'd like to send a bottle of Perrier Jouet Fleur Blanc de Blanc '99 over to Mr. Castilo's table, with my compliments on a well-run race."

"Certainly sir, whom shall I say it is from?"

"If he asks, point out this table and mention that it is from a gentleman who shares his love of freedom." The message was vague enough to rouse curiosity instead of suspicion. At least Jonas hoped that would be Castilo's reaction. Making contact with a target didn't happen like a James Bond film—there was no script indicating how it would go down. The businessman might simply drink the champagne with the rest of his party, then leave.

Jonas sat back and watched as the chilled bottle was delivered to Castilo's table. He received it with a smile, and tilted his head to listen to the waiter deliver the message. The waiter discreetly pointed out Jonas's table, and when Castilo looked across the floor to the upper tier, Jonas raised his wineglass in salute. The Cuban inclined his head and motioned for the waiter to pour for his delighted wife and guests.

Jonas watched Castilo summon a bodyguard to his table and whisper in his ear. The stocky man returned to his position, opened his cell phone and began texting, or at least that's what he wanted to appear to be doing. Jonas knew he was being photographed, and he also figured that they would be getting his name from the reservation book, as well. So far, everything was going according to plan.

After several minutes, the waiter returned. "Mr. Heinemann, Mr. Castilo requests the pleasure of your company at his table."

Here we go, Jonas thought, pushing his chair back and rising. "I would be delighted."

17

"Jonas has initiated contact with the target." NiteMaster spun around in his chair, the piercings in his eyebrow glittering in the light. "We're getting hits on the cover story, as well." He brought up various Web pages, one a relatively bland corporate site, one from the ATF and several from other foreign news sites, each of which had an article on Mr. Ferdinand Heinemann. The company site was for a European import-export business, similar to Castilo's, but the other mentions of Heinemann's name told a very different story.

Watching in the virtual ops center, Kate only nodded, scanning the wealth of created electronic data available on their operative. With the Web becoming an instant background resource available to anyone with a cell phone or laptop, it was vital for Room 59 to provide an in-depth history for each operative's cover story. For this, hackers worked behind the scenes in the world's major search engines, tweaking hit algorithms to ensure that the false pages would pop up immediately in any search. A company Web page was easy, but faking news reports and other believable media usually took time. However, the three hackers had smoothly established Mr. Heinemann as a living, breathing person—at least on the Internet.

What a story they had woven, Kate thought. According to reliable sources, Mr. Heinemann operated a successful import-and-export company out of Munich. However, a bit more digging revealed that he had been investigated—but never charged—for illegal arms smuggling and sales by the U.S., German and French governments, and had been rumored to be involved in various black-market deals for the past twenty years.

It's amazing how the Internet gives instant credibility to things, simply by letting people find it for themselves on a computer screen, Kate thought. What could be located by a simple keyword search would be enough to plant the notion in anyone's mind about Mr. Heinemann, but there was one final straw that anyone seriously checking a cover story would probably think to do, as well.

"Incoming call for Rhienland I.E." KeyWiz adjusted his headset mike and looked to Kate for confirmation.

She let it ring three times—after all, it was a thriving business—then nodded.

"*Guten Tag,* Rhineland Import/Export, how may I help you?" Kate winced at KeyWiz's accent—he was laying it on a bit thick. "I'm sorry, sir, but Herr Heinemann is on vacation. I'm afraid that I am not at liberty to say where he is at the moment. Yes, I can confirm that he is overseas. Yes, he does enjoy greyhound racing—it's a life-long hobby of his. May I inquire as to whom is calling? Very well, sir."

While KeyWiz was handling the phone call, El Supremo traced the cell phone call to its source.

"Originating in the Palm Beach Kennel Club restaurant," he reported.

"I think he may have been outside the bathroom—I thought I heard someone flush. No message. Guy said he'd call back later. Damn, I love this *Mission Impossible* stuff," KeyWiz said." He held up his hand, and NiteMaster and El Supremo did the same, in a virtual high-five.

"Good work, gentlemen. Let's keep monitoring the sites for any other hits—who knows, this bait may attract some other targets, as well. Also, I want analysis done on everyone at that table, who they are, their relationship to Castilo, anything and everything we can dig up on them," Kate said.

Judy spoke up. "Kate, I've got Denny on another line. Something's gone wrong on the Hawaiian operation—our operative just landed himself in jail."

"What? Oh, that's great—I hope he didn't blow his cover. Conference me in, and let's see what we can do." Kate kept her gaze on the dot that was Jonas as he walked to a pair of tables in the racetrack's restaurant. *Good luck, Jonas.*

18

Rafael Castilo rose to meet Jonas as he approached. "I understand that we have you to thank for this excellent champagne."

"Your fine animal made me a tidy profit, and when I recognized you, I felt it was only right to share some of my good fortune." Jonas extended his hand. "Ferdinand Heinemann."

Castilo took it and pumped firmly three times, then let go. Up close, his dark brown eyes were even more penetrating, even through the barrier of the sunglasses. Jonas felt himself being appraised, and returned the other man's stare with a steely one of his own, friendly enough on the outside, but all business when confronted with a fellow predator in the corporate jungle.

"Rafael Castilo, and this is my wife, Javier." He made introductions around the table, with Jonas filing the names and faces away for future reference.

Just then a waiter brought Karen to them. "Darling, you must play those hunches more often." She handed him the folded sheaf of bills, exposing them just enough so that Castilo saw the outermost hundred.

Jonas tucked the wad in his pocket. "Now you have the chance to thank the owner of our good-luck greyhound in person, my dear."

Castilo's eyes lit up. "So you are the companion of this stunning woman." He took her hand and kissed it, with Karen acting suitably charmed.

"It is my honor, yes. May I present Joanne Seneschal. Joanne, this is Mr. Rafael Castilo, an American competitor of mine," Jonas said with a smile.

Castilo's eyebrows raised slightly, and he glanced toward the bathroom.

Perfect. Now he's trying to figure out who I am, how I compete with him and where his bodyguard is with the background check on me, Jonas thought.

"Oh, Ferdinand, always thinking about work, even on vacation." Karen's words were playful as she turned to Javier. "It's a pleasure. I don't know about your husband, but I cannot get this one to talk about anything other than business for more than five minutes, I swear—"

Just like that, Karen had Castilo's wife in the palm of her hand. She turned to the rest of the group, providing a slight but definite barrier separating them from Jonas and Castilo.

"*Señora,* you must join us for a glass of this excellent vintage. Carlos, two more glasses." The waiters had already brought over two chairs and Castilo said, "Please, sit. I hope you'll pardon my interest, but I haven't seen you around the club, and I come most every week."

The waiters filled the glasses now, and Castilo raised his. "Care to do the honors?" he asked Jonas.

Jonas considered for a moment, then raised his glass, catching everyone's eye. "Here is one from my homeland. May bad fortune chase after you for the rest of your days— and never catch you."

The surprised looks on everyone's faces dissolved into chuckles and nods and the crystal clinked in celebration.

"To answer your question," Jonas said, "as if my accent didn't give me away, I am on vacation from my import-export company in Munich, and am also doing a little side business, exploring the feasibility of bringing organized greyhound racing back to Germany. So I thought, what better place to begin than in Florida, where I can also work on my tan, as well?"

Castilo nodded and grinned. "You have definitely come to the right place, my friend." His bodyguard appeared over his shoulder, leaning down to whisper into his ear.

Jonas leaned back in his chair and sipped champagne, watching for Castilo's reaction to the report without appearing to. The Cuban didn't even pause, just nodded and thanked his man, who resumed his position a few feet from the table.

"Please forgive the intrusion," Castilo said politely.

Jonas held up his hand. "There is nothing to forgive. After all, I was the one who interrupted your gathering."

"Think nothing of it. Now, you had mentioned wanting to bring organized greyhound racing to Germany."

And with that, the conversation turned to dogs, organized gambling, the exporting trade, with Castilo and Jonas each recounting tales of strange shipments and dicey situations that had the table roaring with laughter. Briefly, they talked politics. Karen kept her side of the table abuzz with celebrity sightings in South Beach and other tidbits of gossip. As she regaled the table with an involved story about a well-known Miami drag queen, his resemblance to a current Hollywood hunk and an embarrassing mix-up at a Palm Beach hotel, Jonas caught Castilo eyeing him more than once. Then the businessman leaned over.

"The message the waiter delivered with the champagne said that it was from a gentleman who also possessed a love of freedom."

"Yes, I must confess that I recognized you as soon as I walked in. I have followed your success in our industry for the past several years, and in doing so, I have learned something of your background, as well," Jonas said.

"Keeping your friends close and your enemies closer?" Castilo's grin didn't come close to his eyes.

"It may have begun as something like that, but the more I learned, the more I admired what you have done. You are a true success story, in America, Germany or any other country. Besides, with both of us taking it on the chin from the Chinese, why waste time fighting over scraps from their table, eh?"

Castilo frowned. "Perhaps Europe is knuckling under the Asian invasion, but we here in the Western Hemisphere do not intend to surrender without a fight."

"Well spoken, indeed. When I realized I had a chance to meet you, I didn't hesitate."

Castilo leaned back and sipped his champagne. "Fortune favors the bold."

"Perhaps, but I think chance has as much to say in determining success or failure in any enterprise. If I had not come here today, or if you had not, then neither of us would be sitting here drinking this excellent vintage."

"Also true, but you still have not answered my question."

Jonas drained his own glass. "True enough. During my research, I learned of your beginnings in America—the exile from Cuba and the rest."

To his credit, Castilo scarcely flinched at the mention of his homeland. Anyone else would have thought he was just shifting in his seat.

Jonas continued, "I know what it is like to live under oppression, to grow up not even knowing what freedom is. You and I, growing up in Cuba and East Germany, could not have been that different. Some people, they bow to the autocratic state, reveal their necks and live lives of quiet desperation. But men like you and me, we seek something more, to make a better life for ourselves and, if time and resources permit, a better life for others through our work."

Castilo burst out laughing, making everyone else at the table look over. "Mr. Heinemann, you certainly had me going for a moment. I escaped Cuba, indeed, left behind that Communist bastion for a new life in America, where I could control my own destiny, true. But that was solely to become a wealthy businessman. Others may mock and insult this country, but for me it truly was paved with gold, and I am enjoying it as much as I can, every day."

Jonas was taken aback for a moment. The ebullient businessman before him didn't seem anything like a devoted freedom fighter. But perhaps that is what he wants me to think—at least in public.

Castilo rose, and the rest of the table rose with him. "This has been an interesting conversation, my friend, and one that I would enjoy continuing another time. But I'm afraid that business calls, and while you're enjoying yourself here in our fair state, I should be maximizing my advantage in your own country." He laughed, and Jonas chuckled with him.

The rest of the party headed for the door, Karen still chattering with Javier. She caught his eye and raised her eyebrow.

Jonas motioned with his chin at the door, indicating she should leave. He walked out into the humid summer day with Castilo, who paused at the door. "Tell me, Ferdinand, do you enjoy a good cigar?"

"I indulge on occasion, but have not yet sampled the variety here," Jonas said.

"Then please, before we part, I insist that you join me. I'm afraid that we could not do so in the club, since they have banned smoking inside, more's the pity. Besides, knowing my wife, she will most likely be talking with your lovely companion for the rest of the day if we are not careful." Castilo's knowing expression made it clear that he understood Karen was not Jonas's wife.

"How could I refuse?" Jonas allowed himself to be led to the pearl-gray-and-black Rolls-Royce Silver Shadow stretch limousine. They stepped into the air-conditioned interior, and Jonas made himself comfortable on the soft leather seat, near a small wet bar. Castilo faced him, with one of the ever present bodyguards, a broad, stone-faced man with short blond hair, sliding in next to him.

"Although I did confess that I left Cuba behind, there are some things from my former homeland that I still treasure." Castilo opened a panel in the bar, revealing a small humidor. "Cohiba Piramides Millennium Reserve. You will not find its like anywhere else."

Jonas accepted the thick, slightly conical cigar, along

with a proffered cutter. He snipped off the tip of the head and then, holding the foot just above the flame, rolled it until it lit satisfactorily. He drew slightly, then released the aromatic smoke to the side. "This is incredible."

"I thought a man of your tastes would enjoy it." Castilo lit one of his own. "And now that we have talked and are enjoying these fine Cohibas, perhaps you would care to tell me—"

Jonas couldn't help but notice the black semiautomatic pistol the bodyguard had drawn from his holster and set on his crossed leg.

Castilo released smoke from his mouth. "Why have you, a man accused of international arms dealing, really sought me out, Mr. Heinemann?"

19

"You sure that's where you want to go?" the motorcyclist asked.

"I have come to Havana to hear the men of our government speak," Marcus replied, his tone taking on the slightly awed reverence of a stolid, rural Communist. "If you cannot take me there, then I will find someone who can."

"All right, all right, just relax, I can get you there." He jerked a thumb at the empty seat behind him. "Get on."

Marcus hopped on the back of the Harley and held on to the fender, knowing the man would be insulted if he held on to him. He just hoped that no rocks would fly up and cut his fingers. The man revved the choppy engine and released the brake, taking them away from the bus station, down Havana's streets and toward Revolution Plaza.

They crossed out of Old Havana and into the plaza proper. Even from a distance, Marcus saw the iron face of the Guevara on the Ministry of the Interior Building. Across from that was the white, fourteen-story monument to Cuba's national hero José Martí, the nineteenth-century author, statesman, poet and freedom fighter, with a white marble statue of the man himself in front of it.

His research had revealed that there were speeches in the plaza every Wednesday, and he was pleased to see that this day was no exception. Thousands of people had already assembled in the square, and addressing them was an aged man with glasses and salt-and-pepper hair. Marcus recognized him instantly. *The man's brother himself. I wonder what's brought Raul out to speak today?*

Marcus made his way through the crowd in the plaza, entertaining a brief fantasy of taking the elevator to the top of the Martí monument and taking aim at the speaker through the scope of a Weatherby Mark V rifle. *It would be fitting to end his life from the monument of Cuba's greatest true hero,* he thought.

Marcus took out a pair of sunglasses and put them on. Activating the tiny built-in camera, he recorded Raul Castro speaking, and slowly looked from left to right at the other military personnel near the infamous chair where the senior Castro usually gave his long-winded speeches. Raul wasn't nearly as charismatic a speechmaker as his brother. It sounded as if he was already winding down, exhorting the assembled people to do more for their country, that Cuba would prevail against all enemies and other such standard propaganda.

Marcus spotted his man in the row of military officers standing behind Castro, matched him with the grainy photograph he had received, just to make sure. It wasn't difficult to spot him, since he stood several inches above the rest of the soldiers all listening intently to their commander. Marcus activated the camera's zoom, making sure to get a good picture of the man's face. Normally he would have tried to follow the man in order to make contact with him, but with no immediate transportation available, that wasn't going to happen. Marcus also didn't think he could get close enough to bug the man with a tiny transmitter, so that he could track him down later.

I wonder if he's listed in the phone book. It wouldn't be the first time we've found targets that way, he thought.

At one end of the plaza, a small commotion attracted Marcus's attention, along with other nearby watchers. A small contingent of what looked to be anti-Castro protesters were marching toward the space, holding signs and banners and chanting loudly. At first the throngs in the square didn't seem to take sides with or against the marchers. Many simply stepped aside to let them through. Marcus watched people of all ages, from young men and women—obviously students—to middle-aged and older people, all of whom lent their voices to the cry for freedom.

"A free Cuba now!"

"Allow the people to speak!"

The chants were clear, demanding that Cuba be freed from its decades-long oppression, and that the people be allowed free speech, a choice of government and the right for individuals to own businesses.

However, another group was swiftly organizing into what looked like a mob to challenge the protesters. Shouts reverberated throughout the plaza. The two groups squared off on one side. Marcus glanced toward the chair where Raul Castro had been just a moment ago, only to find that he had disappeared, along with the majority of the military personnel. In their place, however, nondescript trucks had pulled up to the square, disgorging several dozen plainclothes men.

Although Marcus thought the activists were possibly crazy to challenge the Cuban lions in their den, he also admired their guts for coming to this bastion of the government to demonstrate for what they believed in. As he watched the government supporters distract the protesters by hurling insults, letting the new arrivals organize, he realized what was about to happen.

They're going to get their asses stomped, he thought, looking around for police to intervene. Not surprisingly, there were none in the area. Marcus knew that this was a common tactic. "Ordinary people" would break up the protests, so no one could claim that the police were brutalizing civilians.

Although Room 59 directives explicitly forbade operatives from getting involved in matters of civil strife or unrest, Marcus couldn't simply stand by and watch innocent people get beaten for trying to gain their freedom. He also knew that he couldn't jeopardize his mission by assisting the protesters. If he was arrested in a country already isolated, no one from Room 59 would help him. He'd be completely on his own.

The protest-breakers had assembled, and the progovernment crowd let them swell their ranks. The large group walked forward, outnumbering the freedom protesters by at least three to one. The demonstrators refused to be intimidated, however, and linked their arms together, chanting even louder.

As one, the front row of the government men rushed the protesters, surging into them with flying fists and feet. The protesters tried to hold together, but broke apart under the onslaught. People started fleeing the plaza, running every which way. Marcus dodged several of them while trying to still keep an eye on what was happening. The protesters weren't fighting back, only defending themselves. However, the government men weren't under any such restriction, and were kicking and punching people—protesters and innocent bystanders alike—with abandon.

Intent on the confrontation, Marcus hadn't noticed that the conflict was coming perilously close to him. But when a stocky man dressed in a sleeveless flannel shirt and stained jeans shoved a woman who had to be at least fifty years old to the ground and was about to kick her in the ribs, he couldn't stand by any longer.

In two steps Marcus moved right behind the attacker. Grabbing his cocked foot in one hand, he swept the man's other foot out from under him with a low kick to his ankle. The thug howled and dropped to the ground. Marcus followed up with another kick behind the ear, bouncing the man's head against the pavement and knocking him out.

His actions had been noticed by a pair of government thugs, both of whom moved to intercept him. Marcus saw them coming at the same time that two of the protesters bent down to help the woman. Placing himself between her and the attackers, he met them head-on.

The two men didn't circle or feint, but charged in together. One of the men was slightly ahead of his comrade, and threw a straight punch at Marcus's face. Ducking the blow, Marcus responded with a straight shot to the man's abdomen. The man gasped and staggered off balance. Marcus side-stepped and landed another shot to the man's right kidney, making him drop to one knee, clutching his gut.

While Marcus dealt with the first thug, his uninjured partner had drawn a knife and slashed at Marcus's chest. He drew back in time to see the man reverse direction and come after him again with a backhanded sweep at his ribs, leaning over his buddy, who wisely dropped to the ground. This time the point snagged in Marcus's shirt, ripping it open.

The ex-Ranger knew he faced an experienced knife fighter, and had to finish it before anyone came to his attacker's assistance. The knife fighter feinted high, then lunged forward, aiming for Marcus's stomach.

He let the man come at him, the blade slicing within inches of his stomach before he grabbed his wrist and turned into the attack so that they were side by side for a moment. Marcus pulled the man's arm forward as he planted his left foot and yanked him off balance. His opponent twisted around Marcus's hip, slamming to the ground, his flying feet cracking into his partner's face, sending him back down, as well.

Marcus twisted the knife out of his attacker's hand and kicked it away, then glanced back to make sure the woman had gotten up and away. He didn't see her, but couldn't tell if she had escaped or been taken by the government agitators. What mattered now was that he got out of there fast.

Hearing sirens in the distance, he released the still-prone man and trotted away, losing himself in the rest of the scattered crowd before either of the two could get up to pursue him. Even though the plaza was large and open, Marcus made it to the edge of the area and walked calmly to an alley, which he immediately ran down, in case anyone was following him. Twisting and turning down the narrow roads and paths between the buildings, he didn't attract any more attention. He looked like just any of the hundreds of people who had run from the plaza moments ago.

Several blocks away, Marcus slowed to a walk and strolled down a thoroughfare, calming his rapid breathing and bringing his heartbeat back under control. Checking his watch, he saw that there were a few hours before he could check in with his findings. I should try to find Valdes's home—he's got to get off duty sometime. Or maybe it would be best let things die down around here first.

Spotting a cantina ahead, Marcus ducked into it and ordered a *mojito,* tipping generously. He sipped the sweet, tart drink and leaned against the wall as he watched white police Peugeots scream down the road toward the Plaza de la Revolución.

20

Jonas drew on his cigar again before answering. "You are a very suspicious man. Surely you're not going to risk ruining this fine cigar by making me drop it on the floor after your man shoots me for no good reason," he said calmly.

Castilo exhaled a thin stream of smoke. "I hope that won't be necessary. Just call him my insurance. After all, it's not every day that someone who moves in your particular business circles and someone who moves in mine come together. When it happens, I consider it more than just chance."

Jonas savored his Cohiba—no matter what, Castilo did have excellent taste in cigars—and leaned back in the leather seat, resting one arm on the back of the seat. "That's a fine-looking pistol. I hope you take care of it," he said to the body-guard.

"Well enough to handle you if necessary," the bodyguard agreed affably in a deep voice. There was no menace in his tone. Like any professional, he simply stated his intent.

"A S&W 1911 .45 ACP, the scandium alloy model, to cut

down on the weight. Eight rounds plus one in the pipe, and I see you've modified it with the Crimson Trace grips—how do you like it?" Jonas asked.

The bodyguard lifted the pistol again, keeping his finger away from the trigger, but putting enough pressure on the checkered rubber handgrips to activate the laser sight, which speared Jonas's chest with a small red dot. "I do a two-inch group at twenty-five yards, but at this distance, it would be considerably messier."

"Not to mention what those slugs would do to my jacket, the seat and possibly your employer's driver, as well," Jonas replied.

"I have no doubt that when the smoke cleared, William would be just fine in the front seat, while you, no doubt, would be much less so. But I didn't invite you here to make idle threats, so I'll ask you again. Why have you sought me out, Mr. Heinemann?" Castilo said.

"First, I want you to know that I did not mislead you during our conversation inside. I am in the import-export business, and I am very interested in bringing organized greyhound racing back with me to Germany. I also meant what I said about you and I—the type of people we are. And I think you were just playing me in front of everyone else," Jonas said.

"Speculating, that's all you're doing right now. I don't know what you've heard, but I'm a businessman, nothing more. And now, if you'll excuse me, I have business to attend to." Castilo motioned to the bodyguard, who holstered his pistol and opened the door, letting the bright Florida sunshine lance into the dark interior of the car.

Jonas reached out and pulled the car door closed. "I wasn't finished. In the course of my *other* business, I kept hearing rumors, hearsay, call it what you will, about a major operation that will be happening somewhere in the Caribbean, and soon. As a businessman, much like yourself, I heard enough different people saying the same things that I decided to come to Florida and see what I could find out for myself."

"And who told you such a thing might occur?" Castilo asked.

Jonas held up a finger. "I'm afraid that I cannot reveal my sources. However, they were acquaintances of Mr. Pierre Lalond, late of Florida, before his unfortunate departure for less pleasant climes."

"Oh? And if I were to mention the name Sahak Sohan, it wouldn't be unfamiliar to you?" Castilo asked, mentioning another prominent arms dealer.

"It is difficult to do anything in certain circles without hearing about him. He is one of the best at his profession, of course."

Castilo exchanged glances with his bodyguard. "You claim to be a businessman, yet I see something else. You know what happened to Pierre, and I think you've come to Miami to take advantage of the vacuum he has left behind."

"I've always said that good business is where you find it. In this case, it seems that Miami—and perhaps places farther south—would be very good for business, indeed."

Castilo fixed Jonas with a sharp stare, as if trying to see through him. For his part, Jonas tried to look as relaxed as possible. He had played out his line, baited the hook with just enough suggestion; now all that remained was to see if Castilo was hooked.

"Let's say that I knew someone who had need of your

other services. Why wouldn't you simply contact them directly?" Castilo asked.

"To paraphrase Sahak, everything in this business is done either through a middleman or a government. I don't think this kind of operation would be sanctioned by any government. Therefore, a private organization is handling it. And, while I know many, there are just as many that I don't know, and therefore require an introduction from someone that both sides trust."

Castilo chuckled. "Oh, so you trust me already, do you?" He nodded toward his bodyguard. "Let's not forget who was recently holding the pistol."

"Would you really have ordered me killed, in your car, after dozens of witnesses saw us talking in the restaurant together? Excuse my directness, but I don't believe I was ever in any danger."

"Perhaps, perhaps not. I have resources here, and your disappearance could be attributed to any number of possibilities."

Before Jonas could answer, his cell phone rang. He opened his suit jacket to reveal no weapon. "With your permission?"

Castilo waved a hand. Jonas opened his tiny phone. "Yes? Yes, my dear, we're just finishing our conversation.... I've been enjoying a very good cigar with Mr. Castilo.... Of course, I'll be out in just a moment.... Yes, please bring the Porsche around." He snapped the phone closed and held it up. "She does love the toys. So, would you be eliminating my companion, as well?"

"It would be a shame for that to happen to one as lovely as she." Castilo smiled and tilted his head to one side, as if considering. "Very well, for her sake."

"Maybe I'll let her know that she saved me from a fate worse than death," Jonas said as he reached for the door handle.

Castilo frowned. "I thought we weren't finished with our conversation."

"Mr. Castilo, I have presented as much to you as I am willing to at this time. Now it is up to you to decide what you wish to do with this information, whether it can help you, or whether you decide to ignore it, in which case may I say this afternoon has been a pleasure." He started to get out of the car, but paused as if considering something. "Do whatever checking you need to do into my transactions. I'm sure you will find plenty of people willing to recommend my services." He extended a business card. "My cell number, should you change your mind. Perhaps we can have drinks on my yacht and discuss this further. My man makes a killer Stinger."

Jonas stared into Castilo's eyes as he spoke, and was rewarded by a raised eyebrow. "And if I had some very thirsty friends?" the Cuban asked.

"Oh, he could make at least fifty if necessary, ten pitchers' worth."

Castilo nodded as he digested this new information, and Jonas knew he had him. "As I said, give it some thought. I'm in town for the next week. Enjoy your afternoon, gentlemen."

Jonas left the car and strolled to the purring, sleek, silver Porsche 911 Turbo. He felt Costilo's stare on his back as he walked to the passenger side and got in, relaxing in the air-conditioned interior.

"Enjoy your cigar?" Karen asked as they pulled away.

Jonas carefully tapped it out in the ashtray. "It would be a shame to waste such a fine Cohiba. But yes, I think we're in. All I have to do now is wait for his call." He turned to look at her through his Dior sunglasses. "How would you feel about a little ocean cruise tomorrow?"

21

Damason maneuvered his Lada into the cramped parking lot of the temporary headquarters his army unit was sharing with the police while they were working together. His head buzzed with what he had just seen—the protest in the plaza and the government's typically heavy-handed response. But what excited him even more was what was safely stowed in a place that only he knew about. The Dragunov.

That, more than anything, was proof that what he was involved in was real, that the plan was actually happening. Until now, it had seemed to be the airy dreams of people living far away, in the United States, who, try as they might, could not truly affect what was happening in Cuba. But when he had held that solid weapon in his hands, the reality had sunk in. The architects of the operation to free Cuba had the ability to smuggle this weapon into the country and guide him to it. That was power. And with that power behind him, Damason could take that next crucial step toward freeing his homeland. A step closer to making sure that no matter what his people had to say about their government, they could say it freely, without fear of reprisal.

Not like that afternoon, where he had been forced to escort his commander away from the plaza, leaving the protesters to suffer under the clenched fists and heavy boots of the pro-government men. Damason had brought up the idea of having the army oversee demonstrations as a way to keep the peace once, but it had been shot down immediately. His superiors said those who weren't happy with the way things were got what they deserved. Damason hadn't been surprised at this callous attitude. He had always known that his commanding officers used the system to get whatever they wanted.

He walked into the stifling building to find Garcia inside the door, greeting him with a crisp salute. "Sir, the women have been transported to a safehouse and the efforts to re-unite them with their families are ongoing. Several have already been put in contact with their various embassies."

"Excellent. How is the peacock taking this?"

"If anger was gunpowder, there would only be a smok-ing crater where Sergeant Lopez-Famosa y Fernandez stands right now."

"I cannot say I am disappointed that he will not get to take his usual gratuity for rescuing those women."

"Also, Colonel Hermosa is in your office, and has re-quested that you be brought to him immediately regarding a matter of utmost importance."

Damason didn't check his stride, but frowned at Garcia. "Unusual." Normally Hermosa couldn't be pried out of his office chair, preferring to give orders by telephone from the comfort of his plush office near the plaza. "He gave no in-dication as to what it was regarding?"

"No, sir."

Damason halted at his office door. "Well, I'll find out soon enough. Dismissed, Sergeant." He paused, gathering his thoughts and reassuming the guise of a loyal Communist revolutionary before knocking on the door.

"Enter."

Damason opened the door and beheld Colonel Alejandro Armenteros y Hermosa coming dangerously close to pulverizing his wooden chair. His sweating, corpulent body was stuffed into his tailored uniform, making him look like a beach ball swathed in olive green that had sprouted flabby arms and legs and was topped by a florid, pudgy face.

"Ah, Major, come in, come in. Please, close the door."

Damason did, although already he could hardly stand the odor in the room. He knew even if he aired it for the rest of the day, it would still smell. Swallowing, he came to attention and saluted, his hand faltering a little as he realized that the leg of his desk was askew, leaning to one side, as if it was about to come off. The fat pig must have sat on it! he thought, alarmed. If the desk did came apart, and Hermosa found the phone, it would all be over. Even Hermosa wasn't that stupid that he couldn't put two and two together. All Damason could do was try to keep his superior's eyes from wandering over the desk. "*¡Sí, mi coronel!*"

"Yes, yes, at ease. What I'm about to tell you is to not go beyond this room, do you understand?"

Damason nodded. Hermosa loved the sound of his own voice and Damason had learned early on to just shut up and let the man speak. He tried not to betray his discomfort as Hermosa leaned forward, planting his pudgy elbows on the creaking desk.

"Given the *unpleasantness* after today's speech in the plaza, our *comandante* has decided to take a short trip to inspect some of the agricultural holdings of the people. He wishes to ensure that the people all over our great country are still committed to the revolution." He held up a sheet of paper. "Here is the itinerary of the trip. Because of your exemplary service in Havana recently, I am assigning you the task of coordinating security with the other provinces that our leader will be traveling in. You may select one other man from your brigade to assist you."

A broad smile crossed Damason's face as he gave his crispest salute. "It will be my pleasure, Colonel!"

"Good, good. I knew I could rely on you, Major." With a wheeze, the colonel pried himself out of Damason's seat, pulling himself up using the desk, which groaned under the pressure. "Let me know if you need anything for the detail, and I will see what I can provide. Also, you should really get this desk fixed. It looks like it is about to fall apart."

With that, he waddled out of the room, leaving an exhilarated Damason in his odiferous wake. The major closed his door, suddenly uncaring about the cloying odor left in his office, or how close he had come to being caught. He locked the door and leaned against it in dizzy exultation.

Truly, God is on our side, for who else would deliver my people's enemy to me in this manner? he thought. He walked to his desk and sat there for a moment. Then he wrenched the desk to one side, grabbed the cell phone and battery pack, fit them together and tried to control his shaking hands long enough to dial a familiar number to deliver the wonderful news.

22

Kate paced back and forth in front of her Perceptive Pixel touch screen, which, along with her viewglasses, was one of the most vital pieces of technology she used. Taking up most of one wall in her office; the huge screen enabled her to keep track of various ongoing operations around the world without having to spend twelve hours a day in virtual reality. She could manipulate between operations, bring up data files at a glance, move things around in 3-D and connect almost anyone in the organization to anyone else, all just by touching the screen.

But as impressive as it was, she knew no technology was a substitute for eyes on the ground. While she could use the touch screen to zoom in on a city block in downtown Moscow if she wanted, or order a Predator III UAV launched anywhere in the world in about an hour, without the context from someone who knew exactly what was going on, all of that data was just that—pictures or bits of information that were useless without the right interpretation.

She returned to the screen and was about to review status

reports from the Southeast Asia sector when the entire screen flashed green, indicating that field operatives were reporting in. Kate drew four windows on the screen and connected to all of them. The faces of Judy, Jonas and Marcus filled three of the screens, with the fourth available to display other information as necessary.

"This is Primary. Everyone have clear access?" she asked. There were nods and murmurs of assent. "All right, Alpha, due to your narrow window, let's proceed with your report first."

Marcus had already uploaded his digital film file for analysis. "I knew there was a weekly address by the government at their usual place. When I went to observe, I found our subject there as part of the assembly. I did not have the opportunity to make contact with him, as the event was disrupted by protesters demonstrating against the government. They were met by progovernment forces, and some violence ensued—"

"Yes, we saw that." Judy sounded like a cat about to catch a mouse. "Also, your footage showed that you took part in the riot. Care to explain how that happened?"

"Per SOP, I attempted to leave the area, but was attacked by two agitators and was forced to defend myself before I could exit the area," Marcus said.

"Yet the first person that you struck had his back to you and looked to be engaged in attacking a civilian—not a threat to you at all," Judy said.

This time there was a pause before Marcus answered. "I took the appropriate actions necessary to leave the area."

"And put your cover and your mission at risk by getting involved in local matters that were not part of your objective."

"I wasn't about to stand by and let an innocent person get stomped into the ground for doing what she felt was right!"

"Alpha, that is exactly the kind of behavior that we cannot tolerate on assignment—" Judy began.

Kate stepped in to head off a full-scale argument. "Fortunately, no long-term harm seemed to be done. We'll discuss the appropriate action upon your return. Please continue," she ordered.

Marcus composed himself before speaking. "Since I lost sight of the subject before contact or tagging could occur, and our available data does not list his whereabouts, I could use a follow-up avenue. Something other than risking my neck here asking questions out in the open."

Kate brought up the satellite photos of the riot, with the real-time shots of the military convoy leaving the plaza. "Our people are going over the satellite photos of the speech and the demonstration now, but it's going to take some time to trace their route, much less track where individuals may have gone once Castro had reached his destination. The important thing is that our contact is still alive. However, why he hasn't contacted us is what concerns me at the moment."

"Kate, may I see the data file Alpha recorded? It may hold some clues as to what is going on with the contact," Jonas said.

Kate and Judy had a quick, silent conference. Both agreed with a slight not that it would be best to bring Jonas in completely. Kate drew a fifth window and brought up a data file, showing the pan across the standing lines of officers. She froze the file and zoomed in on the face of a major in the Cuban army. "Our contact was a man named Damason Valdes."

Kate took a closer look at the serious officer, with his dark hair and unusual blue eyes, and thought he looked familiar.

Jonas didn't say anything for a long time, just stared at the photo with his lips compressed in the tight line. Kate gave him a few more seconds, knowing that a first read of a subject was usually best done in silence. However, when she thought he had taken enough time, she cleared her throat. "Beta, your initial thoughts?"

"Sorry, he just reminded me of someone I knew a long time ago. Typically, when a double agent has been compromised, they are removed from their duties for immediate interrogation. However, I don't see anything here that leads me to believe he has been compromised to his superiors, which means one of two things. Either they've made him, and are trying to keep him in place in hopes that he'll lead them to other members of his resistance cell, or they haven't, and there's another reason why he has broken contact with us."

Judy nodded. "There are several groups working toward an independent Cuba, both in the U.S. and in-country, but for Major Valdes to suddenly stop communication with us, someone else would have to dangle a fairly large carrot to bring him over to their side."

Kate brought up the latest summary of their last communication. "Major Valdes had previously been a useful source of information on the status of the military and related areas under their control. Lately, however, our analysts found a growing undercurrent of dissatisfaction from him about the regime, that change is too slow in coming, and even the progress the military has made in bringing foreign business and tourists into the country hasn't benefited the people. So, what if someone made him a better offer?"

Jonas grasped her implication first. "Put him in a position

to remove a head of state and accelerate a true revolution. That would most likely mean civil war, with factions of the government and the military going at it, with the population caught in the middle."

"That certainly doesn't fall in line with plans for the region," Judy said.

Kate motioned for silence. "Let's get all of the facts before we decide on a course of action. Jonas, we monitored your initial contact at the greyhound club. Please fill us in on the rest of your meeting."

Kate wasn't sure, but she thought Jonas seemed relieved to have the topic of conversation move elsewhere.

"Certainly. As we were leaving, subject invited me into his car for further conversation. Once there, his bodyguard produced a weapon, as the record will show. Subject then asked why an arms dealer would contact him directly, indicating that they had researched my background, and asked why I had contacted him. I reiterated my cover story and mentioned I was investigating rumors of an operation occurring in the Caribbean. Subject also accused me of taking advantage of the recent power vacuum left in Florida by the arrest of several prominent men in Mr. Heinemann's occupation. I alluded to wanting to expand my business and mentioned a current weapons system I had that people he knew might be interested in. I left him with my cell number and an invitation to join me on my yacht. As of yet, I have not heard from subject, and expect that he is doing more research on me right now."

Kate sent a message to the cyberjocks to see if any other data had been accessed on Heinemann or his company. "Do you think he is involved?"

"In a plot to free Cuba? Very probably. If I get a second meeting, which I expect will happen within the next twelve hours, I will do my best to confirm that."

"All right, until we know more about Beta's subject, I want you, Alpha, to see if you can find out anything on your own. We'll get you whatever data on him that we have as soon as possible. Do not get involved in any other local incidents, do you understand?" Kate said.

"Yes."

"Beta, is there anything you can do to push the meeting up?"

"Initiating contact again at this time would accomplish nothing. I'm sure our subject will call—we just have to be patient. If he's as interested in the weapons as I believe he is, he'll be in touch soon. The potential enemy force has several gunships, and that system would be worth its weight in gold to an incursion force."

"Very well. Alpha, I expect contact every four hours with progress reports. We'll crunch that data as soon as possible and upload it to you. Primary out."

Kate tapped the two windows for Jonas and Marcus, making them vanish as the connection was broken. She kept Judy's open. "What are your thoughts?"

"I'm thinking that Samantha may have been right. In my professional opinion, Marcus is too hot-headed for an operation like this." Judy was looking off-screen as she replied, and Kate figured she was reviewing Marcus's file. "If we weren't already in the middle of it, I'd suggest pulling him out now, but it's too late. We cannot have operatives running around like knights attempting to rescue anyone in need. Damn it, he knows better. The mission is what's important, not risking getting captured by the police. It's bad enough that our Hawaii operation is a half step away from being scrubbed because our operative got too close to her targets. As it is, she's endangered the mission, and now we have another one on the edge because Marcus can't control his macho instincts. I think when he gets back, he should go through the entire psych evaluation. We need to see if he really is Room 59."

"I'll take that under advisement. However, in the future, leave comments about an operative's performance for the after-mission review. I don't want them second-guessing themselves in the middle of duty," Kate said.

"If it wasn't addressed immediately, who knows what Marcus might have done under the guise of appropriate actions. I don't like having to upbraid operatives in the middle of missions, especially since they're supposed to be above that kind of behavior," Judy said.

"Regardless of the circumstances, Judy," Kate said, her tone frosty, "you were out of order, and I don't want to see that again. Are we clear?"

Judy took in the steel-hard look in her superior's eyes, and gave the barest nod. "Perfectly, Kate. Hopefully it won't be an issue in the future."

"It had better not. I'll pull an operative from active duty—any operative—before endangering a mission. What did you think about Jonas's report?"

"Funny, I was about to ask you the same question. Does he know something he's not telling us? And if so, will that endanger the operation? It's bad enough we've got one operative on a loose leash. We don't need another one—especially a department head—running around half-cocked, as well."

"No, we don't. Listen, when I first contacted Jonas about this, he mentioned wanting to be involved in this operation—"

"That was the end run, right? I just want to make sure I follow the chain of events properly," Judy said.

Kate stifled a sigh. "Yes, before the board meeting yesterday morning. That led to his pushing for running the op himself—"

"So if you had reservations, or were concerned he had a personal or some other interest in this, why didn't you say so before then?"

"Because all I had then is exactly what we have now—vague suspicions. I'm not going to bar an operative from a mission because of a look, or a strange pause in the conversation. That isn't enough. We need proof—like what Marcus provided on himself, unfortunately for him—before we suspend or discipline anyone. The one thing I'm not going to let this agency become is a nest of vipers all striving to take each other down for personal gain or petty rivalries." And you can take that as a veiled threat if you want, Kate thought.

Judy's expression didn't change at all as she replied, "That's the last thing I want, as well. However, you and I also have to keep our eyes on the larger picture, which is accomplishing the assigned mission with the most appropriate personnel. Now we suspect that Jonas may have a personal motive in working on this assignment." She paused for a moment. "I'm sure there's no hope of just coming out and asking him, is there?"

Kate shook her head. "That would be about as effective as asking you the same question. Jonas is a professional, first and foremost. He'll bury his feelings so deep neither of us, even with all our experience, would be able to see what's really going on. More importantly, he's already made the initial contact, so to pull him out now would cause too much suspicion and likely spook Castilo. Like it or not, we have to continue as planned, at least for the time being. I'm moving both operatives to round-the-clock monitoring, so at least we'll be informed if anything untoward happens."

"Not like we'd be able to do anything about it if either of them does take off on their own," Judy pointed out.

"Then it's in everyone's best interests to make sure that doesn't happen." A flashing icon caught Kate's eye. "Gotta run, Judy, the boys are calling—probably got a hit on the Heinemann data. I'll keep you informed."

"Thank you, Kate, I'll do the same."

Kate closed her link with Judy and opened one with the hackers. "What have you got for me?"

KeyWiz's avatar—a goateed, twentysomething geek in a wizard hat and long gray trenchcoat—popped up. "We intercepted this call twelve minutes ago. An unnamed caller inquiring about our man Heinemann to a black-market dealer he knows in Belgrade. We hacked the call, matched it to a ninety-eight percent positive voiceprint and gave him the bona fides for ol' Ferdy. As far as the caller knows, our man is as legit as the day is long. Our operative should probably get a callback within the hour."

"Excellent work, Key. Notify the others that Alpha is to be moved to twenty-four-hour overwatch status, with immediate notification if you see anything unusual happening."

"Overtime gig—bonus. We're on it. If either of these guys even looks at someone else the wrong way, we'll let you know."

"Thanks." Kate cut that connection and let the touch

screen go blank. She walked back to her office door and opened it, then sat down in her chair, staring at nothing in particular.

"Busy day, huh?" Mindy poked her head around the corner.

"Yeah, you could say that. This was one of those days when I wish I could open my office windows and let a bit of air in."

"Everything all right?"

Sure, except I don't know whether one of my operatives is able to execute this mission without his personal issues getting in the way, she thought. But all she said was, "Besides a couple of minor personnel issues, everything's fine."

"Why don't you take a break and grab a bite? I've got some crostini broiling, and was gonna throw together some angel hair, plum tomatoes and a bit of pesto and white wine."

The mere mention of food made Kate's stomach growl, reminding her she hadn't eaten anything since breakfast. In fact, she hadn't left the office area in almost eleven hours. "Yeah, I think that's a good idea. Besides, you can catch me up on the latest episode of *Crime Wave*."

"Ooh, you'll love this one. Two gangbangers in Phoenix went at it in a drive-by, and—"

Kate kept one ear on Mindy's play-by-play as she got up, leaving her empty chair spinning in her wake. She followed the younger woman out the door.

23

Jonas didn't like waiting. While he recognized it as a necessary part of his job, that never made the time spent anticipating his opponent's next move any more pleasant. It was all too easy to overanalyze a situation, to spin wilder and wilder hypotheses about what might happen until an operative could think himself into freezing at a critical moment, or miss that crucial piece of data that meant the difference between completing a mission successfully or watching it get blown wide-open.

But for Jonas, waiting for Castilo to call meant that he had nothing to do at the moment but ponder the past, and what might have been.

June 19, 1973

JONAS LAY on the ground, covered by palm fronds, scope to his eye, pistol in his other hand. He was not only watching for Marisa, but any patrolling Cuban soldiers. He didn't want to risk bringing the entire unit running with a shot. If he had to take one down, he'd figure out a way to do it as silently as possible. The pistol would be a last resort.

Every minute that ticked away made him more nervous. He kept expecting to hear a shout of alarm from one of the soldiers—or even worse, a scream from Marisa. The jungle's heat and the horde of insects marching over him didn't improve the situation any, either.

A minute rustle in the brush to his right made him slowly swivel the long night-vision scope that way. A hunched-over form crept through the foliage toward him. Jonas kept his hand on his weapon and didn't move from cover, not until he was sure.

"Psst. Karl?" It could have been a man or a woman hissing his name. Jonas trained the scope on the person's face, revealing Marisa's attractive features. Jonas didn't move until she came within three feet, as he was still watching the brush behind her, making sure she wasn't flushing him right into an ambush. She came closer, two feet, one foot, right in front of him.

Setting the scope down, Jonas rose and wrapped her up in his arms, one hand going over her mouth. She stiffened for a moment, then relaxed, not even making a peep.

"For god's sake, don't ever do that again!" he hissed. "If you had been discovered—"

Marisa bit down on his fingers, surprising Jonas so much that he whipped his hand away. "If I had been discovered, I would have been a girl lost in the woods. But if you had been discovered, you would be dead. It was the simplest way to get the information we need," Marisa said.

"Why didn't you let me know first, instead of just running off into the forest? I could have shot you when you returned, you know."

He swore he heard the smile in her voice. "I didn't discuss it with you because you would have said no, and there wasn't time to argue. And you wouldn't have shot me because the noise would bring the soldiers. You had to do exactly what you did—take me by surprise, and, I hope, realize that I am anything but a man when you did."

She pressed against him to emphasize her point, and for a moment, Jonas was stunned by the thought that she might be flirting with him. Dismissing the ridiculous idea, he grudgingly conceded her point. "Very well, what did you find out?"

"The truck is about forty yards to the east-southeast, concealed at the side of the trail. The two men guarding it are under radio silence and are not even allowed to use any lights. They appear to be the point guards, who are supposed to let the others know your team is approaching, then slam the back door shut on them."

"A simple, if effective, trap." Jonas tried putting weight on his injured foot, wincing at the stab of pain. "We need to eliminate them without allowing either to contact the others. Take me there."

He sank to the ground again, packed up his equipment and weapons, took back his machete and crawled after her to the overgrown road. Marisa crouched next to him while he got out the scope and examined the truck. It was tucked into a niche at the side of the trail and masked by cut saplings and brush. It was an early 1960s Russian-built, three-and-a-half ton Zil, with the back converted from a flatbed into a troop carrier by adding rough sidewalls. Although Marisa had said the two men were supposed to be under lights-out, he saw the glow of lit cigarettes from inside the cab. The green-white pinpoints of light were like miniature stars in the scope's eyepiece. He shook his head in disgust—that security lapse would have gotten any member of his team kicked out of the unit.

They pulled back into the trees again. Jonas put the scope away and closed his eyes, trying to regain his night vision. He put his lips close to Marisa's ear. "Have you ever killed a man?"

She tensed for a moment, then shook her head.

"Can you? And be honest, I cannot have you freeze at a critical moment," Jonas whispered.

Again she paused, then nodded.

"All right, here's how we'll do it. You will approach the passenger side. I will take the driver. You *will not move* until I do. When I've eliminated the driver, the other soldier's natural instinct will be to help his partner, then get on the radio. Either way, he'll turn away from you and present a clean target. When you hear the commotion, step onto the running board and stab him between his shoulder blades. If he is still sitting upright in the seat, then reach in and stab him in the stomach if possible. Otherwise you'd have to aim for his upper chest, and your blade might deflect off a rib. Do you understand?"

Marisa nodded.

"Again, do not move until I do—you'll know when. When we separate, begin counting to five hundred, and be in position by the time you reach the end. When I've finished my count, I'll take out the driver right away, and you must be close to the truck and ready to go by then."

She nodded again.

"Good luck." Jonas released her and Marisa vanished into the black jungle again. Jonas gave her twenty seconds, then crawled slowly forward, parallel to the front of the truck, keeping the silent count in his head all the while. About ten yards past the vehicle, he crept to the edge of the road and peeked out, making sure he hadn't attracted any attention. He put an arm into the overgrown path and held it there. No reaction came from the truck. Jonas put his other arm out. His internal count hit two hundred. He slid his right leg out, then his left. Still nothing. Moving one limb at a time, Jonas crawled across the knee-high grass, slipping into and out of the deep ruts in the road. His foot throbbed, his hands and knees ached and he was being bitten all over his face, neck and fingers. But he ignored all of that, focusing every bit of willpower he possessed on getting back into cover so he could get to the truck.

Step by step, he covered the few yards from one side of the road to the other, always keeping an eye on the two soldiers. He crawled into the foliage as his internal count edged past three hundred. He was still fifteen yards away from the truck, and had to be even more cautious. Squirming through the brush on his belly, placing every hand and knee with care, he slithered through the tall grass and bushes until, as his count approached five hundred, he saw the truck's rear tire through the brush.

Jonas heard the squeak of an opening door, then the rustle of boots crushing grass as someone walked toward him. He froze, his hand inching toward his sheathed machete as the steps grew louder, then stopped right in front of where he was hidden.

He heard a sound, like metal rustling, followed by a pattering noise on the leaves and grass around him. Drops of acrid-smelling liquid dripped on his neck and back.

The bastard's pissing on me! Jonas held his nose as the soldier finished and zipped up. There was no choice now. Reeking of urine, Jonas knew he'd never be able to sneak up on the soldier once he got back into the truck. Drawing his machete, Jonas burst from the jungle and lunged at the soldier, ignoring the flare of agony from his sprained ankle.

The man whirled around to see Jonas, blade lifted overhead, coming straight at him. Eyes widening in the darkness, he raised his arm to block the weapon while inhaling to yell for help. Jonas's free hand scrabbled for the man's mouth, trying to cover it before he could make a noise. The soldier's blocking hand found his wrist and pushed the machete away while his free hand locked on Jonas's throat and began squeezing. For a moment, the two men struggled silently against each other, only their hoarse pants for breath heard in the night air.

His vision starting to gray at the edges, Jonas knew he had about twenty seconds before he passed out. He released the machete, letting it drop on the Cuban soldier's head. The man made a grab for the weapon, and Jonas used the distraction to move his right arm up in a circle block to pry the man's hand from his throat while grabbing his sleeve and jerking him forward as he slammed his forehead into the man's nose. All the while he kept his hand clamped over his opponent's mouth.

The soldier arced back, a black trail of blood spraying from his face as he pistoned his knee toward Jonas's crotch.

Jonas sensed more than saw the blow coming, and shifted

out of the way so that the other man's leg smacked hard into his thigh, numbing the muscle. The wiry Cuban used his hold on Jonas's wrist to try to turn him against the truck while opening his mouth wide to attempt to bite Jonas's fingers. Jonas resisted the throw, but released his hold on the man's face and instead tried to launch a palm strike at his chin. His opponent dodged out of the way and sucked in a huge lungful of air to shout for help.

Jonas jammed his forearm into the guy's mouth, cramming it so full of flesh and cloth that he couldn't close it. He kept pushing forward, driving the man back and then against the side of the truck, making it rock with the impact. He felt the man's fists pummel his midsection, and tightened his stomach against the blows. The Cuban clawed for his eyes, but Jonas had five inches on him, and was able to keep his face out of reach. Jonas threw his knee up into the man's stomach, connecting solidly beneath his rib cage. The soldier sagged, choking for air, and Jonas kneed him again, making sure he couldn't get up. Holding the man between the truck and his forearm, he lifted his opponent's head up and drove three knuckles into his larynx, crushing it. The man wheezed, and Jonas let him drop to the ground, both of his hands clutching feebly at his injured throat.

Jonas didn't stop to finish him, but grabbed his machete from where it had fallen and hobbled to the cab of the truck, jerking the door open and raising the blade to find—

The other Cuban soldier, his chest stained black with blood, was hanging half out of the passenger door, dead. Fearing the worst, Jonas limped around to the other side, expecting to see a third body lying in the grass.

Marisa sat next to the truck, holding her dark, blood-stained hands away from her. She looked up at him, and Jonas saw tears in her eyes. "You said he couldn't make any noise, so when he started to check on his friend I stabbed him, only he came at me, and I just kept stabbing and stabbing him, but he wouldn't stop—"

Jonas walked to her as quickly as he could, knelt down and took her in his arms. "No, you stopped him. He won't be coming after you, or anyone else again. It's all right, you did just fine."

A RINGING CELL PHONE JARRED Jonas out of his reverie. He flipped it open. *"Ja?"*

"Mr. Heinemann, this is Rafael Castilo. I hope I haven't caught you at an inconvenient time."

"Not at all, Mr. Castilo. In fact, I was hoping to hear from you. I can only assume this call is in regards to our previous conversation."

The businessman's voice was like oiled silk. "You are correct. I would like to accept your invitation, if it is still open, and would very much like to sample one of your man's drinks. It sounds very appealing."

"I think that can be arranged. Will you be bringing any friends with you?" Jonas asked.

"Not at this time. If I like what you show me, then I will be able to put you in touch with them. Shall we say six o'clock?"

"Excellent. Why don't I have my people meet you at the Key Biscayne Yacht Club? My runabout is berthed there, and they will bring you out to the yacht, where I insist that you dine with me. I do hope your lovely wife will be joining us?" Jonas asked, even though he already knew the answer.

"I'm afraid she has a prior engagement. Until six, then," Castilo said.

"I'm looking forward to it." Jonas snapped the phone closed and opened another one, calling Kate to let her know that his fish was about to jump into the boat. But as he waited for the connection, his mind kept wandering back to Marisa, and her deep blue eyes.

24

Marcus tamped down his anger as he stalked through the Havana streets.

Who does that high-toned British bitch think she is, sandbagging me like that? If she's ever been in the field longer than an afternoon, I'll eat my goddamn phone. I handled that riot just fine, didn't even come close to getting caught. Next time I'll turn off those damn glasses before doing something that could be construed as not within her bloody mission parameters.

With an effort, he put his feelings aside and got back to the problem at hand. All right, back to business. I've got four million possibilities in a city with no phone books. I've been in worse spots. He racked his brain, trying to figure a way in. Cuba didn't have any corner Internet cafés he could just stroll into. Something Kate had mentioned in the briefing clamored for his attention, an off-the-cuff remark about the military becoming more involved in Cuban businesses. That's how to find him, he thought.

Marcus hailed a small three-wheeled cab and told the driver, "Hotel Saratoga, please."

The cabdriver looked at him strangely, but Marcus nodded and discreetly held up a palmful of pesos. The cab took off so quickly it rose up on its two back wheels, and Marcus had to brace himself in the back to keep from falling over.

Fifteen minutes later, he stood across the street from one of Havana's recent success stories. According to his information, the Saratoga dated from the late nineteenth century, but had closed by the time of the revolution and was left to rot for a half century. Recently restored with modern amenities, it was now one of the city's top destinations. On the western edge of the historical center, it afforded a fantastic view of the *Capitolio Nacional,* Cuba's version of a capitol building, which looked remarkably like a certain white marble domed building in Washington, D.C.

Looking at the eight-story building's elegant, neoclassical facade, Marcus was reminded even more of the crumbling neighborhoods he had passed, only several blocks away, on the way over. He knew that it was the same in cities all over the world, yet the disparity kept gnawing at him. At least I now know firsthand why my parents left. They certainly didn't want to raise me or my brothers here. But for each one that was able to escape, hundreds, thousands more were stuck, struggling to live every day as best they could.

Just a few yards away, however, a steady flow of well-dressed European, Canadian and even American tourists walked in and out of the Saratoga, either uncaring of the plight of the people, or perhaps just considering it part of the local color. Marcus checked the street for policemen, then casually crossed the road and walked past the front of the hotel, heading around back. As he expected, there was a large, ancient truck unloading crates of vegetables. Marcus edged closer, biding his time until no one was around the back of the flatbed. He walked over, grabbed a crate of lettuce, hoisted it to his shoulder and entered the hotel kitchen.

The long, large room was frantic with activity as the staff prepared for the evening dinner crowd. Steam rose from several large pots and pans of sizzling vegetables and meats cooked over the open flames of stainless-steel industrial stoves. White-uniformed chefs barked orders at hapless assistants who weren't doing whatever they were doing fast or well enough.

Marcus walked through the room, looking like just another faceless laborer. He found the walk-in cooler for the vegetables and set his crate down next to the rest of them and headed back out, but instead of turning right, toward the exit, he turned left and headed out of the kitchen, into the ground floor of the hotel.

The corridors were small and cramped, but Marcus slipped past people coming and going, none of whom gave him a second glance. He knew the first rule of infiltration— look as if you belong, and even more importantly, as if you know exactly where you're going. He navigated the warren of passageways until he found the way to the front lobby. He was looking for the manager's office, who would certainly have a computer attached to their central network. The Saratoga most likely had a business center, but he didn't want to attract attention by using it and risk drawing unnecessary attention from security.

Although he might have been able to pass himself off as

a Spanish tourist, he had Cuban papers, so that story wouldn't hold up to determined scrutiny. With the high level of tourist apartheid, he couldn't afford to draw any attention to himself. As strange as it seemed, he decided this was the less risky plan—he just had to wait for the right opportunity.

The manager's office was near the long front desk on the far side of the bright black-and-white-tiled lobby. The area bustled with people coming, going or just relaxing. Marcus slipped across the room until he found a small table behind a tall potted fern where he could watch the manager's door. He had just settled when a dozen Japanese tourists walked through the door and mobbed the front desk. The desk staff began processing their reservations and summoned translation help. Pretending to be engrossed in a tourist magazine, Marcus waited until the manager came out to assist with the line of guests.

Marcus palmed his phone and extended a small metal strip from the bottom. The Saratoga may have recreated old-world charm for its decor, but the security was pure twenty-first century, with key cards needed to access the doors. His phone contained a program that would bypass the security of most card or combination door locks. He stepped around the tall column that formed one corner of the desk, and walked confidently to the manager's office. Shrouded in shadow, the door was hidden from direct sight of the guests and the staff who assisted them. He slipped the metal prong into the door slot and activated the program. There was a soft click, and Marcus opened the door and slipped inside.

Compared to the opulence of the lobby, the office was

spartan, with a plain metal desk, wheeled office chair, metal file cabinet and Marcus's goal—a fairly new computer next to a laser printer. Marcus circled the desk and set his phone next to the computer, bringing up another program to connect to the hotel's network. He accessed the computer and began searching for the words "*Mayor,*" "Damason" and "Valdes" in any databases, e-mails or any of the various files across the country. He figured there had to be a listing of officers' addresses somewhere. The data-miner program would find and download any files with those names. He waited for several tense minutes.

The phone flashed softly twice, signaling it was finished. Marcus slipped it into his pocket and stood—just as the office door opened.

Framed in the doorway was the manager of the hotel, his mouth dropping open in shock. "Who are you? What are you doing in here?"

"It's about time you got here. I've been waiting for twenty minutes." Marcus came around the desk and held out his hand. "Jose Prado, with the Ministry of Tourism."

The words had the desired effect, as the manager took his hand and shook it gingerly. "What is this all about?"

"We've had complaints about a group of high-class prostitutes harassing the tourists here. They don't look like the usual working women, which is why they've been getting away with it." It wasn't the best cover story, but Marcus needed to draw attention away from what he had been doing at the computer, and he figured the notion of working girls around his hotel would put the manager on the defensive immediately.

"This is the first I've heard of it. Our security would have notified me immediately," the manager said.

Marcus shook his head. "Normally, that is true. However, we suspect that one or more of your employees are also involved."

The manager's face darkened and Marcus got the sinking feeling he'd pushed his luck too far. "What? I'll get to the bottom of this right now. Let's just get my head of security in here and see what he has to say about this." Reaching for the phone, the manager glanced at Marcus again, suspicion warring with helpfulness. "Let me see some identification."

Apparently, suspicion had won. Big mistake, Marcus thought, but said, "Of course," as he reached for his nonexistent credentials.

As the manager picked up the phone, Marcus grabbed his wrist and twisted it, making him drop the receiver.

"What are you doing?"

Marcus released his wrist and brought his other hand, now clenched into a fist, around and buried it into the man's stomach, turning his shout for help into a strangled wheeze. As the man doubled over, Marcus stepped back and rabbit-punched him, sending him down to the floor.

"Well, that was inconspicuous," he muttered, heading for the door. Opening it, he was confronted by a white-shirted desk clerk. "What's going on in here?" the clerk asked.

Marcus stepped aside to let the youth see the prone manager. "I was waiting for him, and he came inside and collapsed. You'd better get some help."

The clerk's eyes narrowed with suspicion.

"Stay here." He went for a phone on the front desk, and as soon as he did, Marcus was out the door and trotting down the corridor toward the kitchen. He heard a shout from behind him, but kept going. Only when he heard footsteps pounding behind him did he break into a run. He was almost to the kitchen when the double doors opened, and three assistant chefs came out, chattering among themselves.

Marcus heard "Stop that man!" behind him, and reached out to grab the nearest to the kitchen by his white smock. He yanked him around and threw him down the hall while the other two watched in shock. Kicking the door open, he looked over his shoulder to see the assistant careen into two men who could only be security. They managed to dodge him and kept coming, yelling at him to stop.

Marcus scooted through the doors and glanced around for a distraction. He spotted a large, pot of boiling soup stock. Grabbing one handle, he gritted his teeth as the hot metal seared his hand, but tipped the container over just as the guards hit the door, sending a wave of boiling liquid cascading their way. He shoved the pot off the stove, as well, and turned, heading for the back doors.

The only problem was that instead of scattering for cover like normal people, three portly chefs stood in his way. The first one brandished a knife, the second held a large marble pestle and the third one wielded a hardwood pepper shaker easily two feet long and thick enough that it could probably crush a man's skull with one blow.

Marcus leaped up onto the metal table, running down its length and scattering prepared meals and ingredients in his wake. Shouting furiously, the chefs tried to pursue, but he had a couple steps on them, and jumped down just as the first one came at him with the knife. Marcus shoved a large cutting board full of sliced peppers off the table at him. The vegetables flew under the man's feet, making him slip on the tile floor and blocking the other two, as well.

Running for the exit, Marcus almost collided with a guy bringing in another box of produce. Once outside, he darted between the truck and the hotel, sprinting across the small lot as fast as he could, leaving the shouts of the furious security guards and chefs behind.

Almost all of them. Marcus spared a look back to see two of the guards still chasing after him, shouting at him to stop. He ran as fast as he could down Dragones Street, hoping to lose his pursuers in the neighborhoods a few blocks away.

The shouting alerted a pair of police officers halfway up a cross street. One joined the chase immediately while the other ran to his white Peugeot at the far end of the block. This just keeps getting worse, Marcus thought. Reaching an intersection, he turned right, looking for smaller side streets where he could lose his pursuers in the urban maze. If the police car caught up with him, however, he was done.

He was still on what looked like a main street, with scattered pockets of people walking along the sides of the road, past brightly colored shops. The only good thing so far, he thought, was that no one seemed the least bit interested in assisting the police in stopping him. Marcus bolted into an intersection and heard the blast of a horn as a pristine 1959 purple-and-white Chevy screeched to a halt, its chrome bumper mere inches from his leg.

In for a pound, in for a ton, he thought. Although he knew that car theft was a serious offense in Cuba, it was better than the absolute jail time he'd get if caught right now. Going to the driver's door, he yanked it open and grabbed the driver by the hair, pulling him out with a startled yell.

"Sorry, *señor*," Marcus apologized as he slid behind the wheel and floored it, shooting across the intersection just as the security and police came pounding around the corner. He heard the rising siren of the police car, and concentrated on losing the cops as quickly as possible.

He crossed the intersection and drove for another block, then turned left onto a smaller street, praying that he wouldn't encounter another vehicle coming the opposite way, as there was barely enough room for his car. At the next corner he took a right, then went two more blocks and turned left again, heading deeper into the decaying heart of Old Havana. He slowed, trying to maintain the speed limit and look as if he was driving casually. The siren mocked him with its closeness, but he hadn't seen the police car behind him yet, and figured he was about to make his escape.

But as he turned right down a narrow street, he found the way blocked by another white Peugeot, its lone blue light whirling as it slowly advanced. Marcus heard the howl of an approaching siren from behind him, and slammed the accelerator to the floor. The engine groaned in protest, making the entire car vibrate as it was pushed to a speed it probably hadn't seen in decades. The two officers' jaws dropped as he approached. They held up their hands as if they could stop his charge by force of will alone. Marcus said a silent apology to the car and its owner again as the distance rapidly shrank between the two vehicles.

With a jarring crunch of glass, plastic and metal, the speeding Chevy rammed into the French hatchback, sending the lighter car careening back into the intersection. Other than the bone-shaking impact, the Chevy didn't seem remotely affected by the crash, although Marcus was sure he had caused some cosmetic damage. He wrenched the wheel sideways, breaking his car free from the police vehicle, and took off down the street. At the nearest intersection he turned left, then right at the next, then left again, driving into an even seedier part of town. At the first street that didn't have anyone on it, he pulled into an alley so narrow he couldn't open the car doors. He turned off the car, rolled the window down and slid out. He waited a few minutes before walking down the alley to the other end and strolling casually away. He tensed as another police car sped past him, its siren wailing, but it didn't slow down or give him a second glance.

That was too close, Marcus thought. He scratched his head, thinking he'd have to change his appearance to avoid suspicion, as enough people had gotten a look at him to put out a general description to the police. But first he had to put as much distance between himself and the scene as possible.

As he walked, he palmed his cell phone and scrolled through the information he had gleaned from the hotel's computer. On the next-to-last file was Major Damason Valdes's personal information, including his parents, father unknown, mother deceased, along with a home address in Havana.

Marcus smiled as he read the information. I wonder if Ms. Uptight would have thought any of that fell under my mission parameters.

25

I have to admit, a man could certainly get used to this, Jonas thought.

He stood on the sundeck of the *Deep Water*, sipping a weak whisky and water—he had to stay in character, after all—and enjoyed the magnificent sunset. Above the placid water, the sky was aflame in hues of red, orange, gold and pink as the sun slowly sank. The faint cries of circling seagulls and the tang of salt in the air added to the relaxed atmosphere.

"Nice view, isn't it?" Karen appeared behind him, clad in a stunning one-piece white swimsuit that revealed enough of her slender body to start any man's thoughts drifting. She held another highball glass, which she clinked against his. "An ill-gotten penny for your thoughts."

Jonas was dressed for his role, too, wearing a cream linen shirt, beige linen slacks and hand-woven Italian loafers. His sunglasses were the same Christian Diors and around his wrist was a sleek NOMOS Glashütte watch. "I was just thinking if this is what the criminals are enjoying, I may have chosen the wrong profession."

"Are you suggesting that saving a nation, or the world, doesn't have its perks?" Karen asked with a sly grin.

"So far, I think working with you has been the best thing about this mission." Jonas's grin faded as he saw a white dot appear on the horizon. It quickly grew into the same Tiara yacht he'd used to drop Marcus off near Cuba two days earlier. He saw three men and one woman on board. "Almost show time."

Karen pressed one side of her pair of designer sunglasses. "Target is approaching. Everyone assume their positions."

The entire nine-person crew of the *Deep Water* was composed of Room 59 trainees in their final weeks of course work. Jonas and Karen had pulled a few strings and got them on board as part of their training to handle undercover situations. For the most part, they were to carry out whatever their assigned crew duties were, and nothing more unless either Jonas or Karen ordered otherwise.

The pleasure boat approached the rear of the larger vessel, and was met by two crew members in white shirts and navy shorts. In the cockpit was Rafael Castilo, his bodyguard and two more members of the crew, a young man and woman. Jonas had requested that this particular pair pick up the businessman to set his mind more at ease. He was sure that either of them could have handled the bodyguard, if it had come to that.

The massive man exited the boat first, inspecting, checking everywhere, one hand near his holstered side arm without being too obvious about it. Jonas raised his appraisal of the man another notch. "I'm surprised he allowed Castilo to come here at all. They're outnumbered five to one, with limited escape or evasion avenues," he said quietly.

"Maybe he's just that confident," Karen said.

"Maybe. Would you do me a favor and see about dinner? I should greet our guest."

"You just want me to make a suitably distracting entrance later, don't you? On the upper deck?"

Jonas smiled. "Right. That's why men will never win the gender wars—women are too adept at reading our simple minds."

Jonas walked down the narrow set of stairs to the aft deck. "Rafael, so good to see you." He nodded at Castilo's protector, as well. "I trust the ride over was pleasant."

Castilo sighed, glowering at his bodyguard. "Once we got aboard, things were very comfortable, but nothing like this." The businessman looked around with the nonchalance of the very rich. "This is a magnificent vessel." His comment was more of a formality than anything else.

"I'm sure she must pale in comparison to others in the area, and in the Mediterranean she's practically a rowboat," Jonas said.

"I'm sure she holds her own. What's her speed, twenty knots?"

"Twenty-one is the standard. Perhaps you'd like to enjoy a short cruise after our meal. It's a bit late for the sunset, but I've had a light supper prepared."

"We'll see. I noticed that your boat hasn't docked in the harbor over the past few days." His tone made the statement more of a question.

"I find the harbor a bit claustrophobic when I'm here. Also, I don't wish to draw too much attention to my comings and goings, which is why I prefer to stay out here and commute in when necessary."

"Of course—the better to discuss business, yes?" Castilo said.

Jonas allowed himself a small, satisfied nod. "Quite. Shall we?"

He followed Castilo and his bodyguard to the upper aft deck, where service for four had been laid out on a round, cloth-covered table. As they approached, the sliding-glass doors opened and Karen stepped out. She had wrapped a colorful flower-printed sarong around her waist, offering tantalizing glimpses of her tanned legs. "You remember Joanne?"

"Impossible to forget." Castilo lifted her hand to his lips, gazing at her all the while.

Karen returned his direct look without blinking. "Thank you, Rafael. It is a pleasure to be appreciated once in a while." She shot Jonas a half kidding, half serious look. "Dinner is almost ready, gentlemen."

"Thank you, my dear." Jonas turned back to Castilo and gestured to his guardian. "Are you— I'm sorry, I don't believe we were ever properly introduced." He held out his hand to the bodyguard, who looked down at it for a second before taking it and shaking, his grip firm but not crushing.

"You can call me Theodore."

"And I am Ferdinand. Please, join us. There's no need to be on the clock out here. I wouldn't be much of a businessman if my potential clients kept meeting with accidents," he said with a genuine smile. "Besides, I always enjoy the company of someone who may have used some of my wares at one time."

Theodore's eyes flicked to his boss, who nodded almost imperceptibly. The quartet sat down, with Castilo seated to the right of Karen, who sat next to Jonas. Theodore took the fourth chair. Jonas glanced just for a second at the tropical floral arrangement in the middle of the table and the tiny camera that was recording everything Castilo said, along with every move he made.

Two crew members came out, bearing bowls of spicy conch chowder that they set in front of each person. The soup was followed by a light salad, then medallions of beef in a port-wine reduction, accompanied by lobster tails and drawn butter.

When he saw the main course, Castilo chuckled. "Let me get this straight. You consider surf and turf to be a light supper?"

Jonas raised his glass of wine. "What can I say—I'm German. To us, this *is* a light supper." His tone was light, but it was Karen's enthusiastic nod that made everyone laugh, even eliciting a brief smile from Theodore.

Throughout the meal, Castilo was charming and gregarious, whether he was flirting with Karen or holding his own on every topic, domestic or otherwise, brought up at the table. The strange thing was that Jonas could almost see himself liking this man. He was intelligent, quick-witted and showed a streak of ruthlessness that a successful businessman had to have to survive in today's harsh economic world. Although his tone was light, Jonas sensed he was impatient to get to the real reason they were there. However, Jonas continued his role of expansive, relaxed host, knowing that the longer Rafael had to wait, the more eager he would be to move the deal forward.

And besides, it's not like this delay is all bad for him, either, he thought, glancing at his fellow operative. Karen was her usual radiant self, playing Jonas's slightly bored mistress of the ship. She bloomed under Castilo's compliments and did her best to wrap him around her finger. She also sulked just a bit when Jonas gently admonished her for being too forward with their guest, but all was quickly forgiven by dessert, a flourless chocolate cake that resembled a dense mousse, accompanied by Guatemalan coffee.

Theodore, on the other hand, accomplished the unusual task of dining while barely looking at his plate. His manners were impeccable, and his dishes were as clean as if he had once served time—which Jonas expected he had—and wasn't about to waste a single bite of food ever again. Jonas attempted to draw him out in conversation, as well, but his replies were polite but closed. He apparently considered himself still on duty. He did not drink in Karen with his eyes, as most red-blooded men did, but observed her dispassionately, as another possible threat to his employer. He also kept a close eye on the servers every time a course was presented or cleared. Between the two men, Jonas was more concerned about projecting the right image to Theodore—that of a successful black market businessman. He figured Theodore had most likely traveled in circles closer to Heinemann's, and therefore would also probably be more suspicious than Castilo. His overall impression, like at their first meeting, was that Theodore would be a good one to watch your back. That could make things problematic down the line if he really was as good as he appeared to be.

The sun had long disappeared by the time they had finished, and Castilo patted his stomach in contentment. "Thank you for an excellent meal."

Jonas patted the armrest of his chair. "When my crew brings her over from the Mediterranean, I always make sure that a top chef is aboard, as well. Now, how about an after-dinner drink?"

Castilo's eyes lit up. "That would be excellent."

"I'll join you," Karen said, rising.

"Not this time, I'm afraid, my dear. Rafael and I have some business to discuss, and you would be so dreadfully bored," Jonas said.

She pouted, the expression doing delightful things to her full lips. "Someday, I swear, I'm going to make you go a whole day without discussing business." She stepped over and gave Castilo an expansive hug. "It was a pleasure seeing you again. Please give my regards to Javier. I do hope I will have the chance to see her again."

"I'm sure she would enjoy that, my dear. You are, as always, enchanting to the last. *Buenos noches.*"

"Good night." She pecked Jonas on the cheek and flounced into the saloon, the sarong swirling around her legs.

The three men watched her go, Castilo with a sly-smile curling his lips. "She appears to be quite a handful."

Jonas smiled. "Sometimes my dear Joanne requires both, but she is nothing I cannot handle." He motioned to the stairs behind them. "Shall we?"

He led the two men to the upper saloon, now softly lit by recessed lighting. On a low table in the center of the room sat a long olive-green aluminum box with rounded corners, with the metal security bands intact. It was stamped with Rocket Ammunition With Explosive Projectile on the top and the letters FRD on the end.

Castilo's eyes widened when he saw the case. Jonas smiled. "Would you care for something from the bar?"

"In a minute. Our business has waited long enough."

Jonas walked to the table and stood in front of the case. "Rafael, before I show you what I have to offer, I want you to know one thing. I meant what I said yesterday. My business may seem motivated simply by greed, and on the whole indifferent to the suffering of humanity, but I view my services as providing necessary equipment to people. I do so in the hope that, should they have to resort to using force, the munitions I supply may shorten, or even prevent a conflict if possible."

Castilo listened to his words with a slight frown. "I have met many businessmen, each with their own reasons for doing what they do. However, this is the first time I've ever met an arms dealer with a heart of gold."

Shrugging, Jonas walked over and picked up a small wire cutter, offering it to the other man. "As you can see, these haven't even been taken out of their shipping crates. I thought you'd like to do the honors so you can see for yourself that everything is intact."

While Castilo eyed the long metal box with interest, he shook his head. "I will confess that I do not have your experience in these matters. If you please?"

"My pleasure." Jonas walked to one side of the box and pointed to a hexagonal metal disk at the end. There was a circle inside the disk divided into four blue sections by two crossed black lines. "As you will see, the humidity indicator shows that this box has not been tampered with. That shows that this system has not been opened or repackaged."

"Perhaps, but the true proof is in seeing what's inside with my own eyes," Castilo replied.

Jonas unlocked the heavy metal padlocks on each closure and removed them, then broke the wire seal between the lid and the bottom of the case and opened it. Nestled within was the finned tube of a missile launcher. "Gentlemen, this is the FIM-92A Stinger-RMP Block I surface-to-air missile. Approximately fifteen and a half kilograms when loaded, with a speed of Mach 2.2 plus, a ceiling of three miles and a range of eight miles, it is suitable for engaging all types of low-flying air- or rotorcraft."

Castilo and Theodore walked over to the case and stared at the innocuous length of metal and plastic inside. Theodore broke the silence first. "Where are the gripstocks? Normally those are shipped separately."

Jonas nodded. "If you'll check under the table, there is another case that contains the gripstock with its integral Identify Friend or Foe circuitry. Each weapon system is sold with five missile rounds apiece, along with the necessary instructions for use."

Theodore pulled on a pair of thin black leather gloves and slid out a smaller green metal case, opening it to verify Jonas's words. "And the battery systems are fully operational?"

"Absolutely. However, I hope you'll excuse me if I do not propose a demonstration at this time."

"What about end-user certificates?"

Jonas frowned. "That would be interesting. I don't think the mujahideen really cared where these went. They were just happy to receive payment for them once these items were no longer needed."

Both of the men looked up at Jonas. "Is that where these came from?" Castilo asked.

Jonas spread his hands. "I'm afraid I cannot say anything more. If a nation is interested in purchasing these, then I'm sure something could be worked out. However, I didn't know you were representing a country at this time."

Castilo straightened from where he had leaned over to get a better look at the missile system. "I do represent a country, even if it does not know that yet. If we were to assume that I could put you in touch with a buyer, what would the total cost be?"

"Due to their proven effectiveness and relative scarcity, I would have to charge a serious buyer a quarter of a million dollars for each set, consisting of the weapon system and five missile rounds."

Castilo looked at Theodore and nodded at the double doors. The bodyguard slipped out the entryway, standing outside as if guarding access to the room. "I think I'll have that drink now, if you please."

"Of course." Jonas crossed to the bar. "Rémy Martin?"

Rafael waved a hand in assent, his gaze not straying from the boxed Stinger launcher. Jonas poured two snifters of the cognac. He approached the other man slowly, holding out the crystal snifter. "Join me?"

Castilo nodded, accepting the glass and walking over to a set of armchairs arranged around a small low table in the corner. He sat down and swirled his drink, sniffed appreciatively, then took a slow swallow.

Jonas sat back and did the same, letting the silence draw

out. There was nothing to be gained by trying to force the conversation—if there was one thing Jonas knew about the other man, it was that he would talk when he was ready. It really is a shame what has to happen here, he thought. It is rare enough to find another person to enjoy a companionable silence with in the first place. However, now that he might be on the cusp of finally getting what he was here for, he wasn't about to jeopardize that for anything.

The two men sat across from each other for several minutes in relaxed silence. Finally Castilo set his glass on the table and regarded Jonas. "You are one of the most interesting people I have met in a long time, Mr. Heinemann."

"Oh?"

"As I'm sure you have done research on me, I have also looked further into your background. You have a habit of preferring to support certain, shall we say, underdogs in areas around the world, particularly those struggling against Marxist regimes. The United Nicaraguan Opposition and UNITA in Angola are just two examples of your more interesting dealings."

Jonas dropped his gaze to the table, as if considering his reply. "Having suffered under a dictatorship for much of my life in my homeland, I do not wish to see such regimes strangle men and women who deserve better. However, you should keep in mind that I was also well compensated for each of those transactions. Profit is still a powerful motivator, and if I can help in a region, even better."

"Of course. Nowadays, there are few such windmills to tilt at anymore. China is far too large for such a tactic, and hopefully it is crumbling under its own population's desire for capitalist reforms, even as the government clings to its outmoded Communist tenets. An impossible dilemma, in my opinion, which will eventually bring about its downfall." Castilo rose and paced around the room. "That leaves only one other true Communist bastion in the Western Hemisphere."

"Cuba," Jonas said quietly.

"One that has subjugated millions of people over the last half century, killing hundreds of thousands, imprisoning tens of thousands more and reducing what was once the jewel of the Caribbean to a gaudy, crumbling shell of its former glory."

"You'll have to excuse my imperfect grasp of history, but I assume you're not talking about Batista." Jonas knew where Castilo was going, but figured it couldn't hurt to get him a bit more righteously riled.

"God knows that man was as bad as Castro—only the U.S. ever saw it differently. But no, the revolution simply replaced one dictator with another. The Castros and Guevara promised freedom, then gradually took it and much more away from the people."

Jonas sipped his cognac before replying. "And he has been remarkably adept at preventing change, even holding off the U.S. government for all this time."

Castilo snorted. "The Washington bureaucrats have no idea how to handle a true zealot. They are more comfortable getting other groups to do their dirty work—like the Contras—with terrible results for both sides. No, the time for diplomacy—from the U.S., Europe or elsewhere—has passed. There is only one course of action that can free the embattled people of Cuba." He turned to stare at Jonas. "It is time for the people of Cuba to rise up and reclaim their country. And if that requires the ultimate action to be taken, then so be it."

26

"Who *is* this guy?"

Judy had joined the small group in the virtual ops room, holding a mug of steaming tea, in VR as in real life. Kate hid her smile at the sight—like a lot of the baby-boomer generation who'd had to accept instead of grow up with the computer revolution, Judy preferred to have the simulated world mimic her real one as much as possible. Kate would never find her flying without normal, mechanical assistance or deep diving without a pressurized suit, when those VR programs eventually became available. As for Kate, well, she'd be more inclined to try one or more of those things—just for fun.

"I assume you mean besides the obvious answer." The two women watched Jonas talking with Rafael Castilo on the main screen. The businessman leaned over to examine the Stinger missile launcher in its case, while his bodyguard opened a smaller metal case on the floor.

Judy's elegant eyebrow rose. "Naturally. What I meant was that the boys have been diving into his background for the past few hours. We found the usual things, memberships in business organizations, the chamber of commerce and a long record of aboveboard, large donations to nonviolent organizations like the Cuban American National Foundation and the International Committee for Democracy in Cuba. But there has been no hint of him doing anything this rash."

"Perhaps he got tired of the diplomatic way of doing things." Oddly, Kate felt she could almost empathize with him. After all, that was part of the reason she had left the CIA, when she had discovered that the once proud counterintelligence and espionage agency had turned into a tech-heavy bureaucracy, with layers of political and territorial minefields to navigate if anything concrete was to be accomplished. And if an officer needed to work with another federal agency, well, good luck. However, that resignation was what had put her on the track for Room 59, where she could accomplish the necessary things that needed doing. *Like remove a dictator?*

So far, their operatives had never been called upon to do anything like that. They had destroyed more than one nascent revolution before it could challenge its country's government, but they had not been assigned to remove a sitting dictator—yet. But if that scenario ever arose, Kate knew she wouldn't hesitate to organize just such a mission. God knew there were plenty of people around the world who could be helped by the thirty-cent solution.

That's probably what Castilo thinks, as well, she thought. Perhaps he wants to be hailed as the liberator of Cuba—to have succeeded where so many others have failed for so long. It's got to be tempting—but tempting enough to risk everything he's built? Kate mulled that over while she listened to Judy's assessment.

"We'd be able to indict him on conspiracy to transport and sell stolen U.S. government property, treason and perhaps even conspiracy to commit murder. Once the Justice Department started digging, I'm sure they could link him to whichever PMC he's using."

"Excuse me, ma'am, but it appears that this Theodore guy is already connected to a private military company."

Now Kate's eyebrows raised. "The bodyguard? What've you got?"

El Supremo, his eyes red-rimmed yet bright from almost twenty-four straight hours of creating, sifting and collating data to parcel out to various personnel for analysis, brought up a screen with a picture of the man's face while information scrolled past. "He's a member of a company called Threat Evaluation And Response, or TEAR, Inc. They're headquartered in England, with branch offices on every continent. Been around for about a decade—one of the old guard, apparently."

"Do they have the capability to field a force large enough to invade Cuba?" Kate asked.

"See for yourself." The hacker brought up another screen that appeared to be the home page for the company. Prominently displayed among cited assets was the ability to field a brigade-size force anywhere in the world in seventy-two hours.

Kate's eyebrows stayed up. "Really? And the way they do that is by…?"

"According to news reports from several Third World countries they've visited, they either subcontract to local talent or bring in mercs from nearby areas and set them loose. Naturally, they've also been accused of profiteering, involvement in black markets and crimes against civilians," El Supremo reported.

"Naturally." Judy set her cup down. "It is amazing what can be accomplished—or destroyed—if enough money is waved around."

Kate noticed Judy didn't comment on the location of the company's headquarters. "So, what would happen if a few thousand ill-trained mercenaries—excuse me, private military contractors—took over an entire island?"

Judy mulled it over. "They wouldn't be able to fend off its armed forces alone—they'd need help from someone on the inside. Maybe from the military itself. Even so, there would be plenty of assets to seize, equipment both civilian and military. Wherever the target is, it would be a free-for-all, with civilians in the middle as a civil war broke out between loyalists and other factions."

"And it appears this operation is almost ready to begin, if the intel is correct. I'd like to put out some feelers on Web chatter, see if anyone's been tapped to fill this contract of theirs. Given their target, a force that large won't be easy to hide."

"That sounds good, Judy. Let me know what you come up with," Kate said.

"Ma'am, you might want to listen to this." NiteMaster drew their attention back to the big screen, where Castilo stood over Jonas. "He's talking about another revolution in Cuba."

"Thanks." Kate stared at the screen, watching the two men converse, and hearing intimations of a plot unfold that was every bit as bad as she feared.

27

Jonas raised his snifter to his lips and drank, holding the liquor in his mouth for a moment while he absorbed the import of Castilo's words. At length he swallowed and set the glass down. "That is an ambitious undertaking. The other thing Castro is known for is his incredible longevity."

"Yes, yes, I've heard it all, the foolish plans by the CIA, the other nations taking their shots. All too complicated, too circumspect. Poisoning his milkshake, for god's sake! No, it must be simple, uncomplicated and direct." Castilo returned to his seat and plopped down into it, an expression of savage glee lighting up his face. "Everything is falling into place, and soon the people of Cuba will have the chance to take their destiny back into their own hands. And you, my friend, have given us an important weapon in the fight against that disgusting Communist regime." He lifted his glass. "To a free Cuba!"

Jonas toasted with him, his mind racing, particularly about how to elicit the key information about the plan without raising suspicion. "It would truly be a glorious day to see the sun rise over a free Cuba, yet I must confess that I have my doubts that such a massive undertaking can be accomplished, even with help from the inside. It just all sounds too good to be true."

Castilo polished off his cognac and leaned back, suddenly expansive. "I'll tell you what—while I cannot go into details, of course, I can deliver proof of what I have said tonight, so you may see that this is real. I can also arrange for all of these to be taken off your hands. However, the delivery would have to be this evening. I know that is short notice, but I hope that is acceptable?"

Jonas laughed. "You seem to presume that I would be sailing around with the rest of this package on my ship, where it might be found by any inspecting Coast Guard vessel."

"It might, were you within the coastal waters of the U.S. I assume nothing, but am only letting you know what your potential customer will want. If that is a problem, then perhaps we should reconsider the entire deal."

"No, no." Jonas cut him off, trying to appear eager without seeming to, the very model of a businessman who wanted to unload his illegal inventory as quickly as possible. "It just might be a little complicated to do this so fast, that's all. Depending on when they wish to pick up the items, I think we can work something out. However, I must insist that the client bring the complete payment with them. I will accept U.S. dollars, British pounds, Euros or diamonds, the quality of which I will verify myself."

Castilo rose and extended his hand. "Then we have a deal. I will notify the buyers, who will be in touch with you to arrange transfer and payment."

"Excellent. I look forward to consummating our arrangement. And once your homeland is free, I hope we can do more business in the future."

"Perhaps. My people will be in touch. This has been a very pleasurable evening, Ferdinand."

Jonas rose with him. "For me, as well. Come, I'll walk out with you to the aft deck." He led Castilo through the rear of the ship to where the powerboat was waiting, Theodore falling in behind him like a silent 250-pound wraith. The two deckhands made the launch ready, and Jonas watched them board, knowing he had only gotten part of the story. As the Tiara pushed away from the yacht, he raised a hand in farewell, and was answered by a similar wave from Castilo. Theodore stood with his arms crossed, staring at Jonas. The pleasure boat accelerated into the night, fading to a small speck in the darkness.

"So, how was your meeting with the boys?" Jonas turned to see Karen, dressed in slacks and a black brushed-silk blouse, leaning against the railing.

"His clients want all of the Stingers. They'll be calling a bit later to set up delivery. Tonight."

"Kind of in a hurry, aren't they?"

"Yes, but from what little Rafael told me, the operation is about to start. Who knows, perhaps these are the last things they needed to ensure they'd be able to gain a foothold on the island. There's something we're missing, though. Rafael thinks there won't be much of a problem bringing freedom to the huddled masses simply hanging around waiting to be liberated. Sounds like he's got a bad case of Iraqitis."

"You're phoning in, right?" Karen asked.

Jonas glanced down at his phone. "Funny, I'd have thought Kate would have called by—" An orchestral version of the German national anthem rang out. "I spoke too soon. Have you swept the boat?"

Karen nodded. "The moment they left. Nothing showed up—they're very confident—or just sloppy."

He flipped the phone open and put it on the table as Kate's face appeared on-screen. "Good evening, Kate."

"Well, we got halfway there. He wanted to tell you about the grand scheme, didn't he?"

"I think he found me a kindred spirit, and the dose of Oxystim in his wineglass didn't hurt any, either." Although a real truth serum still hadn't been developed, DARPA scientists had created the next-best thing—a drug that stimulated the brain's production of oxytocin, a hormone neurotransmitter that increased feeling of trust between the subject and anyone they interacted with. It wasn't foolproof, but studies had shown a significant increase in the quality of information gathered from people under its influence. The mess crew had been assigned to coat the interior of Castilo's glass with it before dinner, and from what Jonas had seen, they had pulled it off flawlessly. "I have to admire his resolve to keep it to himself. I think stronger measures will be necessary to get the details."

"Understood. So the PMC wants to pick up the cargo tonight?"

Jonas nodded. "They're sure in a hurry."

"There's something you should know about the bodyguard." Kate filled him in on Theodore's relationship with TEAR.

"That's very interesting. Now we know who's brokering

this deal. I wonder if Rafael is aware of Theodore's connection, or if his bodyguard just dropped the name of the PMC to be *helpful.* Either way, it looks like we'll have some potentially hostile visitors later this evening."

His second phone rang, and Jonas picked it up. "Hold on, Kate, I think this is them."

"Take it, we'll be monitoring on this end."

He put the phone to his cheek, noting that there was no transmitted picture on his screen. "Hello?"

"We are the party that is interested in the equipment you have for sale. We were referred to you by a mutual friend."

"If this is true, then you also know what that gentleman's hobby is," Jonas said.

A soft chuckle came over the line. "Very good. He enjoys watching the greyhound races. At the Palm Beach Kennel Club, if memory serves."

"Excellent." For a moment, Jonas wondered if he was talking to Theodore through a voice synthesizer. "You wish to set up a time for transfer and payment?"

"Correct, and I must insist that the transaction occur this evening."

"That is very tight. However, it can be arranged. Let us say midnight? I can text you our GPS coordinates, if you wish."

There was a muffled conference, then the voice came back on line. "That will be acceptable." The voice rattled off a number. "Send your position whenever you are ready."

"I look forward to making your acquaintance soon."

The speaker didn't reply, but simply broke the connection. Jonas switched back to Kate. "We're going to have company at 2400 hours."

"Satellite triangulation shows the call originated about fifty miles to the south-southwest, near the Keys. They aren't too far away," Kate said. "Karen, put the entire crew on overwatch. They might pull a double cross or strike early, attempt to get the cargo without paying."

"Should we break out weapons?" Karen asked.

Jonas responded, "Let's not arm the crew openly. We don't want to spook our boys, the hostiles or both. Distribute the pistols and make sure everyone keeps them covered. Also, everyone should know where the hidden weapons are and try to stay near them if possible.

"Kate, how do you want these people handled? If the deal was to go through without a hitch—which I doubt—then the cases are bugged, so they can be easily tracked. However, if they try to pull something—"

"You and your team are authorized to respond with whatever force is necessary to retain your cargo and capture or eliminate the hostile force," Kate said.

"Understood. We'll report in after the meeting."

"Right, and, Jonas, Karen—be careful."

"Always." Jonas cut the connection and turned to Karen. Her mouth was set in a grim line. "Let's prepare a suitable welcome for our guests, shall we?"

28

"I didn't know you were a nautical man, Major."

"There is much you do not know about me, Sergeant."

"That is true. I do know, however, or strongly suspect, that if we take this boat onto the open ocean, we may not return."

Nodding, Damason had no choice but to agree. The craft they had been assigned might once have been a fisherman's skiff. Perhaps twelve feet long, to call it white would have been a relative term, as the entire hull had been scraped clean by years of water and salt air, leaving only bare wood behind. The once smooth planks had been attacked by barnacles, and boring worms had left pits and scores of tiny holes along the sides. The outboard motor had to be at least thirty years old, and the dented, rusty cowling appeared to have suffered through every single day. Damason shuddered to think what the engine itself looked like underneath.

"Sir, with respect, I still think this is a very dangerous idea."

"Acknowledged, which is why you're coming with me." Damason was just as wary about their upcoming meeting.

They were both dressed in civilian clothes for this night run, but were armed under their loose shirts.

Only a few hours earlier he had shared the news about the supreme commander's tour of facilities outside of Havana. The person on the other end had been pleased, but then had informed him of the upcoming meeting, and stressed that he wanted Damason to attend. When he had protested, saying he needed to be available in the event of sudden changes to the leader's schedule, the voice had stated that Damason needed to meet the people he would soon be working with over the next weeks. The tone had made it clear this was not a request, and Damason had been left with no choice but to agree.

As much as they were concerned about meeting with their illegal contacts, they were just as worried about the clearance they had received for the trip in the first place. Damason had bulled it through by saying he wanted to view the coastline from the sea to ensure that there would be no possibility of an assassin shooting at their supreme commander from the ocean. His colonel had approved and gave him papers stating he was to have carte blanche access to anything that the Cuban Border Guard had available. But even with the signed documentation, Damason had already thought of several ways the whole thing could go awry, starting with the possibility that the Border Guard wouldn't have any suitable boats for an ocean trip. Even worse, that they would have a boat but no fuel was a more likely possibility. After a brief meeting with a guard on duty, which included the requisition of enough gas for their trip, Damason and his sergeant now stood in front of the boat that was supposed to carry them. They were staring at it in disbelief.

"You're sure we have a clear route to sea?" Damason asked.

Lopez looked pained. "Major, I am embarrassed that you would even ask such a question, but yes, I have the Border Guard's planned patrols this evening. I don't know whether God is looking over our shoulder, but apparently there is a large group of citizens that will be attempting to leave the homeland tonight. The majority of the guard in the area will be on hand to take them into custody."

I know, I called in the tip to make sure they were caught this evening, Damason thought. Normally he tried not to get involved in people fleeing the country, but he knew tonight had to go smoothly, and the distraction would remove most of the patrols from the equation. He shook his head, knowing Lopez would assume he was sad about the impending capture—which he was, but it was also because of the guilt he carried, as well. "Soon that will no longer be necessary."

"Amen, Major, amen. I thought the Coast Guard was seizing boats from refugees and drug runners," Lopez said.

"What they haven't sold outright, they're using elsewhere." Damason examined the waterline in the wan light, trying to see any bubbles or rotten wood. Finding nothing out of order, he took a deep breath as he stepped aboard. He was surprised to find that the deck was solid and dry under his feet. "Seems sound enough."

"Then let's get this potential death trip started," Lopez said. He untied the bowline and tossed it into the boat, then jumped in after it—making Damason wince as he landed on the deck with a thump. The vessel shuddered a bit, but held together.

"Always a positive attitude with you, Sergeant," Damason said.

"If you liked that one, you'll love this—I hope the engine doesn't explode when I try to start it." He filled the external tank and wound the old-style pull cord around the starter. "Here goes." Tugging with all his might, Lopez almost fell over as the old engine clattered into relatively smooth life, with no smoke or sputtering. It was very loud, but if that was the only issue, Damason wasn't about to complain.

"Sounds decent enough," he shouted over the racket. Pointing Lopez to the bow of the boat, he took the tiller and twisted the throttle. The decrepit-looking vessel responded, if not on a dime, reasonably well enough that Damason thought they might actually make it back in one piece.

He piloted the boat out of the harbor and headed due north, relying on Lopez's guidance to avoid the coastal patrols. The intelligence was right on the money. The channel waters were deserted, with only widely scattered lights on the horizon. The engine settled into a steady thrum, and the boat cut through the water with ease. Damason kept a sharp eye on the engine, looking for smoke, leaks or anything else that might suggest a long swim back. But so far, the boat handled well enough. The only downside was that he suspected the engine's deafening clamor might eventually split his skull open.

Damason looked up to see Lopez waving at him, then point to a pair of flashing lights, one white, one blue, off the starboard bow. According to his contact, that was the signal for the party he was supposed to meet. He turned the boat toward the lights.

Five minutes later, he pulled up alongside a forty-foot cigarette boat, its stylish hull painted midnight-blue and black, making it look like a huge arrowhead in the water.

There were three people aboard—a large white man with close-cropped blond hair, along with two other very dark-skinned men. None were visibly armed, although Damason had the feeling they were all carrying some kind of hidden weapon. All of them had the wary nonchalance of men who had killed before and would do so again with relative ease.

Lopez tossed the rope to the other boat, but none of the men moved to pick it up.

"Who are you?" the solidly built man called out.

"A man who wants to change his country's direction," Damason said as he stood with his hands on his hips.

The blond man nodded and grabbed the rope, pulling the two boats together. He held out his hand. "Welcome aboard. I'm Theodore."

"Very well, you can call me Daniel. This is Julio," Damason said, pointing to Lopez.

The other two men eyed Damason's boat with incredulous expressions. One of them asked Theodore a question in a singsong language, which he used to answer the man, as well. "He says you must be brave, to come all the way out here in that."

Damason smiled, not showing his teeth. "All Cubans are as at home on the water as ducks."

The other man said something, and held out his hand. Damason shook it, and the man laughed, the humor not even coming close to his eyes. Theodore also smiled a bit as he translated again. "He says it is good to meet you, because now he knows there is at least one person he knows not to kill once we are ashore."

Damason pointed at his sergeant. "What about him?"

Theodore asked the man a question. He replied by holding his hand out palm down and waggling it back and forth. "Apparently they like you, but he may be on his own." He smiled, showing large, white teeth. "That is good, because your friend will have to stay here."

Damason's hackles rose. "What do you mean by that?"

"We'd like you to accompany us on a little trip north. We have to pick up some cargo, and our leader has instructed us that you are to come along. However, since we cannot take that—" he waved at the boat with a dismissive hand "—your friend will have to remain behind. Don't worry, nothing is going to happen to you. You're far too important to the operation. We should be back in about three, maybe four hours."

Damason glanced at Lopez, who stood casually, his feet planted on the bobbing deck, one hand at his side, one hand behind his back. He knew that if he gave the order, Lopez would draw his pistol and do his best to kill all three of these men, even if he died in the process. He walked over to him.

"I want you to stay here—" Lopez looked as if he was about to cut him off, but Damason held up his hand. "If I am not back in four hours, you are in charge of the operation. All of the information you need is in my desk. The equipment you would need is in the air duct in my office. Carry out our plan as far as you can, and trust in God that the rest will happen. The mission is larger than any one of us, and must succeed, no matter what stands in our way."

"Yes, Major." Lopez started to cross back to the small skiff, but Damason stopped him, speaking again in low, rapid Spanish.

"And if for some reason I do not come back, be sure to find and kill these three bastards."

Lopez nodded and stepped into the small boat. Damason knew he was taking two huge chances. If his sergeant had been playing along with him all this time, he could return to find soldiers waiting to arrest him on charges of treason, conspiracy and much, much more. But Damason was sure that wouldn't happen. He and Lopez had been through too much together—hell, he had already given the man enough information to have gotten him arrested ten times over now. The only reason he wouldn't have done so already was if he was trying to get as many conspirators as he could in the sting. Damason shook his head. He certainly hoped that wasn't the case.

The other chance was accompanying these men on what seemed to be a risky mission for very little gain. However, whatever he had to do to prove his devotion to their cause, he would do if it was within his power.

"Let's go." He took a seat in the corner of the boat and didn't look back as the powerful engines rumbled to life, and the speedboat roared north into the night.

29

Jonas stood on the aft deck again, surveying the water around them with a pair of Yukon Ranger digital night-vision binoculars. He knew the bridge crew was on the radar to watch for approaching craft, but he also believed in using every available asset, and often there was no substitute for eyes on the deck.

His cell phone vibrated at his side. Jonas kept scanning the waters around them as he activated his wireless earpiece. "Yes?"

It was Carla, one of the two-person boat team he had sent to return Castilo to shore. "Subject and escort are away, but, um, I'm afraid we won't be returning to the boat for a while." She sounded embarrassed and frustrated.

"What's the matter?" Jonas asked.

"The engine's been compromised."

He heard muffled conversation, and then a "Damn it!" followed by a thump.

"Tell Brett to stop kicking the engine—that boat's not ours. You have any idea what's wrong?" Jonas asked.

"Brett thinks the big guy sabotaged it somehow, even though he was in *plain sight the entire time*—" from the extra emphasis on the words, Jonas figured they were being said for Brett's benefit as much as his "—but he can't figure out how. Everything looks fine, but when we tried to leave the dock, the engine wouldn't turn over."

"Not bad, not bad, indeed," Jonas muttered.

"Sir?"

"All right, both of you calm down. What's your take on this?"

He heard a deep intake of breath. "That there's no such thing as coincidence. If they are planning an assault, then removing two of the crew would make their job easier—less potential hostiles," Carla said.

"Right you are. I want you both to secure the boat—get the harbor patrol's help if you have to. Once ashore, I want you to go to the address I'm going to text to you, and begin surveillance. Keep your distance, and above all, don't get made. Someone will relieve you by dawn. Otherwise, if that doesn't happen, go to the second safehouse. Watch for tails. They shouldn't be following you—there's really no reason to—but stay alert regardless."

"What if the primary leaves the building?"

"If you know it's him, and I don't mean you just saw his car, but you visually ID him, then follow. Unless someone contacts you first, call in at 0800 hours, and we'll go from there."

"Yes, sir."

Jonas cut the connection and called Karen, who answered on the first ring. "Yes."

"Theodore sabotaged the Tiara, leaving two stranded ashore."

"Bad company is coming," Karen said.

"Yes, inform the crew quietly, and have everyone vest up. They all need to stay on their toes—these guys will be playing for real."

"You got it."

Jonas flipped the phone closed and returned it to his belt, then kept an eye on the dark, calm waters around the ship. Now that his hunch had been confirmed, there wasn't much to do but wait. That hadn't been a problem for him for many years, but he imagined the younger operatives were running through their own internal scenarios about what might go down and how they might react to it. Room 59 operatives came from all walks of life—law enforcement, intelligence, military, diplomatic corps—and for some that meant extensive weapons and unarmed-combat training before joining, for others, the bare minimum. All trainees went through rigorous self-defense and firearm courses, held at a training facility so secret that they didn't even know its location. For some, this would be their first exposure to armed assailants who would probably try to kill them. Of that group, some would rise to the challenge and some wouldn't. It was the nature of the beast. Jonas only hoped that none of them got killed while trying to do their jobs. Karen and he would do everything they could, but when it came down to it, the mission was the primary goal, and if any of them didn't understand that, then they were in the wrong line of work.

As he looked out over the dark waters, Jonas remembered a time when he had been a bit scared on an operation, not for himself, but for someone else—during a mission that had happened not too far away.

June 19, 1973

JONAS HELD the shuddering Marisa close. To her credit, she didn't sob or cry out, but just wept into his shoulder for a minute, then pulled away, clamping down on her emotions with iron control.

"Sorry," she whispered.

"It's all right. The first time I had to kill a man, I threw up, so you've already got me beat." His attempt at humor was feeble, but it distracted her for the moment. "I'm afraid we're not done yet. Can you give me a hand?"

She nodded, wiping her hands on the dew-laden grass, then stood. "What do we have to do?"

Jonas grabbed the body of the dead guard and pulled him out of the truck cab, letting him fall to the ground in a limp heap. Marisa grimaced, but didn't look away as he stripped the man of his pistol, canvas web gear and extra magazines.

"Let's get him into the bushes." He helped as much as he could with his ankle, but Marisa proved surprisingly able to haul the body, dragging him into the undergrowth without complaint.

When Jonas commented on her ability, she replied, "I cut and haul sugarcane all day. He's just floppier."

They went around to the other side of the truck and disposed of the other guard, as well. Hobbling back to the cab, Jonas took stock of their new weapons, two loaded AK-47s with two extra magazines apiece, the Makarov pistol with two additional magazines, two bayonets and four grenades. He tried contacting the team again, but got nothing but static.

"Well, now we've got a chance to stop them. At the very least, we'll make enough noise and fire to warn the team off, and meet them at the secondary extraction site. I don't suppose you've ever fired an AK?" Jonas asked.

She shook her head.

"All right, I'm going to give you the basic rundown." In five minutes he taught her about the safety, single-shot versus automatic fire and how to reload and cock the weapon. "Don't worry about aiming—you'll be supplying what we call suppressive fire."

"Just trying to keep their heads down?" she asked.

"That's right. Snug the butt into your shoulder and keep it tight. Don't forget to lean into the rifle a bit, as the autofire will kick. Fire short bursts, then, when the weapon is empty—" He watched as she removed the banana magazine, inserted another and pulled the charging lever back, readying the rifle for action. "Very good, and don't forget to move after emptying each magazine. Look for muzzle-flashes from the clearing, and aim in that general direction. If you hit anyone, great. If not, no big deal, they'll take cover either way."

"What about you?"

"I'll be on the other side, trying to take out as many as I can. The exploding truck should draw most of their attention. The key will be to try to make them think they are under attack from an equal or larger force." He handed her the pouch filled with four magazines, which she slung around her shoulder, and the Makarov in its holster and belt, which she strapped around her waist. "Just a few more minutes, and we'll be ready to go."

Jonas knelt at the external side gas tank, took the cap off and wedged a grenade firmly into the hole, making sure the pin faced away from the truck body. He tied a long piece of cord to the pin and got into the cab. "Walk a few paces behind the truck until we get about fifty yards from the clearing, and keep an eye on me. When I jump out, you head into the jungle. Go right—I'll go left. Shoot and move until you're out of ammunition, then fall back to the clearing where we found the truck. If anything goes wrong, fall back to the clearing and hide. Wait ten minutes, and if I don't return or you see soldiers coming, get out of here."

Marisa took it all in with short, sharp nods, her wide blue eyes fixed on his. Jonas ran through the plan one more time, and couldn't come up with any other refinements. "Just remember, shoot and move and keep low at all times. Good luck."

He was about to climb into the cab when he felt a hand on his shoulder. "Karl."

Grimacing at the fake name, Jonas turned around. "Yes?"

"You be careful, okay?" She hesitated, then leaned forward on her tiptoes and kissed him quickly on the mouth. She tasted like sweat and hibiscus, and it was a sensation he didn't want to end.

"We'd better go. Stay behind the truck and watch for my signal." Jonas didn't know what else to say, so he turned back to the cab and climbed painfully inside. Once there, he placed his sniper rifle between the seat and the door and tied the cord to his wrist, making sure it snaked between the door and the cab frame. He measured the distance between the gas pedal and the seat, then tied the haft of the bayonet to its scabbard so that the blade protruded from one end, making a rough weapon about eighteen inches long. He set that on the seat beside him, then braced himself for a good deal of pain as he put his injured leg on the clutch.

Gritting his teeth, he started the truck, hearing the rough rumble of the engine as it sparked into life. He depressed the clutch with his left foot, trying to ignore the white flare of pain in his ankle. With a minimum of fumbling, he got his right leg on the gas pedal and jammed the gearshift into first, then eased off the clutch and got the lumbering truck moving, hauling on the wheel to steer it out onto the trail.

Panting with the effort, Jonas checked that Marisa was following him as they started up the path. He could barely see her in the dim red glow of the taillights, but she was following a few yards behind the truck, the AK-47 rifle large in her hands. Jonas steeled himself, then pushed the clutch down again, biting back a growl of pain as he shifted into second. The radio on the seat next to him crackled into life, a puzzled voice asking in Spanish what he was doing. Jonas pushed harder on the gas pedal, the truck shuddering as it accelerated to twenty miles per hour. He didn't turn on the headlights, but drove blind, letting the truck find its way down the rutted path. The tone of the voice on the radio grew more strident, demanding that whoever was in the truck respond immediately.

Jonas could see the clearing, a dark, empty space in the tree line. He switched on the truck's lights to blind the men who would be looking down the path, making sure to look away from the glare so as not to blind himself. He goosed the gas pedal, then jammed the modified bayonet between the pedal and the seat to keep the truck moving forward. Opening the door, he grabbed his rifle and stepped out onto the running board, using the door as a shield. Pulling the pin with his teeth, he hurled a grenade in front of the truck, then jumped, trying to use his good foot to at least break his fall so he could tuck and roll away.

Jonas landed hard, but his uninjured foot took the impact, and he rolled away on the ground, tucking his rifle across his chest as he went. He felt the tug of the cord on his wrist, then it went slack, and he hoped that just the pin and not the entire grenade had come free. He came out of the truck in a prone position and kept rolling over and over, his rifle aligned vertically with his body. All the while a small voice in his mind counted down the seconds from five to one.

Jonas came to a stop and covered his head with his arms. The two grenades exploded almost simultaneously, along with a much louder report as the truck's gas tank followed suit. The heat and shock wave washed over him, and metal parts hit the ground around Jonas, but none landed on him. Bringing the rifle to his eye, he looked to the right of the inferno, scanning for targets.

The truck had made it into the middle of the clearing before erupting into a huge, greasy ball of flames that illuminated the surrounding jungle, casting dark shadows of the running men in the flickering flames. At least one soldier had been caught in the initial blast, and he screamed and capered madly as flames sizzled on his back and legs. Others shouted orders and questions, trying to make sense out of what had just happened. Jonas dropped his sights onto a shouting man's chest, drew in a breath, held it and squeezed the trigger, not needing to compensate for wind or anything else at that range. As soon as the bullet left the barrel, he moved, rolling to the left again as the man jerked in shock, then fell forward to the ground.

He heard the distinct popping of an AK-47 firing on his right, then a scream from the clearing. More shouts, tinged with the high tone of impending panic, echoed across the open space. Jonas came to a stop a few yards away from his first position and brought his rifle up again. His eyes had mostly adjusted to the light, and he saw a dark form move from one side of the old sugar mill to the other. He put three rounds through the building, spaced about a degree apart, and was rewarded with a shout of pain from inside.

The rest of the Cubans were firing, but from what Jonas could see, they had no idea where the incoming shots were originating. Automatic fire filled the clearing, perforating leaves and shattering branches everywhere. He put two 3-round bursts into an area where two muzzle-flashes appeared intermittently, and saw one stop, but couldn't tell if he had hit the soldier, or if he was just reloading.

Jonas didn't know how well trained the soldiers were, but he knew eventually someone was going to regain control and order the men to circle around both sides of the clearing to flank their attackers. He needed to make sure the rest of the forces couldn't get that organized. Rising onto his knees, he pulled the pin and threw another grenade to the left of the sugar mill, trying to bounce it into the nearby jungle. The ordnance made it most of the way before erupting, but his movement must have caught someone's eye, because Jonas immediately took fire from across the clearing. He hit the ground as 7.62 mm bullets chewed through the foliage around him.

He pushed back into the jungle, then rolled right again, taking cover behind a banana tree, its trunk scored from bullets. Jonas realized someone must have taken command of the unit, since the indiscriminate shooting had stopped. He moved to the other side of the tree, but couldn't see anything past the broken palm fronds and shattered trunks. Suddenly, he heard something that chilled his blood.

Off to his right, the undeniable scream of a woman echoed through the jungle.

A LIGHT IN THE DISTANCE flared through the binoculars, and Jonas lowered them, blinking away the spots dancing across his vision. He raised them again and looked just to the right of the light. A boat was coming at him, fast.

Jonas grabbed his cell phone and hit the number that would contact every member of his team. "All right, everyone, our target vehicle is approaching at seven o'clock. Deck team, be ready to secure the vehicle when it comes in, and escort the group to the upper aft saloon. No one is to make any kind of overt move unless you confirm hostile intent. Karen, report to the aft deck."

He closed the cell phone and kept the glasses trained on the cigarette boat as it cruised around the *Deep Water* once, then pulled up to the aft platform. There were four men inside, and three immediately climbed aboard the yacht, leaving one to watch the cockpit.

Jonas walked inside the salon and put the binoculars away under the bar, then walked over to the Stinger missile case, which had been repacked and closed. Next to it was the smaller metal case containing the gripstock. Jonas sat in a chair and waited for the men to appear.

A minute later, one of the crew opened the door and said, "This way, gentlemen."

Theodore trooped in, carrying a small aluminum briefcase. He was followed by two men Jonas didn't immediately recognize, one a dark-skinned African, and the other a Cuban who, when he stepped into the light, made Jonas's breath catch in his throat.

He slowly rose to his feet, trying to disguise his shock at seeing Major Damason Valdes—Room 59's contact inside the Cuban military—next to the men planning to invade Cuba.

30

Marcus was bored. Totally, unbelievably bored.

For five hours he had been keeping the Valdes home under surveillance, waiting for the major to arrive, or for his wife to leave, or for anyone to do anything. The side street, lined with rows of quietly crumbling two- and three-story homes, many of them subdivided into several small apartments, had been about as busy as an average U.S. city block. Children played, scattering when the police came around on their patrols, then reforming into loose groups to run, laugh and scream in the early evening. Parents had either come home and shooed their kids inside, or called them from the doorway to dinner, the street filling with delicious smells of cooking food, making Marcus's stomach rumble. He had grabbed a hasty meal at the cantina before the debacle at the hotel, but hadn't had anything since except a dry, tasteless protein bar and some water.

Of course, I had to freshen up after my intelligence gathering, too, Marcus thought, running a hand over his newly shorn scalp. After ditching the car, he had found a bodega and had grabbed a pair of scissors, disposable razor and shaving cream, and spent twenty minutes shaving his head bare, then wrapping a do-rag around it. That, a pair of cargo shorts and a gaudy, red, green and blue guayabera shirt had completed his quick disguise.

At first it had been difficult to watch the house without being noticed. Enough people passed through the street that he was sure sooner or later someone would remember a young man no one in the neighborhood had ever seen before loitering in front of an army major's house. The fact that both sides of the street were filled with homes also made his task more difficult, as he couldn't find a cantina and while away the hours with a drink and a sharp eye. So he had changed up his routine every half hour. Moving around, altering his appearance—sometimes he was the bald, shirtless guy, other times he was the sunglasses-wearing, do-ragged man—and taking up different positions on the street, even parking himself right in front of the major's house for fifteen minutes, so he didn't appear to be targeting one particular home. And he always disappeared whenever the police came down the street.

With nightfall, the street had quieted, and Marcus had located a decrepit house that was either abandoned or the residents weren't coming home. He sat on the front stoop, nursing a bottle of sickly sweet, neon-yellow papaya drink, chasing it with swallows of water to remove the taste from his mouth.

Lowering the bottle, Marcus checked his watch and saw it was about time to check in. He looked around to make sure no one was watching him, then flipped open his phone and dialed the number for Room 59. When the automated switchboard answered, which usually took care of wrong numbers and crank callers, he punched in the day's code to speak to Kate directly.

"Alpha? Where are you?"

"I'm outside the subject's house, and have been for the past five hours. There has been no movement, and I have not spotted—"

"No, you haven't, because Beta is looking at him at this very moment about thirty miles off the Florida coast. It seems he's linked up with our bad guys. If Jonas confirms that he's part of their operation, he is to be terminated at the first opportunity."

Marcus took a moment to digest the news just as he saw a woman with two young kids in tow, stopping at the very house he was watching. He slipped on his sunglasses and recorded the trio. "Primary, the subject's wife and children have come home. What you do want me to do?"

"Withdraw from your current location and find a fast oceangoing boat. We may need you to rendezvous with Beta at sea. Will be in touch as soon as we have more information."

"Understood. Alpha out." Marcus turned off the sunglasses recorder and slipped them into his shirt pocket, then strolled down the street, heading for the tourist section of the harbor and the powerful speedboats docked there.

31

Covering his brief lapse in concentration, Jonas slipped his left hand into his pocket and immediately focused on the one person he was supposed to know. "Theodore, this is a pleasant surprise. So good to see you again."

"Mr. Castilo suggested that I oversee the actual transaction, as it were," the bodyguard said.

"By all means, please, come, sit. Would you and your friends like any refreshments before we get down to business?"

Theodore turned and spoke in what Jonas thought was Swahili, then Spanish. Both men shook their heads. Theodore nodded to the African on the left. "This is Nyakio, and the gentleman next to him is Daniel. He's the gentleman that Mr. Castilo spoke of earlier."

Jonas frowned. "Forgive my suspicion, but how am I to be sure that this man is who you claim he is? For all I know, you could have gotten him from anywhere in Latin America."

Theodore didn't appear insulted, but nodded. "A very prudent question." He turned to Damason and asked him in

Spanish to produce identification. Damason asked if that was a smart thing to do, and Theodore assured him that it was safe. Hesitantly, Damason produced his military identification, which listed him as a major in the Cuban Revolutionary Armed Forces. He held it out for Jonas to see, but would not let him take it.

"I hope this will do," Theodore added.

"It is acceptable." Jonas nodded at the young man, who inclined his head in return. "It is a great pleasure to meet you, sir." Impulsively, he reached out his hand. "Please, I would shake the hand of a man who has risked so much to be here."

Damason looked slightly uncomfortable at the idea, but he took Jonas's outstretched hand and shook it, frowning as Jonas clapped his left hand over Damason's and shook heartily. "The pleasure is mine. Please, do not mind me as you gentlemen conduct your affairs."

"Do not worry, this shouldn't take long." Jonas released him and turned back to Theodore. "Do your clients wish to see the merchandise for themselves?" He stepped aside to reveal the Stinger crate, smiling slightly as the other two men's eyes widened in surprise. "I take it they are impressed?"

"Oh, indeed." Theodore set his briefcase down, unlocked it and opened it, revealing neat, banded stacks of one-hundred-dollar bills. "Please, examine the money as you wish."

Jonas reached down past the first layer to take a packet out from underneath. He brought out a nondescript pen and clicked it, then drew the tip across the note. The ink looked bright yellow, indicating that the bill was genuine. The pen was manufactured by a research department of the Secret Service, and was ninety-nine percent accurate, much more so than the simple iodine pens used to test currency in convenience stores. The note also passed his touch and visual examinations, so unless it was one of the superbill forgeries that had been in scattered circulation for the past decade, he was holding real American currency. And if his math was correct, Jonas estimated there was another one and a quartermillion dollars in the case.

"This is a good start, but you are a bit light. I see only the first half of the amount agreed upon," he said.

"Of course, but we prefer not to carry such large amounts of currency around. We would like to take these cases with us as our down payment. A vessel will come by within the next hour, drop off the second half of your fee and pick up the rest of the cargo. Please be sure it is ready, as they will not wish to stay out here any longer than necessary," Theodore said.

Jonas wasn't thrilled with the arrangement—but it would arouse suspicion and probably kill the deal if he were to disagree. A real arms dealer might even take the million-plus in the case and split, a tidy profit for a night's work and only one Stinger. Something about the arrangement niggled at the back of Jonas's mind, but he couldn't tease the intuition into a full-blown thought. Instead, he played his part and smiled. "Naturally. Once I have the rest of the funds in hand, the transfer shouldn't take more than ten to fifteen minutes. Would you like some assistance getting this one down to your boat?"

"I think the three of us can handle it, but thank you," Theodore said. He motioned to the two men, each of whom came over and picked up one end of the case.

Jonas caught the flash of a frown on Damason's face as he lifted his end of the crate, but it quickly disappeared.

Theodore took the gripstock case, walked to the door, and opened it, letting the two men out ahead of him. Jonas followed, and watched as the trio maneuvered the bulky case down to the bottom rear deck. They hauled it aboard, and Theodore turned back to him before disembarking.

"Thank you very much—these will be a great boon to us in our mission. Watch for a double set of lights on your port side, one white and one blue. That will be the ship to pick up the rest of the cargo, and they will have the other half of your payment." He extended his hand. "It's been a pleasure doing business with you, Mr. Heinemann."

Jonas gripped his hand and shook it. "The pleasure has been mine, Theodore, and I'll be ready for your acquaintances. Have a safe trip back."

"That we will. Farewell."

The man who'd remained behind cast off the line, and the cigarette boat backed away, its engines growling in the darkness. Theodore turned the boat south and accelerated into the darkness.

As soon as they were out of sight, Jonas was on his cell, tucking a wireless Bluetooth receiver into his ear. "Bridge, I want someone on the tracker following that boat at all times. Do not let the Stinger's signal out of your sight. We will be expecting a larger ship in the next hour. All positions stay alert—this is when they're going to try something. Anyone see anything out of the ordinary, no matter how small, report it immediately."

32 II II66 III II I 59II II II III I II

William Hartung finished his third check of the *Deep Water*'s rear platform, his gaze sweeping from side to side and also checking the dark water astern. He found nothing out of the ordinary, but that didn't lessen his apprehension about what he knew was coming. Although he felt this was where he was supposed to be, that everything in his life had trained him for this purpose, at the same time he couldn't quell the nervous butterflies in his stomach as he patrolled the rear of the ship.

Valedictorian of his high school class, along with state-champion wrestler back in Idaho, he'd been top of his graduating class at the UCLA, and then came 9/11. Like many other men his age, William had wanted to make sure that an attack like that would never happen again on American soil, so he had applied to the nascent Department of Homeland Security. After four years there, however, he watched it turn into a sea of bureaucracy and waste. It was also about that time that he uncovered a major plot to bring Al Qaeda terrorists across the Canadian border to strike power plants near the Great Lakes, hoping to cause a chain reaction similar to the blackout of 2003, only much larger. While winning only a certificate of merit from his superior, William's almost single-handed unraveling of the plot had brought him to the attention of Room 59, who had recruited him for their intelligence-analysis division.

Before he could begin, however, he had to complete their intensive basic training, which far outclassed anything the DHS had to offer. This was his last week, and when Judy Burges had requested available volunteers for a two-to-four-day training assignment in Florida, he had gladly accepted. Now, however, the 9 mm Glock 22-C pistol in a clip-on holster under his shirt felt heavier with each step, and he was seriously reconsidering his choice to "see some action," as he had put it, before settling down behind a desk.

His cell phone vibrated and he activated his Bluetooth receiver.

"Lights have been spotted off the port bow. We think this is our contact ship. Everyone stay alert." The voice was that of the operative in change, a stern-looking guy named Heine-mann.

William was sure the name was fake, but wasn't about to ask. He had seen the cigarette boat come alongside, and then the three guys carry a long box back aboard as they left. Something heavy was going down, and he was a part of it. He hoped this would look good on his record; it would be a nice way to begin his career with the supersecret agency.

Everyone confirmed receiving the message, and he replied, as well. "Position Six confirmed. All clear aft."

Taking another look around the platform, William looked across the water on the port side, searching for the pickup ship's signal. He saw twin lights, one white, one blue, about a half mile away. It didn't seem to be getting any closer, however, which he thought was odd. William watched it for several more seconds, but the lights stayed where they were.

Why aren't they coming over? he wondered. A squeak on the deck behind him caught his attention. "Hey, what are you—?"

His words died almost as quickly as he did. The man behind him wasn't another member of the crew, but was instead clad from head to toe in a black wet suit. Before William could do anything, he fired a silenced pistol twice. William's bullet-resistant vest stopped both bullets, one of them breaking his collarbone. He staggered back and clawed the Glock from his holster, opening his mouth to call for help as he brought the pistol up—

The black-suited man took one step forward and put a bullet through William's open mouth, blowing out the back of his skull. The young man from Idaho didn't even register his own death as he fell to the deck. His index finger, however, already on the trigger of the primed and ready Glock, spasmed enough to discharge his weapon, sending a round into the floor. The report echoed through the yacht and across the water.

33

"Shot fired aft! Shot fired aft!" Jonas broadcast to all positions. "P-Six, report! P-Five, cover aft deck. Everyone else, remain at your positions."

Pistol in hand, he left the saloon and ran to the sundeck rail. Although the back of the yacht had been designed in a cutaway style, with every higher level set farther ahead than the one below it, the staggered tops effectively cut his vision. But if he couldn't see their assailants, they also couldn't see him. He climbed down the ladder to the second level, leading with his gun the entire way. Pausing by the right spiral stairway, he tapped his receiver. Just as he was about to speak, he heard the distinctive *chuff* of a silenced weapon, followed by breaking glass. Immediately the loud, twin barks of a Glock answered.

"This is P-Five. Have encountered at least three hostiles on the aft deck, right side. Cannot raise P-Six—" Two more shots sounded. "Hostiles may attempt to gain access through the left side of the ship, repeat, hostiles may attempt access through left side of the ship—" The transmission was cut off again by the sustained burst of a silenced submachine gun stitching holes in the ship wall. "Request backup immediately."

Jonas was impressed by the calm tone of the speaker—it had to be the ex–Las Vegas cop, Martinson. He was about to see if he could move to assist when he spotted the muzzle of submachinegun, perhaps an MP-5, poke up through the open stairwell. It was immediately followed by the hands holding it, then the upper body of a black-clad infiltrator. Jonas ducked behind the solid stairway railing, biding his time. For a moment there was only silence, broken by the soft lap of waves on the hull, and the strong odor of gunpowder on the breeze.

Although he hadn't been in a firefight in more than a decade, Jonas's combat reflexes took over. Every second seemed to slow, allowing him to see and react in a way that seemed faster than normal. He heard the impact of the boarder's foot on the deck, and pushed himself out, falling on his back as he came around the curved railing. His target had been leading with the MP-5 held high, and before he could bring it down, Jonas lined up his low-light sights on the man's abdomen and squeezed the trigger twice. The 9 mm bullets punched in under the bottom edge of the intruder's vest, mangling his stomach and intestines and dropping him with a strangled grunt to the deck. As soon as he hit, Jonas killed the man with a third shot to his face.

"This is Lead One. I have secured the second aft deck. P-Two and P-Three—"

He was cut off again as more shots sounded, this time from the front of the yacht. Jonas looked back out. A second team? he wondered.

And then he realized the plan, and how they had been suckered. "All positions, all positions, they mean to take the ship! Repeat, hostiles intend to take the ship! Lead Two, secure the bridge. P-Three, remain where you are and target any hostiles crossing your area. Will clear from this end and meet you in the middle."

A chorus of affirmatives answered him, but Jonas was already moving. He stripped the dead man of his MP-5 and slipped three 30-round stick magazines into his pockets. As he stood, a small tube came spinning up the stairway, leaving a small trail of smoke as it hit the back wall and bounced onto the deck.

Dropping the MP-5, Jonas hurled himself back around the other side of the stairway railing, clapping his hands over his ears, squeezing his eyes shut and opening his mouth as he landed painfully on his right elbow. The grenade went off with a deafening bang and a white burst of light that Jonas saw even through his closed eyelids. He heard more pistol shots below, followed by the canvas-ripping sounds of the silenced MP-5s firing back. *Martinson's going to get his ass shot off if I don't get down there,* he thought.

Jonas shook his head and pushed himself up, grabbing the submachine gun and checking its load. He figured the stairs had to be covered, so that way was suicide. But there was a narrow space, perhaps less than a yard wide, between the back of the stairwell and the railing of the ship's main level. If Jonas could get down there that way, he could possibly take them by surprise, and he'd also have the stairway as cover. It might also be suicide, but it would certainly be the last thing they'd expect. He crawled around the stairway again and searched the dead body, coming up with two XM-84 flash-bangs.

Jonas grabbed one and set it for the shortest fuse time, one second. It should go off right as it hits the deck, he thought. He still heard the silenced guns firing below him, so somehow the two trainees had kept the rear team from advancing. He crawled to the edge of the platform, checked that his drop zone was clear, then pulled the pin and let the grenade go, pulling back and assuming the fire-in-the-hole position again.

The grenade detonated. As soon as the shockwaves died away, Jonas rolled to the side of the boat just as a stream of bullets ripped through the floor where he had been. He jumped over the stairway, using one hand to keep in touch with his cover so he didn't jump too far out and miss the boat entirely. The moment he sailed into the air, he saw a huge problem—one of the assault team had had the same idea of using the stairway for cover, and had moved right under him.

Unable to stop himself, Jonas stuck his feet straight down and tried to aim for the guy's head. The intruder glanced up, so surprised by what he saw that he forgot he had a gun in his hand for a moment. He had just started to bring it up when Jonas's deck shoes crunched into his face. Jonas kept going, forcing the man's head back and pushing him to the deck with the weight of his body. The mercenary collapsed to the floor, unmoving.

Jonas didn't stop to check him, but stepped on the man's gun arm, snapping his wrist as he steadied his own MP-5, tracking anything moving on the aft deck. The second team member rolled on the deck, clutching his bleeding ears, his tearing eyes screwed tightly shut. Jonas cleared the rest of the area, then came out and slapped the frame of his gun against the man's skull, knocking him unconscious. He then cleared the rest of the area, stepping over Hartung's corpse as he did so. Only when he was sure there were no hostiles lying in wait did he activate his transceiver.

"P-Five, this is Lead. Lock word is *tango*. Have secured the aft deck. Report."

"This is P-Five, key word is *salsa*. I took a couple in the vest, maybe cracked a rib, but I'm okay. What should we do?"

"Take P-Six's area and defend it. Hole up in the rear saloon, and keep watch as best as you can. As soon as we've secured the ship, someone will come and relieve you."

"Got it. I'll be going forward by the left side, so please don't shoot me."

"If you're not wearing black, you'll be okay." Jonas heard steps coming and raised the gun, just in case a hostile was using the ex-cop as a hostage to get to him. When he saw the stocky Native American come around the corner, Glock first, Jonas held up his hand before the other man could draw a bead on him.

Martinson nodded, and Jonas pointed to the motionless man in front of him and the other one bleeding in the corner of the deck. "Arm yourself, search these two and secure them, then hole up. I'm heading forward. Anyone comes back that doesn't give you the key word, kill them."

"Right."

Jonas headed topside, figuring he'd take the high-ground advantage. Scattered shots came from the bow, and he planned to get the drop on the other team. "P-One through P-Four, Lock word is *tango*. Report."

"P-One here, key word is *salsa*. We've got two hostiles pinned at the bow, behind the watercraft. Attempts to dislodge have met with heavy resistance, including flash-bangs. P-Two is down with superficial injuries. We're under cover on the left side of the ship, trying to keep them in place."

"Affirmative. P-Three?"

"I'm moving up on the right side to cut off their escape route."

"P-Four? Come in, P-Four?" There was no answer. "P-Four, if you can't speak, key any button on your phone once." Nothing. Shit, he thought. "All right, P-One, hold tight. P-Three, advance to the corner and keep them busy. I'll be there in a second. Lead Two, if you are in position, key twice."

There was a pause, then Jonas heard two beeps. Good. He climbed onto the roof of the yacht, crept past the radar and radio antennae, then crossed the roof of the bridge, walking lightly. As he came upon the forward observation room, he saw a black shadow crawling up onto the roof below him. Jonas hit the deck and drew a bead on the man. Before he could fire, however, three shots sounded from below him, slamming into the man's side. The intruder jerked as the bullets hit him, then rolled off the observation roof.

That gave Jonas an idea. "P-Two and Three, fire in the hole." He set the timer on his last grenade and skittered it across the roof of the observation deck, the flash-bang disappearing from sight and exploding, lighting the night in a brilliant flash.

"Advance now!" Jonas jumped down to the observation roof and ran forward, training his pistol on the two prostrate, moaning men as the two trainees also came from both corners and covered them, kicking their weapons away. Jonas walked to the edge of the roof and let himself down, then checked the prone body lying underneath the shattered windows. He glanced up to see the other two men, their wrists and ankles neatly cuffed back-to-back in the middle of the bow area.

"Lead Two, this is Lead. Bow is secure. Tally is six hostiles, two dead, four captured. Our side has one KIA, two WIA, one MIA."

"Acknowledged. Bridge is secure," Karen replied.

"P-One, make sure P-Two is stable, then head back and reinforce P-Five, and make sure you give the proper key word. P-Three, you're with me," Jonas said.

Leading the way, Jonas and the trainee swept and cleared the entire ship, room by room. Along the way, they found the body of the young woman who had been at position four, taken out with a clean head shot. Jonas checked her vitals anyway, even though he knew it was a lost cause, then covered her face with a towel and kept moving. Only when he was satisfied that no one else was aboard did he contact everyone.

"The ship is clear—repeat, the ship is clear. Karen, let's head in. We've got wounded to take care of."

"What happens afterward?" she asked on a separate channel.

"I'm going to visit Mr. Castilo and ask him a few questions."

"Do you want to interrogate any of the captives on the way?"

Jonas considered that for only a moment. "Negative. All of them are either deaf from the flash-bangs, concussed or both and besides, I doubt they know anything about what's going down today. No, I need to go to the source."

"I'll contact Primary and update—?"

"I'm the agent in charge, I'll do it," Jonas interrupted. He sent a call to headquarters on a second line. "No doubt Judy will flip over this. Do you still have a fix on that Stinger crate?"

"Yes, it's heading south-southwest, probably to Paradise."

"Naturally. See if you can get this behemoth to go any faster, will you? I've got a really bad feeling that this thing is going down faster than we thought." He gripped the handrail and waited for the connection, willing the yacht to speed them to their destination more quickly.

34

Losing an operative on a mission was always Kate's biggest concern, even though she had long ago resigned herself to the fact that it would happen. She acknowledged the people who joined Room 59 knew the attendant risks, and their training had been designed to make them the most formidable operatives in the world. She also accepted that sending one person directly into harm's way to prevent a catastrophe that could hurt hundreds or thousands of innocents was reasonable. However, whenever she lost an operative it was always painful.

When Hartung's implanted chip sent out the signal indicating he was deceased, NiteMaster had alerted both Kate and Judy, each of whom had arrived just in time to watch the takedown of the last two remaining hijackers. All they could do was watch.

NiteMaster signaled that he had the incoming call, and patched it to Kate directly. "This is Primary," she said.

Jonas's voice was as calm as ever, but he was speaking slightly faster, which was how Kate knew he was angry.

"This is Beta. After our meeting, the buyers tried to take over the ship and its cargo and marked us as expendable. In the course of defending ourselves, two of our trainees were killed and two were wounded. We killed two of the hostiles, and captured the remaining four, who will need transport once we're ashore."

"What's your next move?" Kate asked.

"We're heading to Castilo's home. There are two operatives on surveillance there already. Contact them and pull them out," Jonas said.

"Don't you want backup?"

"Not right now. The rest of the team isn't going to be operational after what happened, and I don't need inexperienced members watching my back. A single operative will stand a better chance of infiltrating the target and getting the information we need."

"How can we help?"

"Two things. First, contact Alpha and have him ready to depart Paradise in the longest-range ship he can get—we may need to insert into Paradise, and this yacht isn't going to be fast enough. Any information you can give him on patrols or any other obstacles would be appreciated."

"He's already been briefed and will be on the way to you immediately. What's the second thing?" Kate asked.

"They brought proof that a Cuban military officer is involved in the mission." Jonas paused, as if weighing how to say what he knew, then blurted it out. "As I'm sure you know, it was Damason Valdes."

"That was a surprise." Kate sighed. "I've issued a termination directive—he cannot be allowed to carry out whatever his handlers intend to have him do."

"Everything I've seen indicates he's involved in a plot to overthrow Paradise's government. That's what I'm going to verify from Castilo, as well as what Valdes's role in it is. When we met, I tagged him with a microbug, as I'm sure we'll need to find out where he's going."

"We'll have real-time surveillance on him by the time you're on the beach," Kate replied. "Be careful out there, okay?"

"Right. We're arriving at the launch point. Will contact after insertion is over. Beta out."

Kate cut the signal and rubbed a hand over her eyes. "Get me the files on Hartung and McMichaels, please, Judy."

"Right away, Kate."

Kate sent a query signal to Mindy and asked her to brew a pot of tea. Her comm screen beeped, and Kate saw that Judy had downloaded the files on the two dead trainees. Sitting, Kate scrolled through the files of the latest two people who had given their lives so that a Third World dictatorship could remain in power.

That's irony for you, Kate thought as she began the unenviable task of briefing herself on the dead.

35

Jonas piloted the twelve-foot inflatable raft through the calm ocean waters, aiming the small craft's bow toward the palatial beachside estate owned by Rafael Castilo. Behind him the black shape of the *Deep Water* was anchored a half mile offshore, enabling him to make the short trip with ease.

Two hundred yards out, Jonas cut the motor and rowed the boat toward the beach with powerful strokes, trusting the raft's dark gray color would be enough to hide it in the darkness. He didn't want to waste precious time hauling it to the tree line or camouflaging it. Despite what had happened, all of the surviving trainees had volunteered to accompany him, but Jonas had ordered them to stay aboard the yacht. It wasn't that he didn't trust their abilities, but two of their colleagues had already died that evening, and he wasn't about to risk anyone else, especially when there was a strong possibility he might be walking into an ambush.

Once ashore, he took a moment to scan the building he was about to infiltrate. Castilo's home was a two-story

Mediterranean-style home with a large pool, terrace and red Spanish tile roof. There was enough foliage surrounding it that Jonas was sure he'd be able to infiltrate the grounds, but the electronic security perimeter was another matter.

Adjusting the multispectrum detection system integrated into his close-fitting Kevlar-weave helmet, he crept across the beach, figuring any systems wouldn't begin until the actual grounds. He hit the tree line, weaving through palm trees, chinkapin thickets and clusters of buttonbush. Using the infrared detection lens, he scanned back and forth until he saw the beam surrounding the groomed lawn. It was about four feet off the ground, and Jonas easily stepped beneath it. He knew why it was that high in the next few seconds.

From around the corner of the house came two black-and-brown Doberman pinschers, their lean bodies streaking toward him as they ate up yards of ground in long, loping strides. The moment they appeared, bright halogen lights flicked on, bathing the pool and lawn in white brilliance.

Stepping back into the bushes, Jonas dropped to one knee and activated the gas filter on his mask as he extended a powerful aerosol canister and filled the five yards in front of him with a cloud of fine white mist. The Dobermans ran straight through it, and immediately collapsed on the wet grass as their legs gave out. They skidded to a stop at Jonas's feet. Both dogs whined feebly, then passed out from the inhaled tranquilizer. Jonas waited for someone to investigate the disturbance, but the grounds remained quiet. While waiting, he pinpointed several security cameras scanning the grounds around the house. He also noticed a small blind spot near the northeastern corner, near what looked like some kind of sunroom.

While waiting for the lights to turn off, he took in the house, changing lenses to a thermal detector suite. The first floor was empty, but on the second, closer than he'd expected, he saw two sleeping forms, their red-and-orange shapes appearing to float in midair against the cold blues and blacks of the walls and floors. The master bedroom appeared to be behind that sunroom, next to the blind spot in the security perimeter. Jonas's instincts again screamed that this could be a trap—indeed, it most likely was. The team that had been sent to commandeer the yacht hadn't reported in, and he was sure Theodore knew that. But this was the best possible chance to learn the details of Castilo's plan.

Jonas began working his way toward that corner, watching the grounds for any sign he'd been discovered. He crawled through the brush and tropical trees until he reached his objective, and still, there was no sign of having tripped any security alarms. Jonas took another minute to scan the wall and rooms where he was going to access the house. Finding nothing out of the ordinary, he slipped a small pistol-like device from a pouch on his arm, aimed it at the light on the wall and pressed a button. The narrow-beam electromagnetic pulse fried the light's circuit, disabling it. Jonas put away the gun, waited for the camera to turn toward the pool, then slipped out of the trees and ran to the corner of the house, gauging the height at the top of the short railing as he closed the distance.

Just as he reached the wall, Jonas crouched and leaped as high as he could, fingers reaching for the lip of the railing, and just grabbing it. Arms trembling, he pulled himself up, aware that the corner camera was coming back on its sweep, and if he didn't get inside in the next few seconds he could be spotted. When his head drew level with the railing, he threw an arm over, clawing for a more secure grip. Bracing his arm on the inside of the rail, he slithered across the railing and collapsed on the tile floor, panting for breath.

This was a lot easier thirty years ago, he admitted to himself.

He listened for any sign that he had alerted anyone. Only the gentle roll of the surf and the night breeze rustling the nearby forest reached his ears. Rising, he moved along the right wall, avoiding the wicker-and-glass patio furniture set in the middle of the room, until he reached the French doors leading to the bedroom.

While some people might have left their doors open to enjoy the cool ocean breeze, the double doors were closed, and Jonas was sure they were locked, as well. He took a small device roughly the size of a pack of cigarettes from a pocket and ran it along the door frame, ceiling and floor, looking for current flow to indicate the door was attached to a security circuit. The meter came up empty, so Jonas concentrated on the formidable-looking doorknob lock. Kneeling, he took out a small leather case, selected the appropriate pick and a torsion wrench and went to work. Since finesse was needed and his movements were so minute, he hardly made a sound. Although it took longer than he'd have liked, after several minutes, the lock clicked open. His thermal imaging told him that both occupants were still in bed.

Switching to infrared, Jonas pushed the doors open slowly and slipped inside, pushing aside the billowing white curtains hanging on the inside. He closed the door behind him and glanced around. Feeling a breeze, he looked up to see a large ceiling fan stirring the air. The master bedroom was spacious, with an ornate antique dresser and armoire against one wall matching the four-poster, king-size bed in the middle of the room. On it, nestled together, lay Rafael Castilo and his wife.

Taking a small capsule from a pocket on his web harness, Jonas walked over to the sleeping couple, broke it and held it under the woman's nose. She frowned and moved her head to try to avoid the scent, then her body relaxed as she passed into deeper slumber. The potent narcotic Jonas had given her would ensure that he and Castilo could speak undisturbed.

Going to the heavy door leading to the rest of the house, he made sure it was locked, then padded back to the side of the bed. Drawing his pistol, with the short sound suppressor already attached to the threaded barrel, Jonas pressed the cold circle of metal to the sleeping man's forehead.

The businessman's eyes fluttered open, then widened in shock. Jonas didn't blame him. The helmet and full face mask were quite intimidating, concealing his features behind a black, vented guard that covered his nose and mouth. His eyes were concealed by the multipurpose goggles with their vision suite. He had no doubt he resembled some kind of futuristic home invader.

"Do not move, or you and your wife will die. Keep your arms at your sides." The mask also contained a small microphone and voice-modulation chip that altered Jonas's normal speaking tone into an unrecognizable one. With a black silk balaclava covering the rest of Jonas's head, Castilo would never know who was behind the mask.

"Who are you? What do you want from me?"

"My employer is not pleased. Not more than two hours ago, the gentlemen you introduced him to attempted to hijack his yacht—and the cargo he was holding."

Castilo's eyes widened, and Jonas activated his visual voice-stress-recognition program, which would analyze Castilo's responses and determine whether he was lying or not to a ninety-five percent degree of accuracy. Based on technology developed in Israel, it had been integrated into masks as soon as the Room 59 techs had gotten their hands on it.

"What are you talking about? I had dinner with Mr. Heinemann tonight and it was agreed that he would provide the Stingers my people needed for the price we had negotiated."

Jonas admired the man's calm—even when threatened with his own impending death, his voice was steady. Even more surprising was that, according to the voice program, he was telling the truth.

"So you knew nothing about the attempt to hijack the yacht and steal the missiles and the money?" Jonas asked.

"Are you serious? I could buy ten of those yachts, and the money was a pittance to me compared to what it would get us. We need those missiles to defeat attacking gunships—" Castilo stopped in midsentence.

"Yes, your plan to invade Cuba. If you didn't authorize the assault, why would we have been attacked after you left? What's the connection?"

"I don't know. Maybe pirates saw your boat, and thought it was an easy target."

"No, these men were organized, professional, well trained and equipped. They couldn't have been anything but mercenaries, which leads straight back to you."

Castilo's brow furrowed as he tried to think of an answer. "I'm sure your boss has enemies—if they know he's trying to take over in the power vacuum in Miami, perhaps one of them decided to eliminate the competition."

"And they happened to arrive within the time frame that we had agreed upon with your man—and use the two lights he had told us to expect?" Jonas stuck the gun under Castilo's jaw. "You are not convincing me."

Castilo shrugged. "The only thing that makes sense is if the PMC I hired decided to eliminate you, to stop the trail of the Stinger missiles from being traced any further."

The voice analysis said that Castilo believed he was telling the truth. Jonas nodded—at least that was possible. "My employer wants to know the details of your plan. Who is involved? How does it begin? What is the event that starts it in motion?"

The frown reappeared, and Jonas sensed the Cuban closing up. "I've told you what I know. The plan doesn't involve your employer any longer. You got what you came for—now get out of here, before my security finds and kills you." He actually started to lift his head from the silk-cased pillow in annoyance, but Jonas pressed the pistol down on his forehead again, pressing him back into the plush bed.

"Your PMC's insistence on having it all has changed our agreement. If your units do not receive the rest of the Stingers, they'll be mincemeat when those Cuban helicopters get airborne. It will be the Bay of Pigs all over again—that is, assuming you don't abort the plan before it even has a chance to start. Now, tell me—when does it begin and what is the catalyst?"

Castilo considered his options for a moment, then shook

his head slightly. "I don't know what you're playing at, but you are not going to stop the plans I have worked toward for the past twenty years—not when they are so close to fruition. I would rather die first."

Another truthful statement. Once again Jonas rued the fact that he hadn't come to know this impassioned man under different circumstances. And he regretted even more what he was about to do.

"You are a brave man, I'll give you that." Removing the pistol from Castilo's forehead, he placed it behind his wife's ear. "But if you do not tell me what I wish to know within the next three seconds, I will pull this trigger."

It was a stone-cold con—Jonas didn't think he would ever kill a truly innocent person, no matter what the circumstances, even if it meant jeopardizing a mission. The question was whether Castilo would call his bluff. If his patriotism was stronger than his love for his wife, then Jonas was in trouble.

"She knew the risks when we got married. She would sacrifice anything for our cause," Castilo said.

Jonas pushed the gun roughly into the back of her neck. "This trigger has a five-pound pull. My finger is already putting three pounds on it. One more flex, and the first thing you'll see when the sun rises is her brains decorating that wall. Three seconds left…"

Castilo tensed, and for a moment Jonas thought he was going to call it, but suddenly his body relaxed. "No—wait!"

Jonas let up the pressure on the woman's head slightly.

"There's no way you can stop it anyway, even if you had people on the island. There are three thousand men on the island right now, ready to move against key positions at a predetermined time."

"What about the army? Surely they won't just sit by and let their country be snatched out from under them?"

"You have already met our man on the inside, who has given us invaluable information regarding the status of their military, their placements, their equipment, everything. We know where we will land the rest of the men, what to take first and, most importantly, how to block communication between various army units. There are also dissatisfied elements of the nation's military who will assist with the overthrow of the government at the proper time. Between the outside forces seizing key facilities and the army tying up other interference, any kind of organized resistance will be disrupted long enough for the internal forces to seize control of key facilities and order the rest of the military to stand down. I'm sure there will be some die-hards who will do exactly as that term suggests. However, the young people, the students, they want change, and that is what we can give them. Once they see that this is really happening, they will flock to our cause."

Castilo's eyes gleamed with the fire of the true political radical. "As for the event that will launch the real revolution—my man inside the army is going to assassinate Raul Castro later this very morning. That is when the true liberation of Cuba will begin."

36

Jonas remained still as he digested the news, but kept his pistol pointed at the motionless woman's skull. "Go on."

"Recently we received word that Raul will be touring agricultural companies outside of Havana, and that our man will be coordinating security. It is the perfect chance."

"So you have a way to get in touch with him—you can call it off," Jonas said.

Castilo shook his head. "No, once he has left the city, he will not be in communication with us until the invasion begins. The timetable is already counting down, and neither you, I nor anyone else can stop it."

His words made Jonas lean back, only for a second, but it was enough. Castilo brought his arms, still under the sheet, up and pushed the pistol away from his wife's head, shouting, "Security! Intruder!"

Jonas pulled away, wrenching his arm out of the other man's grasp just as the door burst open, and another man rushed into the room. Hearing the sound of the door, Jonas had already turned, and tracked the bodyguard as he came in, hoping to catch the intruder by surprise. Jonas's gun discharged, and the man halted in midstride, then collapsed to the floor, his pistol falling from his hand.

"*¡Bastardo!*" Castilo screamed.

Jonas tried to head for the French doors, but was stopped by a strong hand on his arm. Hearing running footsteps in the hallway, he twisted around and brought the butt of the pistol down on Castilo's forehead, laying open his scalp. The businessman released him and fell back against the headboard, clutching his bleeding forehead.

Jonas cut around the corner of the bed and ran for the door. Sensing movement behind him, he dived as a fusillade of shots erupted from the hallway, one of the bullets scoring a burning line across his back. Jonas had planned to roll to the far wall and return fire, but a dead weight smashed into him, pinning him to the floor.

"Damn! I think Castilo got in the way." Jonas heard Theodore's voice in the hallway. "Looks like we got them both."

Jonas played dead, hoping they would relax their guard.

"Clear the room, I've got to get on the horn and see what we're going to do. This may scrub the whole damn op."

Footsteps approached, then Jonas felt his pistol get kicked out of his hand. Someone grabbed his shoulder and spun him onto his back. "What the hell?" A goateed, wiry Hispanic frowned when he saw the mask covering Jonas's face. "Hey, you should take a look—"

Jonas didn't let him say anything else as he set off the flash unit mounted in the mask's forehead. The 250,000-candlepower light burst in the merc's eyes, blinding him. He screamed as Jonas stripped the pistol from his hand, jammed it into his chest and pulled the trigger twice. The bullets shattered ribs and carved through his heart and left him bleeding out on the hardwood floor.

Jonas kept going, shoving the body away and aiming at the hallway, catching a glimpse of Theodore dodging out of the way while shouting for backup. Jonas grabbed his pistol from the floor and ran to the doorway, a gun in each hand. He tucked the guard's pistol under his arm, grabbed the EMP gun and set it to overload, then launched it down the hallway. There was a loud pop and suddenly all of the lights in the house winked out.

Jonas readied his guns and walked to the archway that led to a landing overlooking the large, two-story, cathedral-ceilinged living room. He heard Theodore bark commands while he tried to raise someone on his suddenly useless cell phone. Peeking around the corner, Jonas recognized one of the men as the African who had helped load the Stinger crate on the yacht.

"Goddamn it, I can't get a hold of anyone. Get some night vision over here—the bastard's probably already split. And find out what the hell happened to our dogs! You two, with me," Theodore shouted.

That's a ballsy move, Jonas thought. Although if it was three on one, they'd still stand a good chance of capturing or killing him, most likely the latter. As for himself, Jonas had no wish to get involved in the barely controlled chaos of a firefight, particularly in a confined space. Now that he had paused for a moment, the graze on his back throbbed and his vest and shirt were sticky with blood. He needed a way to even the odds quickly. Taking a quick inventory of his equipment, he came across the large canister of tranquilizer he had used on the dogs, and the plan immediately came to him.

The two men were already at the foot of the stairs, backing each other up in a crisp leapfrog pattern. First one would advance, then crouch and cover while the other one moved forward. Jonas didn't have time to admire their synergy, as they were already halfway up the stairs. He set the nozzle to wide-pattern spray, laid the canister down at the top of the stairs and let it rip.

The cone-shaped cloud of heavier-than-air tranquilizer drifted right into the faces of the men. Before they could react, they leaned groggily against the wall or the balustrade, then both slumped to the floor, unconscious.

"It's just you and me now, Theodore," Jonas called out, his modulated voice sounding eerie in the cavernous living room. Three pistol shots answered his taunt, followed by the thump of running feet. Jonas popped up to try a shot, but the larger man eluded his sight again as he rushed out the main doors. Jonas considered pursuing, but he had bigger problems than the mercenary returning with reinforcements. If he did contact his employer—assuming he really was working with the PMC—and they pulled their forces, the men left on the island would be without any reinforcements. *It would be the Bay of Pigs all over again.*

Staying low, he trotted back through the bedroom to the sunroom. The entire house was still dark, and he shimmied down the wall without a backward glance and disappeared into the forest. He heard shouts from the front of the house as he hit the beach, ran to the raft and dragged it into the surf. Jonas gave the boat one final push and threw himself aboard just as bobbing handheld lights pierced the darkness on the shore.

How in the hell did they find me so quickly? he wondered. He triggered two shots from his pistol, hoping to keep their heads down, then remembered the silencer on the end and cursed. Stabbing the electric start button with his finger, he felt the engine shudder to life. Twisting the throttle, he sped away into the night, ducking low as muzzle-flashes flared from the beach, the shots smacking the water around him. Jonas returned fire, knowing it was futile, and thanking his luck that they weren't carrying automatic rifles.

The sudden scream of an outboard motor as a speedboat raced out of a hidden cove told Jonas his situation had not improved. The boat sped by, and Jonas saw a flash of muzzle-fire as someone took a shot at him with a short-barreled sub-machine gun. Fortunately, they were moving much too fast for the bullets to even come close, but if the pilot had any idea what he was doing, Jonas knew he'd get it right on the next pass.

Jonas opened up the motor's throttle, trying to get far away from the beach while the speedboat came back around. When at last he was caught in the fixed spotlight of his pursuers, he pushed the raft's tiller hard left and dived over the right side, letting the Atlantic waters close over his head as the speedboat roared past to crush the raft without stopping.

37 ⠿ ⠿⠿ ⠿⠿ ⠿ ⠿ ⠿ ⠿⠿ ⠿ ⠿⠿

Damason leaned back in the passenger seat of the 1961 Chevrolet flatbed truck his commanding officer had assigned to him for the duration of his mission. He tried to relax. With Lopez at the wheel, they traveled down the highway that ran from Havana through Matanzas and into the province of Villa Clara, where Raul Castro's first stop was scheduled, a visit to the sugar and tobacco plantations.

The trip of about two hundred miles would take over three hours in the old vehicle, which Lopez was unwilling to push above about fifty-five miles per hour. They were going to be cutting it close as it was, and this wasn't going to help matters. After Damason had been treated like a pack mule by that arrogant blond mercenary, he had been escorted back to his own boat with a minimum of conversation, save a warning to be sure to launch the flare once the assassination was completed. "And if you fail, you might as well turn that rifle on yourself," Theodore had told him matter-offactly. "As I understand it, it would probably be quicker than going through what you'd endure in your own prisons."

"I will do my part. Just make sure that your men are ready on your end," Damason had replied.

Once on his boat, they had sped back to the dock, and then through the quiet streets to Damason's headquarters. There he had collected the carefully wrapped rifle and left instructions for the men who were to handle things in his stead while he was away. He also left an itinerary of his trip that would be completely void if the next seven hours went according to plan.

But as hard as he tried to focus on his approaching task, Damason couldn't get the face of the European arms dealer out of his mind. *It was like he knew me from somewhere,* he mused. *Which is impossible, of course. Still, I would have liked to know what was going through his mind at that moment. And yet, for some reason, he also looked familiar to me.*

Sergeant Lopez, who had been very quiet all during the boat trip back, as well as the ride out of the city, cleared his throat. "Is there anything you'd like to go over regarding our mission while we have the chance?"

Damason turned to his subordinate, grateful for the interruption of his troubling thoughts. "Yes." He unfolded a satellite map of the sugar mill and spread it out on his lap. "Raul will be touring the sugar mill that has been converted to producing alcohol from cane juice. Of course, security will be posted around the building, as well as in the perimeter. I have placed Gonzago here." He tapped a large cluster of trees that would give anyone in them an unobstructed view of the front of the large processing buildings. "I have manufactured evidence of his involvement with the CANF exile group, and will denounce him as a traitor to the revolution, should the operation go wrong. I will maintain my story of having discovered the assassination plot and trying to stop him before he could attempt it. Either way, you will be backing me up, both as a rear guard and a witness, to confirm my story."

"And afterward?"

"All I know is that outside forces are poised to land on the island once they've received confirmation that our target is truly dead. My contact has told me that there are other people in the armed forces who will join this revolution, but we have been kept out of communication with each other, so that if one cell was compromised, it wouldn't lead to the capture of the others. They will block communications between loyalist units and also keep the local militias pacified so that they will not rise up and fight us. The paramilitary forces will strike near Havana and move to seize the capitol building. Once we have that, we can establish the military junta until a new government that is truly of the people can be created."

At least, that is what is supposed to happen, Damason thought. He knew there were hundreds of things that could go wrong, and each one could have a snowball effect on the entire process. But regardless of the final result, he believed the one thing that must happen to bring any change was the removal of one of the men who claimed to have brought it to the people all those decades ago. Damason might not get his shot at the real head of the Communist snake, but assassinating his brother might accomplish the same result, by removing Castro's successor.

Damason kept repeating that simple goal as he stared out into the darkness, coming ever closer to the dawn of a new era for his country.

38

"He's where?"

Kate winced and adjusted the sound on her earpiece. Using a thermal-tracking satellite, she had been ghosting along with Jonas as he had infiltrated Castilo's beachfront home. Although outwardly the picture of calm, her heart was in her throat when she was forced to watch, helpless, as Jonas went down as a flurry of gunshots sprayed through the air from a man in the bedroom doorway. When he turned the tables on that same person seconds later, the three cyberjocks cheered and pumped their fists in the air. They all saw him take out the two other men and exit the house, only to be waylaid by the speedboat on the ocean, which forced him overboard and destroyed his raft. Kate had then called Karen and informed her of his current location.

"Beta is fifty yards from the stern of the boat, so please let the rest of your team know to stand down—the last thing we want is a friendly-fire casualty. You might also want to have a couple of people there to assist him."

"Affirmative," Karen replied.

Kate heard the message go out, and tried not to tap her foot as she waited. She picked up her cup of jasmine tea and brought it to her lips, only to find that it had gone cold during Jonas's snoop.

The cell phone's sensitive microphone picked up running feet, and the authoritative timbre of Jonas's voice as he snapped out orders. "Head to Cuba at top speed."

She heard a rustling, and then Jonas came online. "This is Beta. The Miami contact is terminated. Repeat, the Miami contact is terminated."

"What happened?" Kate asked.

"He had more guts than brains. He tried to tackle me on the way out, and was shot by his own security personnel. Theodore got away, unfortunately. I left the site, but was attacked by a speedboat. I evaded them in the water until they left the area, then swam back to our yacht."

Kate heard Karen's voice in the background. "We're heading due south at twenty-three knots. Did you know you're bleeding?"

"Yes, it's a graze. Please get some peroxide and bandages. You'll have to put a temporary dressing on it. If you can, seal it against water, too."

"How about I just simply heal you completely while I'm at it?" Karen said.

Kate heard an indrawn hiss of breath. "Beta?"

"I'm here. The important thing is that the incursion into Paradise is supposed to happen later this morning—apparently they've been waiting for an event that would bring one of the Castros out of the capital city, and it's happening as we speak. Valdes is the catalyst—he's going to try to kill Raul Castro later this morning. We're heading down there at top speed, so if Alpha isn't moving, he needs to get his ass in gear and meet me so we can stop this. Do you have a fix on Damason's position?"

Kate relayed the question to the cyberjocks, who put a large map of Cuba up on the big screen. "Signal is weak but steady. Currently he's traveling due east, on the A1 highway through the Matanzas province. Possible destinations include the airport at Santa Clara, or the city of Sancti Spiritus, both in the adjacent province of Villa Clara."

"Both good guesses, but right now, that's all they are." Jonas ticked off numbers on his hand. "It's going to take us probably two and a half to three hours to get down there, and that's assuming Alpha acquired a fast enough boat to get us back ashore in time. Put up a map of Villa Clara Province, particularly the north shore."

Kate did so, zooming in on the coastline of the Cuban province, and as she did, it also appeared on a monitor on the yacht. Jonas grunted with satisfaction. "At least there's plenty of small islands to hide in and around—that should cut down on the chances of the border patrol finding us."

Kate caught a signal from KeyWiz. "Marcus is on his way. That should shorten your time considerably," she said.

"Yes, now all we have to do is find a needle in the Cuban jungle. As soon as you've pinpointed their exact location, text me the coordinates."

"You'll have it."

"All right, it's been disinfected, salved and bandaged, so you're ready to go," Karen said in the background. "I won't tell you to go easy on it, since you won't, but that should see you through."

"Thanks. Primary, I've got to get ready. Is there anything else you need from me?" Jonas faced them again through his tiny screen, pain and fatigue drawing his face tight.

"No, Beta, you're cleared to go. You know that you both have permission to terminate Valdes. Use whatever force you deem necessary to stop him."

Jonas visibly deflated for a moment, and Kate thought he was going to pass out. "Beta, are you all right? Do we need to call in someone else on this?"

As quickly as it had happened, the moment passed, and he was the quintessential hardened operative again. "Negative, Primary, I'm on it. Besides, there is no one else. Acknowledge your message—any necessary force has been approved. Beta out."

Jonas cut the connection, but not before Kate spotted what she thought might have been the gleam of a tear in the older man's eye. Before she could comment on it, Judy was onscreen.

"Kate, I think you should take a look at this." She brought up another screen, this one showing a map of the Caribbean Sea. Cuba was featured in the middle, with the various island nations all around it. "We've been trying to find out where this force might be located, thinking perhaps they're coming together on one of the other islands, since there are several that could be potentials in the area. But nothing indicates that anyone has been amassing men and equipment anywhere nearby. There's nothing in the Bahamas, Jamaica or Haiti, which would be a poor staging ground anyway. Nor is there anything on the mainland, either in the Yucatan Peninsula of Mexico, and of course, I cannot see anyone being crazy enough to launch from Florida."

"So while we've found out that a force is poised to strike, we haven't found any evidence that they even exist?"

"Not in the traditional battlefield-encampment sense, no." Judy zoomed in on the map of Cuba, which now included the shipping lanes. "A better possibility would be that, with the recent increase of tourism in Cuba, TEAR might have just flown their forces in as small groups of tourists, waiting until they receive the signal to strike."

"That makes sense. They could disperse until needed, but also take up positions around key areas in Havana and scout certain areas. They would certainly know how to elude the security in the city, and that would be the last thing the government would expect. But where will they get their equipment from?"

"From the only logical source—the harbor. El Supremo, put up that real-time map of the incoming vessels to Havana's port, please," Judy said.

The map·changed colors, and all of the sea traffic appeared as slowly moving paths of light. Ships all over the Gulf of Mexico and the Atlantic Ocean came and went.

"Limit traffic to incoming to Cuba, please," Judy ordered. Hundreds of dots disappeared, leaving only about thirty coming from all different directions. "This is the register for the past twenty-four hours. Any one of these ships could be carrying the several thousand tons of gear and vehicles that a brigade-sized force would need to establish themselves. They're all registered with various Third World countries, and any one of them is coming from ports where it would be possible to load arms and vehicles aboard with no one being the wiser. In fact, it's very possible that there is more than one ship involved."

"Sail right into port and meet your men already there—now, that's gutsy. Too bad their supply line is about to be cut off." Kate opened a channel to the three hackers. "Gentlemen, I need an alert from the Cuban Border Patrol to the Havana harbor, requesting that all foreign cargo ships be detained and fully inspected, under guard if need be, and I need it inserted into their communication network immediately. For the rest of those ships, this will be an inconvenience. But for anyone carrying contraband, they'll be in for quite a surprise. Nice work, Judy."

"Thank you. I just hope that Jonas and Marcus can stop the other part of this, or else we're going to be seeing a very different headline on the morning news."

True, and we'll also have failed to stop what will most be a senseless slaughter, Kate thought. She banished the bleak thought from her mind and raised the three hackers again. "Once you're done with that, I want someone to find out exactly where Raul Castro is going to be this morning."

39

Marcus couldn't help feeling pleased at the approving once-over Jonas had given the speedboat he had acquired from the Marina Hemingway in Havana. "If that doesn't get us there quickly, I don't know what will. Good job."

The watercraft in question was a brand-new thirty-nine-foot cigarette boat painted in elegant darts of white, light blue and black, with inboard twin Mercury six-hundred-horsepower fuel-injected engines. Marcus had just shrugged modestly and said, "No problem."

It really had been easy. Marcus had taken a walk along the marina, which was crammed with a wide array of foreign yachts, including several superyachts anchored offshore. Strolling along until he had found an unattended boat that suited his needs, he jumped in, hotwired it and set off. Guided by the downloaded patrol information from Primary, he avoided most of the border patrols, and even when one spotted him and tried to pursue him, he just pushed the throttle forward and left them eating his wake. Now they were refueling at the *Deep Water* and taking on the necessary gear to make their second incursion into Cuba.

As he carried a hard-sided rifle case aboard, Marcus noticed that Jonas moved more gingerly than before and occasionally a wince of pain crossed his features. He'd also noticed the dark stain on the aft deck, as well as what were obviously bullet holes pocking the back of the ship. He thought about asking Jonas, but instead went looking for Karen, finding her on the platform, checking equipment against a BlackBerry device.

"Hey, you got a minute?" he asked.

"I do, but you don't," she responded.

"What went down here? Jonas looks hurt, and I haven't seen any of the crew except for you two, not to mention the obvious damage. Were you guys boarded?"

"Yeah." Karen filled him in on what had happened earlier, including the casualty count. "They wanted it all, but bit off more than they could chew. We've got them under armed guard below, and drugged, as well—I don't want anyone making an escape attempt or trying another shot at taking the ship." She took a deep breath. "But that's not important right now. You need to get your mind focused on your own mission, not what happened here."

"Right. I'm sorry for your loss," he said.

She glared at him. "Don't be sorry for us. Be sorry for those poor bastards below. And make sure our people didn't die for nothing."

Marcus nodded, taken a bit aback by the cold fury in her eyes.

Jonas walked up at that moment. "This the last of it?"

"Yes. Good hunting," Karen said.

There it was, Marcus thought. That wince again. Hope that injury doesn't slow him down too much.

Jonas nodded, picked up one last piece of gear and stepped aboard the speedboat. Marcus snatched the last duffel bag and followed.

"Keep heading south until you're about fifteen miles out. Anyone gives you trouble—you know what to do," Jonas called back.

Karen nodded, arms folded tight across her stomach.

The older man settled in at the helm and directed Marcus to cast off the mooring line. He fired up the engines and reversed away from the yacht, then turned the sleek go-fast boat south and accelerated until they were speeding across the calm Atlantic Ocean.

Marcus alternated between prepping their equipment, keeping an eye out for hostile ships and watching Jonas pilot the boat. Jonas stood stock-still, guiding the craft with minute adjustments of the wheel, but this time there was no disguise, no subterfuge in him. Dressed in tiger-stripe camouflage, with a matching cap on his head, load-bearing web gear over his chest and a pistol on his hip, he looked like what he was—a professional soldier on the way to execute his duty, one who wouldn't let anyone or anything get in his way.

The younger man finished his premission checklist and readied both Jonas's and his packs. They had over half an hour to go, and there was one nagging question on Marcus's mind. "Can I ask you a question?"

Jonas answered without looking at him. "Yeah, if you keep your eyes open on your side."

Marcus was already scanning the dark waters on his right.

"I know why we're going back. My question is, why not let it happen? Why not let the Castros get capped and the people remake the country and lead themselves for a change?"

Jonas's flat gaze flicked over at Marcus. "*Verdammt,* you been talking to Castilo recently?"

"Hey, I know it wouldn't be easy, but even a few hundred, or even thousand eggs broken would be worth the possibility of establishing a more democratic nation in the Caribbean, one that could serve to project our interests to other nations like Haiti and also put others farther south and east on notice that a change is beginning in the area."

"Spoken like a true Washington policy wonk." Jonas's eyes never left the horizon as he spoke. "That method of regime change has already been tried. The U.S. government overthrew Cuba's government early in the twentieth century, replaced a democracy with a theocracy in Iran, worked with—and then against Hussein against Iran—before invading that little corner of Middle Eastern paradise, helped destabilize Chile, which led to Pinochet assuming power, toppled the South Vietnamese government and several others throughout Central America, all of which led to instability in each country and region."

Marcus opened his mouth to reply, but Jonas cut him off by stabbing at the dashboard with his finger. "Every single time. Meanwhile, countries like Libya have come around to a more cooperative way of thinking, without anyone having to bomb them back to the Stone Age. The point is, odds are that decapitating the head of the snake—and he is a despotic bastard, make no mistake about it—would tear the country apart, no matter what rosy predictions government analysts a thousand miles away have made. Like it or not, there is still a strong faction that clings to the notion of communism being a good thing. There are even students there who think it can still work, despite the ample evidence to the contrary. As much as we don't like it, the only way to really help Cuba is to gradually let nature take its course. The brothers won't last forever, and when they're gone, your country, mine and others will be waiting to help Cubans really help themselves."

Marcus was silent for a long moment, considering his reply. "It's just that—I saw how people had to live over there, while rich European tourists jet in, visit the local culture and jet out again. I know this isn't the only place it happens, but it just seems so wrong, particularly when they insist on following this backward path."

"Well, I think you're correct, but it's also happening all over the world—only in many places, there aren't any tourists. While Room 59 may not be able to do everything, we can at least try to ensure that some places don't get any worse. If given the opportunity to prevent a dictatorship from rising, I'm sure any of us would leap at the chance to nip it in the bud, but what we're heading into—doing what many would see as the wrong thing for the right reason, that's the really hard choice to make. Bottom line is, the more palatable solution is to not accelerate change so quickly that the island destroys itself, but to ensure that when they're ready to make that change—and I think they will be, in time—they can do so without resorting to another violent revolution. I don't know about you, but I've seen plenty of civil wars, and they're never a good thing."

"Yeah." Marcus turned back to the ocean, mulling over what Jonas had said. It was true that the American involve-

ment in manipulating foreign governments had often re-
sulted in worse conditions. But there were isolated victories,
too, he thought, like removing Noriega from Panama, and
taking out Milosevic in the Balkans. He didn't think anyone
could say either of those hadn't been justified. But do one
or two right acts make up for several wrong ones, especially
when the wrong ones mean fighting unwinnable wars for
years on end? That question nagged at him for the rest of
the ride, but try as he might, he couldn't come up with a suitable answer.

40 ǁ ǁ65 ǁ ǁ ▪ ǁ 59ǁ ǁ▪ ▪ǁ   ǁǁ ▪ ǁ▪

When he saw the night-shrouded coastline of Cuba break up
the endless expanse of water, Jonas was unsure how he felt.
Seeing the place that had changed his life so many years ago—
and had just changed his life again earlier that evening, Jonas
was surprised to find he didn't feel sadness or anger or even
nervous anticipation at returning. His mind was calm, evaluating and estimating possible plans of attack, options and
escape routes, even though he didn't have the full information
needed. This was what it was all about, he thought, working
on the fly, improvising when necessary—just like the last time.

June 19, 1973

JONAS FROZE for a second, then pulled back, making sure
he was out of sight. The truck still burned brightly in the
clearing, which was now devoid of any other living thing.

"Hey, you out there!" a voice shouted in Spanish. "We
have your accomplice. Surrender, and she will live."

A part of Jonas's mind said he should withdraw, that the mission had been accomplished and that the girl was an acceptable casualty, especially when weighed against saving the rest of his team from an ambush. He didn't give that idea a second thought.

Rolling left, he had worked about a quarter of the way around the clearing, and was in a position to see into the ruin of the sugar mill, where he figured the soldiers were holding Marisa. Rapid, high-pitched cursing, followed by a loud slap confirmed his suspicion.

"You have one minute to give yourself up. Otherwise she dies!" While the voice kept shouting, Jonas crawled closer, counting on the burning truck and the yelling man to cover any noise of his passing. Peeking out of the foliage again, he got enough of a view through the narrow window on the side of the tumbledown building, and saw shapes moving around inside. He knew he would have only one chance. He peered around for anyone nearby, but saw no movement. The rest of the soldiers probably all took cover in the building, he thought. Grabbing the trunk of a palm tree, he pulled himself upright, then braced the rifle against it, wedging the stock into a piece of bark that had split from the trunk.

"Thirty seconds!" The voice sounded even more furious now, and Jonas's other concern—besides trying to hit a mostly concealed target inside a building—was that the soldier would lose it and kill Marisa anyway. But he forced that thought from his mind and steadied his breathing, sucking in oxygen to try to restore his depleted muscles.

Jonas sighted in on the building and aimed at the upper-right quadrant of the wall. From how the man's voice carried away from him, Jonas pegged him as standing to the left of the doorway, with her kneeling in the middle of the room so he could cover her and yell out into the clearing.

He took one more deep breath, and as he let it out, Jonas's pain and exhaustion fell away, replaced by calm certainty. If he failed now, at least he had tried to save Marisa, and that was the best he could do. His only hope was that she would be able to seize the opportunity he hoped to give her.

At the bottom of his exhalation, he held his breath, and for a moment, his entire body stilled. Jonas lined up his sights, imagining the head and chest of his target inside. He squeezed the trigger. He moved the rifle to the left a fraction and squeezed again, then repeated the action one more time before taking cover by the expedient method of falling backward, pulling his rifle out of the tree as he did so. From the ground he saw a small form lunge out of the mill door as AK-47 fire exploded from every window and door on the building's left side.

Jonas crawled farther into the jungle, pausing every couple of yards to send covering fire high into the mill, trying to keep the soldiers' heads down. He had no idea whether Marisa had made it out alive or was lying somewhere, riddled by bullets. Slinging his rifle, he made his way back to the trail road, heading as quickly as possible to the hollow where they had first found the truck. He heard shouts and scattered rifle fire behind him as the Cubans tried to flush him out of hiding.

He didn't know if it had been a few or ten minutes, but at last Jonas arrived back at the clearing. Nothing appeared disturbed—if she was hiding, she was doing a good job.

"Marisa?" he called out. "It's Karl. Where are you? We have to get out of here—they'll be coming soon."

The bushes parted, and she stepped out, walking unsteadily toward him. Even in the dim moonlight he saw her bruised and rapidly swelling lip and cheek. "Are you all right?" he asked.

"Better now that you're here." She swayed, and he reached out to catch her. "No—I'm fine—we have to get moving."

She slipped her head under his shoulder, and this time he didn't protest, but allowed her to lead him into the jungle on the other side of the path, each of them supporting the other as they went. Flashes of light bobbed along the trail as the soldiers searched for them, but Jonas and Marisa were deep into the thicker jungle, leaving the ambush site farther behind with every labored step.

They walked until both were ready to drop from exhaustion. Jonas's ankle was a mass of white-hot pain from the recent abuse. Even trying to put as much distance as they could between themselves and the Cubans, he had insisted on doubling back and going in circles, laying false trails just in case the soldiers were better at tracking than he thought. When he had mentioned his concern to Marisa, she had laughed softly. "Didn't you know? Only crazy people go into the jungle at night."

As tired as he was, the joke still made him smile. "You'll get no argument from me on that." When he was sure they were safe, he got his map out and figured out their rough location. "We're about a mile from the pickup point, and we need to get the raft and move it to the secondary drop zone. Are you up to getting there tonight?"

"The farther we get away from those bastards, the better I'll feel." She rose and helped him up. They set out, Jonas cutting a path only after they had traveled about twenty yards, so they wouldn't leave such an obvious trail. Fortune favored them and the jungle thinned out as they got closer to the coast. The tang of the salt air began to overpower the fetid smell of wet, rotting vegetation, and Jonas was glad to breathe it in.

They pushed through one more cluster of dense brush and found themselves back where they had started, seemingly a lifetime ago. Jonas limped to the raft hidden in the underbrush and pulled the fronds and cut bushes away. With only two people, and one of them injured, the launch was slow and painful, but at last they got the raft in the water. Jonas broke a low-hanging palm frond in half, making sure the stem attached to the tree pointed west, then helped Marisa aboard, before starting the nearly silent electric motor. Slowly they put away from the shore.

"What now?" Marisa asked.

"We travel to the secondary drop point, drop anchor and wait for a signal from my team." Jonas guided the rubber raft through the calm water about two miles from their original landing site, and found a small island off the main coast where they could hide, yet still see the far shore with ease. He tossed out the small anchor, then settled back against the raft's outer tube, relaxing for the first time since he had come ashore. "If you want to rest, go ahead, I'll keep watch," he said.

In the moonlight, Marisa looked as if she was shivering. "I'm cold," she said.

Jonas hesitated for a moment. "You might be going into shock." He rummaged through the small case in the raft. "I've got a blanket. Here, take it."

He wrapped it around her, feeling her shake beneath his

hands. "Come here." He pulled her next to him, feeling her snuggle up to his dirty, sweaty body. Not having anywhere else to put his arm, he wrapped it around her shoulders, sharing his warmth.

"Karl?" her voice sounded drowsy. "You weren't going to leave me back there, were you?"

"Of course not." The truth in his statement assuaged some of the guilt he still felt at not being able to tell her his real name. He shifted his weight to a more comfortable position, trying not to notice her warm breath on his neck. He glanced down at her, only to find Marisa staring up at him, her blue eyes shining in the moonlight, her lips slightly parted. Almost before he knew what he was doing, Jonas bent his head down and kissed her, lightly at first, but more passionately as she responded to him.

JONAS'S CELL PHONE SHOOK, and he answered it, setting aside the memories. "Go."

Kate's voice sounded in his ear. "Target hasn't stopped yet, but has bypassed Santa Clara, and appears to be heading toward the coast. The good news is that we have a very likely destination. We picked up communications regarding a tour of the Heriberto Duquesne sugar-processing company, which was converted to processing sugarcane juice into alcohol in 2006."

Jonas checked the phone's screen, which showed a blown-up map of the area, with a little red dot marking Damason's position in real time as he came closer to his final destination.

"The road he's on heads right to Remidios, near the plant." Another dot marked the town, along with the plant's location and, more importantly, the distance it was from the coast. "You two have your work cut out for you," Kate said.

"What, that little walk? It's not even fifteen miles from the coast." Jonas showed Marcus the location, and he nodded. "We'll be in and out before anyone even knows we're there."

"For your sake, I hope so. We'll be sending you updated location maps of your target every minute. Good luck."

"Thanks. Alpha and Beta out." Jonas cranked the boat to the southeast and skirted the coast, throttling forward until they were almost flying across the water, his mind totally focusing on the mission that lay ahead.

41

Damason strained his eyes in the early-morning darkness, trying to make out their destination as soon as it was visible.

"Relax, we'll have plenty of time to scout the area before preparing for his arrival." Even as he spoke, Lopez coaxed a bit more acceleration out of the truck.

"Easy for you to say—you just have to watch my back. I've got the hard part, remember?" Damason was more than a bit irritable. The hurried trip out to sea and back, followed by the long ride across the country with no sleep, had not done his mood any good at all.

"It's bad luck to talk about it. Let's just get there and have a look around. I'm sure you'll feel better once we get everything set up," Lopez said.

"For our sake, I hope so." Damason gnawed on an already ragged thumbnail, more worried than ever.

Lopez swung the truck left onto a narrow dirt road, and they smelled the thick, sweet-sour scent of cane pulp in the air. It grew stronger, and a few minutes later they came upon the cluster of buildings that made up the sugar refinery. There were already lights on in the yard and men walking around, no doubt preparing for their supreme leader's visit. Lopez drove past the main group of tin-roofed buildings, continuing up the road to the next corner on his left. Turning, he went around the perimeter of the compound, he and Damason both noting sight lines, copses of trees, outlying building placement, exit roads and various places an assassin could use for cover.

Lopez shook his head as they circled the refinery. "You've got your job cut out for you, sir."

"Yeah." Damason swiveled his head back and forth, not liking what he saw. The main entrance to the processing buildings was right in the middle of the acreage, flanked on almost all sides by other buildings or storage tanks. Three-quarters of the way around, after they had taken another left and were headed back the way they had come in, Damason pointed at the other side of the road. "Slow down."

A rough path, little more than two tire tracks in the grass, led west between two clumps of forest. It wasn't perfect, but as he looked through the foliage to the northwest, he saw that it was as good a line of sight to the main doors as he was going to get. "All right, finish the tour of the perimeter, and let's go meet the head of the facility."

Lopez sped up, following the road as it curved to the left, then straightened out again, and then made one last left turn to drive along the back of the large, corrugated-tin buildings where the sugarcane juice was refined into alcohol. They ended up at the intersection where they had first seen the entire place. He drove up the main road again, turned left into the driveway, and parked the truck near the large group of buildings.

A man dressed in a dirty guayabera shirt with an unraveling sleeve and torn, spotted pants came over to them. When he saw the military uniforms, he stiffened. "Sirs, we did not expect the army to arrive so soon—"

"Exactly, and neither would our leader's enemies, which is why we are here now." Damason swung out of the truck and introduced himself and Sergeant Lopez. "Where is the facility overseer?"

"That would be me, Julio Montoya, sir. We have been working around the clock ever since we received word that our leader would be visiting our plant, and I am pleased to say that I believe everything is ready for his arrival."

"I'll be the judge of that, if you don't mind." Damason fell into the role of supercilious military officer with ease. "My sergeant and I will be inspecting the buildings and nearby grounds for placement of the security detail. I trust we will receive the necessary cooperation?"

"Oh, yes, sir, whatever you need, we will provide." The supervisor nodded his head in fawning agreement.

"Very well. We will take a look around, and will summon you if necessary. You may return to your duties."

"Thank you, sir." The man hustled off to the main building, no doubt to inform the others that the advance guard had shown up. Damason reached back into the truck and pulled out a battered pair of binoculars. "Let's take a look at that area across the yard."

The two men slowly walked toward the far end of the complex, occasionally pointing out an area to each other or conferring on a particular structure. All the while they kept moving toward the large cluster of trees next to the rough grass path leading west.

When they reached it, Damason stepped into the brush and stamped down a space, hidden by a thin curtain of grass, large enough to kneel in while still being concealed. Looking out of the improvised blind, he saw a clear line of sight to the front of the processing buildings.

"Facing east, I'll be aiming into the sun. The only possible advantage would be that the shadows cast by the buildings might give some relief." Damason checked his watch. "The rest of the men will be arriving in the next hour. Let's get positions worked out for the rest of the perimeter, and place Gonzago right here." Damason stared out at the spot about seventy-five yards away where, in the next two hours, a man would step in his crosshairs and fire a shot that he hoped would change everything he knew.

42

Walking through the tranquil Cuban landscape, Jonas was worried.

Upon a final review of the map of this section of coastline on his cell phone, he'd realized they would be better off tying up close to shore rather than near one of the outlying islands. They had traveled along the coast for another ten minutes, then swung the boat around the southern end of Cayo Fragoso Island, anchoring it below a long bridge that connected Cayo Santa Maria with the main island, about ten miles from their destination.

"I still don't see why we couldn't grab a car and take the road over," Marcus said as he adjusted the straps of his face-mask for a more secure fit.

"That's the problem with you young pups. You always want to do things the easy way." Jonas checked the load on his pistol and replaced it in his thigh holster, then chambered a round in his HK MP-5 SD3 submachine gun with integral suppressor. "I don't want to attract any more attention than we already have, and I don't want to announce our arrival five miles before we get there. On the way back, if you want to commandeer a vehicle, I'll see what can be arranged."

"Cute. And don't worry, I'll try not to leave you too far behind during our walk," Marcus replied.

"Don't forget the suppressor for the rifle."

"Already packed, Dad."

"All right, then." Jonas slid the last of his magazines into a pocket on his vest. "Show me what that Army of yours taught you about cross-country navigation."

Marcus snorted. "With this setup, they really didn't have to teach me anything. It's practically cheating."

The state-of-the-art headgear they were both wearing, besides having a tight-beam communication link that worked up to three miles away, featured a heads-up display that allowed the wearer to follow the best satellite-mapped route to a destination using GPS coordinates.

They had been on the move for an hour, and Jonas had been impressed by the younger man's ability. Marcus had taken point and led them unerringly toward the sugar refinery, crossing two crumbling highways and setting a steady, ground-eating pace. He ghosted across the dark plains, and with the sensor suite he was alert to any possible trouble, such as the lone rattling car on the highway. They had flattened into the grass to avoid it, long before the occupants could have spotted them. Although Jonas admired the performance, he was sure that Marcus would have done just as well without the technology.

In fact, everything was going more smoothly than Jonas could have hoped. And that's what worried him. It all seemed much too easy so far. Of course, considering what I went through the last time I was here on duty, perhaps I'm being overly concerned, he thought.

Unlike the thick jungle Jonas had encountered on that trip, this area was made up of lightly forested plains that had been divided into farm fields of various sizes, interspersed with groups of trees and sometimes heavier brush. They were making excellent time, but Jonas wanted to get as close as they could to the refinery before the sun began to rise. And he was even more concerned about getting their job done and getting out of there before daybreak.

And that posed an entirely different problem. It was one thing to infiltrate an area to kill a person; it was quite another to infiltrate with the intent of trying to convince your target—whom you'd already lied to once—not to complete his own mission, which he was certain would free his homeland. And if that failed, Jonas would be left with only one option. But, even though he knew the odds against succeeding, knew he was jeopardizing the entire mission, as well as putting himself and Marcus in even more danger, Jonas intended to try.

Ahead, Marcus held his fist up, and Jonas came to a halt. "Yes?"

"My HUD says we're getting close. Going to have to sneak and peek from here on in." Jonas heard a small click as the other man readied his sound-suppressed MP-5.

"All right, but remember, every minute that passes brings daylight that much closer."

"Tell me something I don't know. Now follow me, and try to keep up." The facemask covered Marcus's mouth, but Jonas knew he was smiling underneath.

"Don't worry about me, I'll be right behind you. Just get us there ASAP."

"Shoot, I'll have us in early and back home in time for breakfast," Marcus said.

I wouldn't count on that, Jonas thought. He trailed his partner as they stalked across more fields, through small and large patches of woods and around the scattered small houses they came across. His enhanced hearing brought Jonas the usual sounds of the early morning, the occasional call of a mourning dove, the chirps of crickets in the fields and the warm, gentle breeze as it rustled through the trees.

A soft beep suddenly alerted him to their proximity to the target. As they had gotten closer, every time Primary sent him an updated map of Damason's location, Jonas had plugged it into the sensor suite's map overlay, so that he and Marcus would know exactly how far away they were. Now, about 150 yards out, Jonas called a halt, sucking a long drink of water from his CamelBak hydration system.

Marcus stopped and crouched down, his cammo turning him into a small hillock on the open field. "What's up?"

"Change in plans." Jonas expanded the map overlay, projecting it until the refinery and its surroundings took up his entire field of vision. "Patch into my map view. I've been informed by Primary that I am to make contact with the target and attempt to turn him before calling the termination."

"They want you to go in and talk to the guy?" Marcus's voice was composed of equal parts disbelief and anger. "That could blow the whole mission. What if he'd rather shoot first than chat?"

"Hey, we're here to do a job, not question our orders." As he spoke, Jonas felt another stab of pain at lying to his partner, risking exposing both of them to even more danger. "It's not my choice, either."

And truthfully, it wasn't, Jonas thought. He would much rather set up a clean kill shot from five hundred yards away and take the guy out at range, then melt back into the night. But he couldn't do that—not without at least trying to make contact first.

"Man, this deal is getting worse and worse by the minute. All right, I've got visual. What's the plan?" Marcus asked.

Jonas marked Damason's position with a red dot. "I want you to circle west and come in through the long stretch of forest to here." Jonas marked a spot on the other side of what looked like a grassy trail, to the west of where his target was setting up his ambush. "That should give you a clear field of fire, and with the thermal scope, you should be able to pick out your target easily. However, you are not to fire unless I give the word, even if I appear to be in imminent danger. Do you understand?"

"I got it," Marcus said.

"I'll give you ten minutes to work your way into position, and then I'll start my approach. If you get there early, let me know, and I'll move out," Jonas said.

"Right." Marcus split off and crept into the gloom, disappearing in a half-dozen steps.

Jonas turned and looked to the east, where the first rays of dawn were just beginning to lighten the horizon, then he hunkered down to wait for Marcus's signal, trying to figure out exactly what he was going to say to his son when he saw him.

43

As Damason had expected, the first security squad had arrived about twenty minutes after he and Lopez had finished their perimeter sweep. He carefully arranged the five-man team around the facility so that none of the men would be able to see each other.

"Men, securing this refinery is a larger challenge than usual, but one that I know all of you are prepared for, because you were handpicked by our leader. I have your assignments, and I expect them to be carried out with the professionalism that marks the very best of our armed forces. Remember to keep the radio channel clear unless you are absolutely sure that you have identified a threat to our leader, or unless I contact you. Are there any questions?"

Silence and five curt head shakes answered him. "Then assume your posts."

He gave them a few minutes to get settled, then went to the truck and pulled out the blanket-wrapped Dragunov sniper rifle and handed it to Lopez. "Let's go."

He walked toward Gonzago's position, the sergeant following a step behind. Ten yards away, he got out his radio. "Gonzago, this is Major Valdes approaching your position."

"Acknowledged, Major, you are cleared to approach."

He crossed the road and stepped into the thicket where the small, wiry soldier blended into the surroundings. Gonzago saluted, a puzzled frown crossing his face. "Major, I was just about to contact you anyway. When I came in here, I found the grass flattened, as if someone had already used this area as an observation point."

"Our leader has obviously chosen his protectors well," Damason said as he took a step closer and lowered his voice. "What I am about to tell you is classified and cannot go beyond the two of us."

The soldier's eyes widened, and he stood even straighter upon hearing the news.

"We have received word that there is a plot to assassinate our beloved leader, and the perpetrators of this heinous crime are part of his own security detail."

Gonzago's eyes widened in shock. "But surely our counterintelligence—"

Damason held up his left hand. "It was through the efforts of our dedicated counterintelligence personnel that this plot was uncovered in the first place. Our leader wants to capture the men responsible for this terrible plan in the act, which is why we're here. Your service and dedication to the revolution are above reproach in every way. That is why I have placed you in this vital position. I am asking you, on behalf of all Cuba, to watch with the utmost attention as he approaches."

Gonzago saluted with a quivering hand. "I will not let our leader down." He turned to resume his position. Damason reached around to clap his hand over the soldier's mouth and drag him away from the front of the clearing. Wrenching Gonzago's head to the left, he raised his right hand and plunged a six-inch blade into the man's neck, severing his carotid artery and spraying a jet of blood into the air. The soldier convulsed once, then went limp, and Damason gently lowered him to the ground.

"Although you did not know it, you have an important role to play in this operation, soldier." Damason rolled him to one side, cleaned his hands, then turned to Lopez and took the rifle from him. "Take your position—make sure no one comes up on me. You know the signal."

Lopez nodded and melted into the underbrush. Damason immediately felt more secure knowing that his sergeant would be about ten yards away. He unwrapped the rifle and inspected the scope, removing the protective caps on each end and making sure the lenses were clean. His one regret was that he hadn't had a chance to test fire the rifle. He had loaded an empty magazine and dry-fired it, to get an idea of the feel of the weapon and its trigger pull, but he couldn't have taken the risk of being discovered actually shooting it. No matter what remote place he would have gone to, the risk of being found out was simply too great. However, at this distance, roughly seventy yards, he knew it was unlikely he would miss. He loaded a full magazine, chambered a round, settled into position and began the hardest duty of all, waiting.

44

Poor bastard, Marcus thought as he stepped into the tree line. He had circled west-southwest, and had picked out the supposedly camouflaged soldier's position with his thermal vision right away, recognizing him for what he was. "Beta, this is Alpha."

"Go."

"I've got a potential hostile in the jungle approximately ten yards west of target's position. Looks like the rear guard."

"Move in and eliminate him silently. Do not jeopardize our position under any circumstances."

"Affirmative. Moving in." Don't jeopardize our position. You mean like Primary is doing? Marcus thought. He resolved to have a talk with Kate about mission priority once this was over. Contact and acquire, indeed. What brilliant bureaucrat came up with that one? I bet Judy had a hand in this. But first, he had a rear door to close and a partner to babysit while he chatted up a rogue military officer.

Marcus plotted his intercept course to come in on the

north side of the man, making sure to stay far enough away so as not to alert their target. Sure is getting crowded in this part of the bush, he thought. He crept forward, placing each foot with maximum care, avoiding twigs and leaves, slowly making his way toward the observer one careful step at a time, checking after each stop to ensure he hadn't been spotted. When he was within range, he raised the sound-suppressed MP-5, checked the fire-selector switch and snugged the extended stock into his shoulder. He took one more step forward, breath shallow, aimed at the glowing red-and-yellow blob in front of him and squeezed the trigger.

45

"Alpha has taken out one hostile. Beta appears to be—moving in on the other one." KeyWiz frowned as he sat watching the patch of Cuban jungle.

"Moving in? How close does he need to be?" Kate studied the topographical map, with the various dots signifying Jonas's and Marcus's positions. She watched as the division head kept edging closer to the red dot of Damason. "What is he doing?"

"Unknown, ma'am."

Kate weighed her options. No new information on Damason had come up that would necessitate what looked like a contact attempt. Operatives in the field had almost unlimited ability to do whatever was necessary to complete a mission, however, this looked like something else entirely. Even in the jungle, Jonas shouldn't have needed to get *that* close to carry out a termination—the man was a sniper, after all. He should be able to tag anyone from several hundred yards out.

Kate's instincts jangled again. Something wasn't right, she was sure of it. "Get me Beta." She knew it was a risk, but at the very least she had to confirm that something hadn't gone wrong.

Kate heard the chime of the outgoing call ring again and again. "Beta is not answering," KeyWiz said.

What the hell is he doing? "Keep trying to raise him, and get me Alpha right away."

Kate unclenched her hands, hating what she was feeling—the rising sense that she was not in control of the situation. "Goddamn it, Jonas, what are you up to?" She opened another screen and brought up the Valdes file. *What is it about him?* she wondered.

NiteMaster signaled her. "Link to Alpha open."

"Alpha, this is Primary. Give me a status report," Kate said.

What she heard next made her jaw drop. "He told you *what?*"

46

Once Marcus had given the clear signal, Jonas had begun his own patient stalking of Damason, slipping through the jungle with ease. The old skills had fully awakened, and his senses thrummed with the rush of information he was taking in—the dank, leafy smell of the jungle around him, the silent placement of each foot, the cautious scan of the trees and brush around him as he progressed. His instructor during GSG-9 training had often described silent infiltration as the most dangerous hunt, trying to capture or kill the ultimate prey, and at that moment, Jonas agreed completely.

He stole through the forest, each step bringing him closer to his goal.

A soft chime sounded in his ear, indicating an incoming transmission. Jonas checked the corner of the screen, grimacing at seeing Primary was calling. He ignored the call and kept moving forward. He was too close to start an argument with Kate, who was no doubt calling to find out exactly what he was doing.

He'd handle that later, regardless of the final consequences.

Taking a deep breath, Jonas kept sliding through the brush. The coming dawn was visible through the canopy, painting the trees in shades of pink and gold under a partly cloudy sky. For the final few steps, he switched off the thermal vision, preferring to use his own eyes. He was close enough to make out Damason hunched over in a crouch as he waited for his own prey. Another signal flashed in the corner of his vision. Marcus was getting a call, from Kate, no doubt. It was now or never.

Pistol at the ready, Jonas stepped out from the brush, about three yards away from the Cuban army major. He was careful to approach from directly behind the other man, not only making sure he wasn't detected, but also preventing Marcus from taking out Damason before he could talk to him.

As he inched forward, Jonas saw a Soviet-era Dragunov sniper rifle held in the other man's hands, as steady as a rock, and no doubt ready to fire. Taking another slow step, he also saw that Damason didn't have his finger on the trigger yet. One last step brought him right behind the waiting would-be assassin, close enough to touch him. Jonas resisted the urge to place his hand on the man's shoulder, and slowly lowered his submachine gun instead.

Placing the muzzle of the suppressor to the man's ear, Jonas whispered. "Do not move, or I will be forced to kill you."

47

Damason froze, not daring to twitch a muscle. His first thought was not for his own safety, but for Lopez. If this man was behind him, then his sergeant must already be dead. "What do you want?" he said calmly.

"First, set down the rifle. I know this will be hard to believe, but I'm here to help you." The voice sounded strange, as if it was filtered through some kind of electronic device. "I'm here on behalf of the United States government."

Damason was sure the man was lying, but he set the Dragunov aside for the moment. "They would never send an American agent down here—too risky," he said.

"I never said I was an American, just that I work with them. Right now, another man is aiming a rifle at your back. I'm the only thing standing between you and him."

"Is he with you?"

"Yes."

"But you have come to warn me? Protect me?"

"From that, and a lot more. Over the past forty-eight

hours, the plan to assassinate Castro has been detected and stopped. There will be no reinforcement from the mercenaries and your contact in Miami, Rafael Castilo, is dead."

"How do you know all of this?" He felt the pressure of the gun barrel behind his ear ease, and looked behind him to see the man stepping back.

The gunman wore a strange mask that covered his entire face, making him resemble something out of a science-fiction movie. But the weapon in his hand never wavered.

The man reached up and pulled the mask off.

"I was posing as the arms dealer who sold your people the Stingers. It was all a setup. Our people are tracking the inserted men even as I speak, and I was sent to stop you by any means necessary."

Damason's jaw dropped, and he stood up and turned fully around. "But the U.S. has been trying to kill the Castros for decades. Now, when there is a real chance for that to happen, you are sent to stop me? I will have Raul in my sights in less than one hour. There will not be anyone here who can stop me. Yet you are doing just that."

"Major Valdes, please, listen to me. This is not the way. Although the death of the Castros would certainly be justified for what they have done to your people, there is a very good chance that it would also tear the country apart in a civil war that could last for months, perhaps years. We've heard of the rumblings of discontent among your generals—how long would it be before one of them decided he could take the whole island over, and place you all right back where you were?"

Damason shook his head. "No, the plan will work—it has to. The people cannot take any more of this—struggling to survive every day while rich tourists come in and support the current government with their money, and nothing comes down to help the people. Castro trains doctors, then sends them to other countries, while our own people are sick every day, forced to languish in filthy, ill-equipped hospitals. People with advanced degrees working as cabdrivers, or, God forbid, prostitutes, because there are no jobs for some, and for others, they cannot make enough to survive."

"But change has been coming—slowly, yes, I admit it—but surely you must have seen it. There are those in the government who feel as you do, I'm sure of it. Once the current leadership is gone—"

"When? When will that be? People have been saying that for forty years, and yet it continues. He continues. They will always continue, unless something is done to change it, now." Damason looked at the man again, a nagging awareness in his mind that there was something very familiar about him, but not able to figure out what. "You came to warn me. I say that if you truly want to stop me, you will have to kill me. Otherwise I am going to pick up that rifle and complete my mission."

"Damason, I'm asking you to listen to reason, not gamble your country's future on a wild plan that has no hope of succeeding."

"Even if the plan fails, I will not. My name will be spoken in the same breath as other true heroes who fought for Cuba's freedom." Damason's eyes gleamed with righteous fervor. "At the very least, I will have done something that no other person, no other government, could accomplish. I will have helped put an end to the dictatorship that has strangled our country."

He turned back to the Dragunov rifle on the ground. "If you truly wish to stop me, then you will have to shoot me." Picking up the rifle, he aimed at the yard again, waiting either for a bullet to punch through the back of his head and kill him, or for an armored limousine to drive up and for his target to appear.

48

"Goddamn it, get out of the way so I can pop this guy," Marcus muttered as he stared through the Leupold Ultra M3A scope of his M24A2 sniper rifle. He had tried contacting Beta before he had taken his mask off, but the older man had turned off his communication system, leaving Marcus hanging in the wind.

After he had told Kate what Beta had said, and what he was doing, she had given Marcus his marching orders in clipped sentences. "Continue your observation." There was a pause. "If Jonas does not carry out his primary mission, you are to terminate the subject. If Beta tries to stop you—" Marcus couldn't help noticing the pause "—he is to be terminated, as well, then you are to depart the area immediately afterward."

Although the orders sounded strange to his ears, Marcus wasn't totally surprised by them. The mission came above everything else, even a fellow operative. If Beta had suddenly gone rogue, for whatever reason, then he was a threat and had to be taken down, just like Valdes. Marcus hoped that wasn't the case. He liked the guy, and didn't want to kill him if he didn't have to.

But why is he wasting time jawing with this dude? Marcus peered through the scope, watching Valdes's face as he apparently argued with the other man. *He's got cojones,* that's for sure. While Marcus could have taken the shot at that moment, he was concerned that Beta might be wounded, as well, or that Valdes might be holding an unseen gun on the other man.

Marcus considered shifting position, but something was nagging at him. *Why did Beta remove his mask?* Marcus was pretty sure the Cuban army major wouldn't welcome with a big hug the man he had earlier thought was an illegal arms dealer. But for the life of him, Marcus couldn't figure out why Beta hadn't simply taken him out. He had him dead to rights.

Marcus stared through the scope, taking in every detail of the man he had been assigned to eliminate. His finger tightened on the trigger and he breathed in and out one last time as he prepared to take the shot.

49

Lowering his gun, Jonas was at a loss. He could not order Damason to stop, and he was sure he couldn't kill him. There was only one card left to play.

"Major Valdes—Damason. Look at me."

The Cuban officer slowly turned and regarded him with a flat stare.

"Earlier I d told you I worked with the Americans. Before that, I worked for my homeland of Germany, and traveled around the world, hunting terrorists. One of the places I was sent was Cuba, back in the early 1970s."

"And?"

"While here, I met a young woman by the name of Marisa," Jonas said.

Jonas saw Damason flinch at the mention of his mother. The soldier took a closer look at Jonas, as if really taking in his face for the first time, his eyes widening. "You cannot mean…"

Jonas nodded, not trusting his voice to say the words. He was drowning in unfamiliar waters, unsure of what to say that could possibly make this man understand everything that had come between them over the decades.

Damason stared at him, his eyes round with shock. "She told me...before she died...how my father had been killed. An accident at the sugar mill..."

Jonas swallowed, his throat suddenly dry. "I—I couldn't stay with her, nor could I get her out of the country. It wasn't possible at the time."

"So you just fucked her and then ran off? You left my mother and me to fend for ourselves in this hellhole of a country, alone?"

"I came back as soon as I could—I tried to find her—" Jonas said.

"You had six years to do that. She died when I was six, leaving me to be raised by the state. You turned me into exactly what I am today, *padre*." The last word held no warmth at all.

"I had no idea that you were even alive. I couldn't find any records of her here—"

Damason flew at Jonas, slamming into his chest, sending him tumbling to the ground, the gun flying from his hand. Snatching up the weapon, the soldier knelt and aimed it at his father's head. "I would think you would be enjoying this more, *padre,* seeing what I have become. You must have killed in your line of work, yes?"

Jonas nodded, trying to suck in enough air to speak.

"As have I, many times. Tell me something—did they all deserve it?"

Jonas thought about that for a moment. He had killed in defense of his country, and in defense of liberty, but could he truly say that everyone who had fallen in his sights had been guilty? "I—I don't know," he stammered.

"In my line of work, I was often ordered to arrest people who were innocent, who just wanted a better life for themselves or their families. Somewhere inside me, I knew that, but I ignored it, choosing to believe they were enemies of the revolution. But there came a time when I couldn't stomach the lies I told myself, and that was when I knew I had to do what was right. So tell me, *father,* is that why you came here? To do what is right? Or are you just here to complete your mission, doing exactly what your superiors tell you to do? Is the fact that we are related just a mere twist of chance?"

"If I had wanted to simply complete the mission, you would already be dead," Jonas said. He heaved a shuddering breath. "Instead of sending my partner in here alone to kill you, however, I came to see you face-to-face, to try to prevent you from going down this road, that once started, cannot be undone."

"You are very, very late to be trying to tell me what I should do. My life is not even my own anymore—it has been shaped and molded by a dictator for his own power. Perhaps if my father had been here, things might have been different."

"But they still can be. You can leave this place, and make a new life somewhere else." Jonas hated the pleading tone in his voice, but if it would get through to his son, he would beg if he had to. "Come with me. It's not too late. You can start over, do anything you want to."

Damason regarded him with a strange expression. "What about my family? You are a grandfather—a grandfather to my children, and I do not even know your name."

Jonas pushed himself up onto his elbows. "My name is Jonas, Jonas Schrader. I can help get them out, too. Your wife and children can grow up in the U.S., in Germany, wherever you would like them to live. I can arrange it all. For the sake of your family, don't do this, don't throw away your life and put them in the same position you were in."

Jonas thought he had convinced him, for Damason seemed to relax for a moment, but then he gripped the MP-5 tighter and thrust the barrel into Jonas's face. "It was you who put me in that position. It is precisely for my children and the thousands of children throughout Cuba who are forced into serving the revolution every year that I am doing this." He sat back on his heels, the weapon drifting off target. "I believe it was an American who said long ago, 'The tree of liberty must be watered with the blood of patriots and tyrants.' I will do my part to help that tree plant its roots. And now I ask you—as your son, who has never had the chance to ask anything of you before—to do the same."

Keeping the submachine gun trained on Jonas, Damason crab-walked back to his original position and turned to watch the refinery again. He picked up the sniper rifle. Jonas pushed himself to his feet and stood for a long moment, staring at Damason. Then he slipped the mask back over his head, turned and vanished into the jungle.

50

"Jesus, what the hell was that all about?" Marcus had almost taken the shot when he had seen Damason turn the tables. "I thought for sure he was going to waste you."

"And if he had, you would have shot him, correct?" The older man's voice was neutral, toneless.

"Damn right I would have."

"Kate contacted you."

"Sure she did."

"Then I suggest you carry out your orders."

"What? Look, I don't know what just went down between you two—"

"What went down is that I failed to stop an assassin who is going to murder a Third World dictator if you do not pull that trigger. Now carry out your mission, Alpha."

Marcus was struck silent by the command. He had killed men before, and the mission was worthy—kill one to save hundreds, probably thousands.

"Do it!" Jonas's voice cracked in his ears.

Marcus steadied himself, settled the crosshairs of the scope on the officer's upper back, exhaled and, when his lungs were empty, squeezed the trigger. The suppressed M24 made a muffled sound as it fired. The target jerked, then slumped over, the sniper rifle falling from his lifeless hands.

Marcus straightened up and replaced the covers on the sight, then slung his rifle. He crept forward to the edge of the clearing in time to see Jonas step back out, his mask in his hand again. He walked over to the still form, knelt and took the body in his arms, enfolding it close to his chest. Although he didn't make any sound, his body shook with silent sobs.

Marcus gave him as long as he could—a minute, perhaps—then came up behind him. "Jonas, we have to go."

His back still to the younger man, Jonas slipped on the mask, drew his pistol and stood up. "Let's move out."

With Marcus in the lead, they headed due north again, slipping through the foliage to the edge of the refinery's perimeter. The sun's rays were illuminating the eastern horizon, with golden-and-red fingers.

Just as they were about to leave the jungle to cross the first field, Marcus held up his hand, and Jonas froze.

"I thought I saw something to the east, but there's a lot of heat bleeding off the factory, so I can't be sure." Marcus gave himself a second. "Can't confirm it—let's keep moving before someone does spot us."

He took a step out into the open, and the pop of an AK-47 on full auto shattered the silence. Marcus spun to the ground, hit by at least three rounds that perforated his clothes and chest. Sudden pain washed over him.

"Marcus!" Jonas hit the dirt and crawled to him. "Hold still!"

"Shit—wasn't planning on buying it here. Funny, my arm doesn't work anymore."

Jonas swung his MP-5 up and peered down the sights through his mask. Rifle rounds spit over his head. They both heard shouting from the sugar mill. Clawing off his mask, Marcus lifted his head just as Jonas fired a long burst, then dropped the MP-5 and picked up Marcus's rifle. "He's down. Now, let's get you out of here."

"No—I'm not going anywhere," Marcus said.

"The hell you aren't. I'm not leaving you here to die. Now, get up!" Jonas yanked on Marcus's shirt, hauling him upright and slapping a pressure bandage in his hand. "Keep that tight on your shoulder. This is going to hurt—a lot." He bent over and threw Marcus over his shoulder in a modified fireman's carry. Marcus found himself staring at the ground as white spots faded from his vision.

"Jonas, you're gonna get us both killed."

"Don't talk, we're getting out of here. Keep that bandage tight against your shoulder."

Unable to speak, Marcus shook his head and held out his hand. Jonas held it tightly as he carried him into the forest.

51

Part of Jonas's thoughts screamed that he was out of his mind to even think he could bring this man out of the jungle alive. He didn't consider the very logical arguments for leaving Marcus behind, but concentrated on putting one foot in front of the other, staying in the tree line and moving as fast as possible.

After about one hundred yards, he crested a small rise and ducked behind it, then cut north and trotted as quickly and quietly as he could, listening all the while for sounds of pursuit. With each step he saw brighter glimmers of sunlight creeping over the horizon, and knew they were really racing the break of day, with more than ten miles to go before reaching safety.

"How you holding up back there?" he asked.

"I think I'm gonna be sick from all the up and down but otherwise, I've been worse. How 'bout you?" Marcus said weakly.

"No problems—we've only got about ten miles to go. Piece of cake."

Jonas didn't hear anything behind him yet, but he knew that didn't mean much. Crossing the highways would be the most dangerous. He figured he had covered another half mile when he heard the roar of a racing engine. Whirling around, he saw an old pickup truck with a man standing in the back behind a light machine gun that had been mounted on the roof. It was barreling down the road on a parallel course to him.

"Company coming, got to set you down for a minute." Jonas dropped to one knee and rolled Marcus off him. He unslung the M24, aimed at the engine, then changed his mind and put a bullet into the gunner and more in the windshield. The sound suppressor made it seem as if the shots had come out of nowhere. The truck lurched forward, then drifted right and rolled off the road into the ditch, where it stalled.

"Marcus, you're not gonna believe this, but we just got ourselves that ride you wanted," Jonas said.

Slinging the rifle, Jonas lifted the younger man, trying to ignore the dark red mess his shoulder was turning into, and carried him to the truck. Depositing Marcus a few yards away, Jonas wrenched open the door, pistol out to finish off anyone wounded. The two men in the cab were both dead. One had taken a hit in the head and one in the neck. The gunner gurgled in the bed of the truck, his upper chest a bloody pulp. Jonas finished him then pulled him out. He smashed out the rest of the shattered windshield, dumped the other two bodies on the ground, started the truck and gunned it back on the road. He hopped out just long enough to hoist Marcus into the front seat, then jumped behind the wheel and floored the accelerator.

"Looks like you got your wish, buddy. The boat's just a few minutes up the coast, and then we'll be out of here and back to the States, where they'll get you patched up and as good as new."

Marcus coughed, the effort shaking his body. "Jonas, my glasses. On the boat—Valdes had a family. Found them in Havana."

"Hey, don't worry—you can give it to me soon enough. But you've got to stay awake for a little bit longer now, all right? Hey, you got a family? Tell me about them," Jonas said.

"Oh, yeah, do I ever…" As Marcus rambled on about his parents and younger brothers, Jonas kept a sharp eye out for any sign of the army or police on the road. The landscape was quiet, although Jonas knew the locals would be out soon, and a truck like this would attract a lot of attention. Driving cross-country was also bound to raise a few eyebrows, but Jonas was more concerned about not breaking an axle or blowing a tire and leaving them stranded.

After several miles, Jonas reached the first road they had crossed on foot a few hours earlier. He turned right, knowing that it would connect with the main highway in the region. A few minutes later, he came to the bigger highway and slewed onto it with a squeal of the aged tires. Jonas slowed to the speed limit as he headed toward the boat.

At last he came upon the coast, and followed it to where the road met the bridge. Marcus had fallen unconscious, but a quick check revealed he was still breathing. Peeking out of the cab for trouble, Jonas found he had company.

Three kids stood on top of the bridge, staring off the side at the long cigarette boat bobbing in the swells. Jonas made sure his mask was securely over his face, then hoisted Marcus over his shoulder, grabbed the rifle in his other hand and waded into the water, causing the children to chatter among themselves.

"Hey, your friend looks hurt! Is he gonna die?"

"Is that your boat? How fast does it go?"

"My father called the border guard! They'll come and take you away!" one of the kids shouted.

"*¡Viva la revolución!*"

The chant was taken up among the other kids, making a chorus that could be heard all along the shoreline.

Jonas ignored them as he heaved Marcus aboard the boat, then climbed in after him. He took a moment to tear his sleeve off and make a rough compress for the other man's shoulder. It was a nasty-looking mass of flesh and blood.

Jonas hauled up the anchor, made sure the prop was clear and started the engine, reversing it until he was able to turn the boat around.

Scanning the horizon, he had just started to plot a path to get out to the open ocean when a man's voice yelling through a bullhorn reached him even over the roar of the twin engines. Jonas didn't look up, but shoved the throttle down, making the boat leap forward, its sleek bow rearing out of the water as he aimed it north.

Shooting across the water, the powerful boat easily left the shore patrol boat behind. However, as he aimed for the gap that would lead to open water, he saw the large bow of a Soviet-built Zhuk-class coastal patrol boat coming toward him on an intercept course. Although it was no match for his vessel in speed, and Jonas knew that the border guards weren't normally authorized to use force to catch people on the sea, if someone enterprising had called ahead, they might suspend those rules for a suspected killer. And any one of those four 12.7 mm machine guns could easily chop his boat—not to mention him—to little shreds floating on the tide.

He turned the wheel right, speeding parallel to the long bridge and into the cluster of small, coastal islands surrounding it. Bringing down a map of the area on his HUD, Jonas plotted a course that would take him away from any boats, and hopefully right into the arms of the patrolling U.S. Coast Guard. Even with Marcus aboard, he'd be able to handle them much more easily.

But the Cuban Border Patrol wasn't done with him yet. From the east came yet another vessel, a smaller go-fast boat that was gaining on Jonas. There were two soldiers in the cockpit, and one shouted at him to power his watercraft down and allow them to come aboard.

Screw that, Jonas thought. The smaller speedboat pulled up alongside. Jonas swerved his boat in a controlled ram, smacking the side of their vehicle in a crash of fiberglass, sending them careening away. Knowing that they would be back like a persistent mosquito if he didn't stop them permanently, he throttled down and got out the rifle, steadying it across the top of the windshield as the other boat circled around to come at him again. Jonas rapidly estimated the range and the windage, then emptied the last five shots in the rifle's magazine, putting all of them into the driver's side of the boat. He saw the driver hunch over, and figured that he had tagged him with at least one bullet. Although the second soldier raised his rifle, Jonas was already speeding away, juking back and forth to avoid any incoming fire.

The Zhuk fell away in the distance as Jonas rocketed into the maze of islands, navigating his way through the watery labyrinth until he hit the Atlantic Ocean and freedom. Once he was sure he was clear, he turned back.

"Hey, Marcus…we made it!"

There was no reply from the still body lying on the seat in front of the engines, a smear of blood slowly growing larger underneath him. Jonas throttled down and stepped over to him.

"Marcus?"

He checked the younger man's wrist, then his pulse in his neck, and found no beat in either place.

"Goddamn it, Marcus, I didn't bring you all this way just to have you die on me, too." Jonas slipped to the deck and held the lifeless body, tears streaming down his face as the sleek cigarette boat rocked gently in the ocean swells.

52

Kate barely kept a lid on her emotions as the limousine wound its way through the colorful streets of Little Havana. Jacob was in the driver's seat, taking in everything as he delivered them to their destination. He pulled up in front of a modest two-story yellow home with a small yard, flanked by two palm trees.

Smoothing her suit jacket as she got out of the car, Kate was hit by the oppressive heat after the air-conditioned interior, but the mingled scents of hibiscus and ocean air were refreshing. On the other side, Jonas got out, as well, his eyes hidden behind dark sunglasses.

"Remember, let me do the talking," Kate said. Like his responses to her other questions or comments, all he did was nod his head. The only thing he had been vocal about was that he was coming with her for this visit, and not even Judy's steeliest glare could dissuade him.

Kate had relented, thinking that it might give him some closure. But the fact was that what should have been a relatively simple operation had turned into a fiasco with three operatives dead and two wounded, all to stop one man.

At least the Stingers have been recovered, she thought. Theodore and his men had been intercepted while trying to head out to sea. The missiles were safely back under Room 59's control.

Under interrogation, Theodore had revealed some surprising things, like the fact that the entire operation had been masterminded by TEAR, and been in the works for more than a year. Their ultimate goal seemed to have been to destabilize Cuba, loot key areas and pull out, leaving the rest of the country to fend for itself. Blinded by patriotism, the Cubans had signed on without knowing the real story.

Everyone had underestimated the ruthlessness of the mercenaries, and people under her command had suffered. Kate vowed that wasn't going to happen again, not if she could help it. She had already tasked Judy with working with the department heads to revamp the training, making it even more stringent. Kate knew operatives would be killed in the future, but it wouldn't be because they weren't prepared.

Taking a deep breath, Kate strode up the neatly groomed walkway, steeling herself to deliver the news. She raised a hand to her head, but resisted the urge to scratch the red wig covering her blond hair. She had done this several times since she had taken over as director, and hated it each time. But there was no way she would delegate this to someone else. Like it or not, these people had died on her watch, and she felt that responsibility all too keenly.

With Jonas beside her, she knocked on the door, which was answered a minute later by an attractive, heavy-set woman in her early fifties. Her black hair was bound in a colorful scarf.

She stared at them with surprise that turned to sudden trepidation.

How is it that they always know? Kate wondered.

"Mrs. Ruiz?" Kate adjusted the rimless glasses on her nose.

The woman nodded.

"My name is Donna Massen, and I'm here on behalf the U.S. State Department. It is my sad duty to inform you that your son, Marcus Ruiz, was killed in the line of duty." She had fought hard with the Room 59 board for this, and they had reached the compromise of creating Ms. Massen after protracted negotiations. Even though Kate had to disguise herself to deliver the news, the Massen persona remained viable for all of the families of those who had died while in the service of Room 59, to contact in case they ever needed anything. Although Room 59 would make sure that the relatives would be well compensated for their loss, it would never replace a missing husband, wife, son or daughter.

Mrs. Ruiz sagged against the door, clutching it for support. "I knew it… I knew as soon as I saw your faces."

"We're very sorry to have to deliver this news, madam." The first time she had done this, Kate almost broke down herself, but had managed to keep it together long enough to make it back to the car. Today she remained composed, but her heart was breaking along with the mother who stood before her, tears streaming down her face.

"All Marcus ever wanted to do was serve his country and help people. Tell me, if you can. How did he die?"

"I'm afraid—" Kate began, but was cut off by Jonas, his voice surprising her into silence.

"Ma'am, I had the honor and privilege of working alongside your son, and I can tell you that he gave his life so that thousands of other people would not die instead. He made the ultimate sacrifice, he did it without hesitation and he saved an entire nation."

Mrs. Ruiz wiped her eyes and looked up at him. "Will we have the chance to see him once more?"

That one Jonas couldn't handle and Kate stepped in again. "Yes—we were able to recover his body. There will be a full military funeral at Arlington National Cemetery, and we'll make sure that you are there, all expenses paid." What a great trip—come to Washington, D.C., and bury your son there, Kate thought.

Marcus's mother sobbed loudly, bringing two boys to the door, asking her what was wrong. She pulled herself together with an effort, looking as if she had aged ten years in the few minutes she had talked to them, and shooed the two children back inside.

"Mrs. Ruiz, I know this must be hard for you, and we don't wish to intrude any more today. A representative will be in touch with you soon regarding some paperwork that will have to be completed." The words, spoken like a dispassionate government official, tasted like ash in Kate's mouth. "On behalf of a grateful United States of America and the world, we are very sorry for your loss." Kate handed her a card. "If there is anything we can do to assist you, please let me know."

Kate turned on her heel and walked back to the car. She got in and leaned back against the leather seat, exhausted. Jonas went to the other side and slid into the darkened interior. Neither said a word as the car pulled away.

"Kate?" Jacob's voice came over the intercom. "We'll

have to hustle if you're going to make that flight to Idaho from Fort Lauderdale."

Kate leaned forward and pressed a button. "Right. Do what you have to." One down, two to go, she thought wearily, staring out the window at the bright, sun-soaked city all around her and feeling so very cold inside.

EPILOGUE

It wasn't easy to find a deserted stretch of beach on the Florida coast, but after a bit of searching, Jonas had located a secluded site that was being developed for yet another high-rise. At the moment it now was empty, with no other buildings around for several hundred yards. He parked the Jaguar behind a rise and trudged up the hillock, the sand shifting beneath his feet. Like so much else underneath me recently, he thought.

Cresting the dune, he saw the Atlantic Ocean stretched out before him, vast and dark and empty. This far up the panhandle, the small waves crashing against the sand were a muddy brown, not the deep blue of farther south. Rising and falling every few seconds, the endless waters could hide a multitude of sins, but tonight, Jonas hoped it would also help wash one away.

After the visit to Marcus's mother, he had headed back for an intense after-action grilling by Denny Talbot, who was as serious then as he had been easygoing when Jonas had first put himself forward to head the mission. Although they had

interrogated him extensively about his decision to approach
Valdes, the question of his relationship to Valdes had never
come up. He stated that he alone had made the decision to
approach the Cuban major, and that Marcus had no part in it.
He wouldn't think of staining the young man's record post-
humously.

The reports had been reviewed by the board, which had
dressed him down for letting the mission almost get out of
control, but had not recommended any disciplinary action
except to disallow any more field operations for him during
the rest of his tenure. Jonas didn't care. He already carried
the guilt of having overseen the deaths of three operatives
as it was, and as for what had happened to his son—for that
he would never forgive himself.

After it was all said and done, Jonas had taken his mandatory month off, and followed it with a leave of absence, which
had been approved without comment. He had suspended his
game programming, saying he would be out of the country for
a while, and then had flown back to Florida, settled in and
begun the slow, careful process of bringing his plan to fruition.
Now, after months of planning, and tens of thousands of dollars
changing hands, the last part of it was about to happen. As he
waited, he remembered the end of the long chain of events that
had led him to this beach in the middle of the night, so many
years later.

June 19, 1973

JONAS LEANED BACK in the raft, still not sure what to say.
What had begun as a simple kiss had quickly turned into
something much more, almost before he even knew what

was happening. Although they both should have been exhausted by their ordeal, instead they had responded to each other's hunger with rising passion, culminating in an urgent, wordless coupling that had left them both spent and gasping.

Marisa rested her head on his chest, her light breathing indicating that she had fallen asleep. It was probably for the best; Jonas wasn't sure what he would have said to her anyway. Weariness was trying to overtake him, as well, but he fought against it, struggling to keep his exhausted eyes on the far shore.

At last he saw a red light flashing from the jungle. Reaching for the emergency light in the raft Jonas flashed the recognition code back, and was answered in kind.

"Marisa, wake up." She stirred against him, then reared up as if shot, a small cry bursting from her mouth.

"Shh, it's all right. The rest of the team is here. We have to go get them." He looked down at his disheveled clothes with an embarrassed grin. She smiled, as well, looking away as they both quickly dressed.

"I don't just— That isn't usually—" she stammered.

"It's all right, I know what you're trying to say, and I understand. Um—this usually doesn't happen to me, either."

His tone made her snicker, and he chuckled, too. "We'd better go." He started the engine and piloted the raft across the water to the pickup zone, where the rest of the team waited for them. As he grounded the raft, Jonas noticed that there was the same number of men as had left. "What happened?"

The commander's face was grim. "Safedy was gone when we got there. We must have just missed him. Come on, we have to go if we're to stay on schedule. What happened at the mill? We saw what was left of the place from a mile away."

Jonas filled him in on the ambush, and what he had done to break it up. Reinmann was impressed. "Good work, and good thinking, especially considering that we used the tertiary route, which is why we took so long. But you had things all wrapped up here anyway, eh?" He clapped Jonas on the shoulder. "Time to go. Everyone aboard."

"Right, I'll be with you in a moment." Jonas got to his feet and hobbled over to Marisa, who was standing off to one side as the rest of the team piled aboard the raft. For a second he was seized by the insane idea to bring her along, but he knew that could never happen. "We have to go."

She nodded. "And I will never see you again."

"I don't know. I will try to come back, but I need to know where you live, so I can find you again."

She whispered the name of a village in his ear. "It's on the north coast, not far from here."

"I will come back and find you, I promise." His back to the other men, Jonas grabbed her hand and held it between both of his. "Thank you—for everything. I couldn't have done it without you."

"*Adios, señor.*" She stepped back, as did he, their hands being the last things to separate. He limped back to the raft and took his position, ignoring the sly looks and teasing whispers exchanged between the rest of the team. The commander signaled them to move out, and they paddled away, with Jonas taking one last look at Marisa before she vanished into the jungle.

WITH A START, Jonas came back to the present, glancing around guiltily.

He *had* tried to go back, but his duty had kept him with

GSG-9 for three more years, and he wasn't able to return until 1976. He had found the village, but the people there said Marisa had gone to Havana, even then a bulging city of more than two million people. Jonas hadn't given up easily. He traveled to the city as often as he could, and searched for her day and night. But he had never seen Marisa's face again, until the first time he had seen Damason's eyes in the surveillance photo taken while he had been in Spain. Then, for a brief moment, he had seen the eyes of the woman he'd fallen for in one night staring back at him again.

Jonas had been involved with his share of women over the years, but none had ever taken the place of Marisa in his heart. He supposed that it was partly a fantasy that he clung to, an idealized image of the woman who had fought beside him that night.

The faint sound of a boat's motor carried to him on the quickening breeze, and Jonas took out a small LED key-chain and held it above his head, activating the bright light that could easily be seen on the ocean. Three short flashes, three long, then three short again. He was answered in kind, and the boat revved its engines and headed to shore.

It was another cigarette boat. The cockpit was crowded with two men, a woman and two little girls, about ten or eleven years old. The man behind the wheel jumped out and met Jonas in the surf, holding out his hand. Keeping his left hand behind his back, Jonas took a small money belt off his shoulder and tossed it to him. The man opened it and examined the bundles of hundred-dollar bills inside. Nodding, he signaled to the other man, who motioned for the woman and her children to get out onto the beach. Jonas waded out to the side of the boat and addressed the woman in Spanish.

"I believe you have something to show me."

She looked puzzled for a moment, then nodded and opened her small purse, pulling out a slip of paper and handing it to him. Jonas unfolded it to reveal one half of a torn picture, showing her on a city street. He brought out another slip of paper and unfolded it, revealing the two girls as they had walked up the stairs to her former home in Cuba. He brought the two halves together to form a complete shot that Marcus had taken with his spyglasses in Havana. He compared the woman standing before him with the woman in the picture, and was pleased to find that she matched, as did as the girls. "Come, I'm not going to hurt you. I was a friend of your husband's."

The worried expression on her face lessened, and she helped her daughters into Jonas's arms, letting him carry them ashore. The girls stood on the beach, giggling as the surf tickled their legs. Jonas told the woman to wait up by the dune in the distance, and he would be along shortly. She nodded, gathered up her girls and headed up the beach. Jonas heard one of the girls ask, "Are we in America, now?"

"Yes," she replied, sounding very tired.

Jonas turned back to the smugglers, who had been paid a hefty fee above their usual rate to insure that these three got to Florida safely. "You were never here, and this never happened. I'll be watching over them, and if I ever hear of anyone asking questions, I'll come and find you, and you won't like what happens next. Now, get out of here."

The smuggler clutched his payoff and splashed back to

the cigarette boat, started its engines and roared off into the night. As Jonas waded back to shore, his cell phone surprised him with its insistent tone. He unclipped it and checked the incoming number, then flipped it open. "I thought I had turned this damn thing off," he said.

"We always have ways of making you talk, Jonas." Kate's voice filled his ear. "Do you have a minute?"

"Actually, Kate, I'm sort of busy right now—"

"Don't worry, this won't take long. Look north."

Jonas turned, and saw a familiar figure walking toward him out of the darkness. Kate appeared on the beach, clad in black slacks, a white blouse and a black suit jacket. "You saw the whole thing, didn't you?" he asked.

She shrugged. "Saw what? As far as I'm concerned, that boat was just dropping off three tourists after a night ride. I have no idea where they came from, and I don't care, either. That's not important right now." She turned and looked out over the rolling ocean.

"Oh?" Jonas turned to stand beside her, looking out at the water, as well.

"I know what happened down in Paradise, and I know about your relationship to Valdes. It took a while—and one of our guys accessing GSG-9's classified files—but don't worry, their secrets—and yours—are still safe." She glanced back at the trio. "They're his wife and children, correct?"

He nodded. "My family. I couldn't let them stay down there, not after what had happened."

Kate touched his shoulder. "I understand, but I wish you'd come to us—there might have been something we could have done to help."

"Like what? Use the forces of an ultrasecret black-ops

department to smuggle three ordinary people out of Cuba? I think Room 59 has better things to do," Jonas said.

"Perhaps. Still, it all turned out mostly all right."

"Except for we were left behind." Jonas stared off to the south, down the beach and beyond.

"Jonas, Damason made his choice, just like you had to make yours. I am sorry it didn't work out better, but you did the right thing, no matter how it must have hurt at the time. But what you said to Marcus's mother was also true—he sacrificed his life to save thousands—just like the sacrifice you made."

"And in doing so, I took away a father and a husband to a woman who will never know why he died. I stood by and watched my own son die, Kate. Hell, I ordered Marcus to pull the trigger. They'll never know that. But I know and I have to live with it for the rest of my life."

"That's the high price of the work we do. In the end, we have to look at the bigger picture, and hope that the sacrifices we ask of one or two people prevent the sacrifice of hundreds or thousands down the road. Sometimes it works, sometimes it doesn't, but we're going to keep trying—and I hope you will, too."

"Does that mean you haven't come down here to fire me?" Jonas asked.

"On the contrary—your position is waiting for you when you're ready."

Jonas glanced at the woman and children waiting for him. "I'll need another few weeks to get them set up, and then we can talk about it."

"No problem. You should get going. I'm sure they're hungry and exhausted."

"Right." Jonas began trudging to the hill, then stopped and looked back at her. "Kate?"

"Yes, Jonas?"

"Thanks—for the time, and the space. And for believing in me."

"Good operatives are hard to find—I didn't want to lose you, too."

He nodded and continued walking to the group on the dune. A moment later, the Jaguar started and drove away, carrying the three recent arrivals to the start of their new life.

KATE WAITED until the sound of the sedan's engine had died away, then hit a button on her phone. "Midnight Team, stand down. I repeat, stand down."

At three points along the beach around her, clumps of sand and grass rose off the ground as three men dressed in black, lightly armored stealth suits from head to toe, their faces covered with high-tech masks, appeared from concealment. Each was armed with a high-powered rifle. They had watched the entire exchange.

"Gentlemen, thank you, you are relieved." The three men melted back into the darkness, and as Kate watched them go, she couldn't help but shiver. If she had given the code word, the trio would have killed everyone on the beach except her without hesitation. Operating in groups of three, five or seven, Midnight Teams were Room 59's last resort, a cleaning squad of unparalleled, ruthless efficiency.

"Jesus, was bringing a team out here really necessary?" Jacob rounded the dune and walked up to her. "I told you Jonas wasn't up to anything that hinky."

"I was ninety-nine percent sure—but after what happened

down in Paradise, I wasn't going to take any chances on that other one percent."

"You aren't going to let the higher-ups know about this, are you?"

"This was personal for Jonas, not business. I figure it's on a need-to-know basis, and they don't need to know. However, we'll keep Jonas at his desk in Europe from now on. Come on, I'd like to get at least a few hours of sleep before the next operation."

"Kate?"

"Hmm?"

"Would you really have given the signal if you thought what he had been doing was wrong?"

She turned to him, her face expressionless. "Jake, you should know me at least that well by now."

His eyebrows raised. "Yeah, I do. Sometimes you are one stone-cold woman—that's for sure. Come on, let's get out of here. I never did like the beach at night."

Jacob didn't offer his arm, as he was too busy checking for any possible threats in the area. The two of them walked back to their vehicle, leaving the deserted beach and the incoming waves that were already removing any evidence that anyone had been there at all.